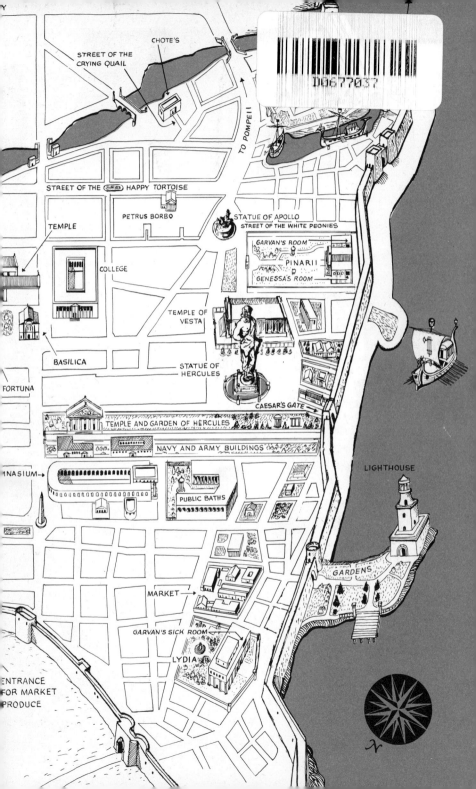

THE FLAME OF HERCULES

RICHARD LLEWELLYN

THE
FLAME
OF
HERCULES

The Story of a Fugitive Galley Slave

DOUBLEDAY & COMPANY, INC.
GARDEN CITY, NEW YORK, 1955

With the exception of actual historical personages identified as such, the characters are entirely the product of the author's imagination and have no relation to any person or event in real life.

Library of Congress Catalog Card Number 55–8408

THE FLAME OF HERCULES

PREFACE

In the early summer of 1709, a Prince d'Elboeuf ordered a shaft sunk in woodland at the edge of a cliff above the Bay of Naples. Water was needed for new building, and under the trees, he thought, might be a spring. Topsoil was cleared, and the workmen struck tufa, a dust thrown out by the volcano Vesuvius, not far off, and set rock-hard by moisture, time, and the sun. Work was slow, a few feet a day, but when the shaft was down about sixty feet, a workman bounced the point of a pickax and stung his hands on a slab of marble. What he said may be guessed, but what he did is fact. He found the site of a buried city, and his little drama was played out, properly, above the stage of its theater.

The Prince ordered the roof holed. The inside of the building was solid with tufa. For seven years, until 1716, men hollowed and dug it clean. All the marbling, statuary, and bronze went to the Prince's home or as gifts to his friends. Other attempts were made after that, but rocky tufa was more durable than men's patience. A little over 200 years later, in 1927, with the aid of the Italian Government, Professor Amadeo Maiuri started clearing the city brick by brick, house by house, and street by street.

Local legend gave the place a name—Ercolano—and told of a city entombed. Theophrastus, in 300 B.C. had mentioned its Greek name, Heracleion. In the first century B.C., Cicero had called it Herculaneum, one of Campania's finest cities. Pliny the Younger, in a letter to his friend Tacitus, had written of an eruption, and had told of ground tremors warning those living in the area, and of the blaze and fury that gave them no time to do more than save themselves. The city vanished on the same day as Pompeii.

That morning, as always, tellers of news in Herculaneum's forum spoke in whispers close to the client's ear to keep poke-noses away.

IN ROME: The Flavian Amphitheater, which some were calling a colosseum, was almost ready and 12,000 Jewish slaves would blood the arena after hauling the last stones to finish the walls.

IN MOROCCO: From the legions in Mauretania came word of fighting with a tribe of Negro giants in the south.

IN POLAND: The Navy had put troops ashore down a river in the wild lands beyond East Germania.

IN THE SUDAN, EGYPT: Nothing had been heard of the legion sent to find the birthplace of the Nile, and their families were advised to mourn.

IN SPAIN: At Caesaraugusta people were stricken with fear by lights in the sky, and it was said that Icarus had landed there, asking for Daedalus, his father.

IN GREECE: Zeus, sire of the gods, pointed in anger at the head of the Cassia family in Achaia, and he drowned himself to wash away misfortune after gaming away his property at dice.

IN SICILY: Poseidon swallowed three ships beyond Syracuse, and a salved mariner told of the god riding a silver stallion on the tallest of green seas with a mile of seaweed curling from his helmet.

IN THE TYROL: Quintus Roscius, a banker of Noricum, found his daughter keeping tryst with a slave in his stables, and killed them. The Aediles freed him because only by such an example might the moral peace be kept.

IN FRANCE: A bullion caravan was raided near Lugdunum by Gallic cavalry, and two legions lost their pay.

IN CHALCEDON: A woman predicted the death of Titus Caesar within the year, and the Proconsul ordered her held for that time and if she spoke truly she would live, and if not she would feed a bear.

The news-tellers ended by calling out that with Caesar, as in every part of his empire, all were held in the fondest embrace of the Great Mother, Diana. Peace and triumph were always hers.

And the client tossed the coin for payment, and if Caesar's head came uppermost, he kept it because the likeness was sacred. But if the profane side turned up, he paid it.

At the banks and exchanges there was satisfaction at news of gold found in Britain. Prices were steady because harvests had yielded well by Caesar's acumen in calling home many of the legions to work the springtime fields. Admiral Pliny's new volume was on sale at the book-stalls in the Forum's shadow. The scholarly Admiral was with his fleet a few miles away at Misenum, and leading citizens had his promise to lecture from the public podium on the marvels of nature.

Titus Caesar sailed that morning for his villa on the crags at Capri. His bodyguard of Praetorians took leave of the city and marched out behind their musicians in splendid phalanx of crimson, gold, and burnished steel.

Down at the quays merchants stood with their scribes ticking off cargoes of precious goods, and shipmasters stood by to see that no tick was lost. The harbor lay downhill and wagons passed under water gates holding the city from high tides, going on, around the walls to the main avenues north to Rome, south to Messina and east to Brundisium. A haze of smoke along the coast marked the town of Pompeii. Furnaces and workshops and bazaars were there, and people untold. But in Herculaneum there was no vulgar trading or making of goods, and few bakers, grocers, butchers, and craftsmen in the arts, enough to serve the city's needs, no more.

Mansions were three and four stories high, set in cloistered gardens, with terraces and porticoes looking over the bay. Drains, sewers, and water pipes were all under the paving. Garbage flung in the street earned a heavy fine. There was no slum. The city fathers were jealous of amenity. They allowed no clutter.

At midday the deep-toned gongs rang, and long lines of chariots
wheeled away from the Forum, taking their owners home for the day's
first meal. Fragrant smells of rich messes came through iron grilles
over kitchen windows, each with a whine of beggars underneath. In
noon silence the sun shone almost with a sound. A dog stood on his
hinds to drink from the fountain, and his lapping was louder than the
sough of cypresses outside the College of Augustales.

On that day the Roman Peace was shared in Roman cities all over
Europe and Asia Minor, and along the entire North African coast.
Palestine was in process of settling after many years of war. Solomon's
Temple was in the dust, and the Hebrew nation was being driven by
the tens of thousands to march wherever the consuls called for labor.
Vespasianus had died during the year. Titus, his son, had been ac-
claimed Caesar, and proved his wisdom by making certain of Africa's
riches in strengthening all the garrisons from Egypt to Mauretania.
Iberia worked at peace under the Eagles. Gaul had come to terms by
diplomacy. Britain was held under the sword, although the Celts
showed themselves not unaware of virtue in the Roman Law. North,
south, east, and west the legions stood guard, and worshiped Mars,
god of war.

But most of Rome knelt before Diana, the Great Mother, of the
flaming eyes and frigid heart. Her priestesses and vestals took the
prayers and the offerings and directed the lives of millions. Other gods
were given respect. Fortuna brought luck, Poseidon held the storms
at sea, Urania looked after crops, and many another did some good.
But in all matters, in every way, only Diana held triumph.

Worship of Mithras, god of light, came from the East along the
caravan routes from Persia, Byzantium, and into Europe through the
valley of the river Danube. The god's plea for gentler dealing among
all men brought converts in every country, and the sting of his scripture roused the best minds and gave the religion solid base in schools
and universities. But most Romans cared nothing for soft speech.
Their territories were won by the sword, and swords would keep them.

Jesus Christ had died some fifty years before in the reign of Tiberius.
Apostles built many churches in Asia Minor, and the spread of their
work to Rome itself roused envy among the Dianists, and hatred in

the temples of Mars. If Mithras were shunned for teaching against harsh action, the Church was abhorred because of the doctrines of Peace and Good Will, which turned swords into plowshares and made warriors like unto little children. Persecution had begun in Nero's time and went on year after year. Christian—once a term of contempt —became a title of honor because of the way the martyrs died.

The scriptures of Christ and Mithras were strangely alike, though only in the Christ was the new, and beautiful, promise of Grace by Salvation. Slowly at first, and then almost overnight, Mithras lost his family to the Church. And because those of Christ were commanded not to worship any graven image, all the temples and altars and the statues of Mithras were smashed. The lord of light turned back.

Rome's superior minds sought the Church, and so did the humblest, freedmen, serfs and slaves. In between, a body of people liked the comforts that Diana seemed to give them so abundantly. Those people held power by the vote. They controlled the Senate.

But all, Senate as well, was controlled by the College of Diana under the aegis of Caesar. Whether abroad or at home, every citizen was assured of Diana's blessing and the Roman Peace, and none more than most of those living in the city of Herculaneum on the morning of the twenty-fourth of August in A.D. 79.

But only a few hours later they were homeless, and the land was buried under boiling mud pouring down from Vesuvius in eruption.

And for almost 1800 years the city lay like a sleeping beauty, awaiting the kiss of a workman's pickax.

THE FLAME OF HERCULES begins in early June of A.D. 79. A war galley flings spray from her blades, beating up the Tyrrhennian coast toward Ostia, seaway and harbor to the city of Rome. The sun is gone, evening comes, and a mariner climbs to the masthead with a lamp. . . .

Richard Llewellyn

Ischia
August, 1954

I

Calm fell when the war galley turned the cape, but the rowers were
helped by a strong tide. They could hear the legionaries on the main
deck shouting a chorus of praise to be safe in home waters, happy at
thought of stamping on the solid stone of Rome's streets.

Two decks below, little light showed in the oar banks. Both lictors
were gone for their evening meal, and their whips hung on the arms
rack in sign that harbor was almost made. The galley-master dozed
at his table, waiting for the call to Senior Mess, and the mallets he
used to beat time for the oar stroke were half out of his hands.

Garvan, the Gaul, chained in the third oar bank, looked at the rack
of spears and swords, thinking what he might do without his chains,
and he spat his hate of the galley-master, the lictors, and every Roman
and all of Rome. But in a wave trough, where sound stopped and
only the waters breathed, the curse came loud as a grasshopper's strid-

ulation, and the galley-master opened an eye direct upon him, and a
smile came to one side of his mouth. His hands withdrew from the
mallet handles, and he stood, taking down his own whip, of rhinoceros
hide tipped with strips of copper sharp as flaying knives. He came
down the steps into the aisle between the two teams, ready to snap
the lash, as always, first this way, and then that until flesh and muscle
flew, and his target lay bloody and voiceless, ready at will to kiss a
foot in brute surrender, or spirit held and the body died.

Garvan called in the Gallic blood of his father for strength to keep
his teeth shut, and his tongue curled and his throat closed to any
sound so that a Roman might not hear a Gaul made less than his
breed. The nearness of harboring, and the rowers' chains made the
galley-master careless of his safety. He had no watchers, and the light
showed only the gleam of his breastplate and the metal fringe of his
kilt. He strolled between the first and second banks and paused at the
third, looking Garvan from head to foot as if he chose where the lash
should take first bite.

But the pause was long enough. A sense, nothing so much as a
feeling, seemed to pass not from mind to mind but from skin to skin,
filling the oar deck with a pulse that brought every rower to scrape his
ankle shackles together.

Garvan watched Khefi the Saracen, with a place in front, slide his
left arm, a muscled serpent, along the shaft of the oar. The length of
the chain allowed him to stretch only halfway into the aisle. The
galley-master raised the whip, and set his feet, bringing himself barely
within reach.

"When the blood drains, remember the order," he told Garvan.
"We work aboard one of Rome's war fleet, not in some fishing caique.
And I'll take that look off your face for the last time. I never did like
a towhead with brown eyes. Never trust a man with brown eyes. So
said our Nero Caesar. There was a lover of the whip!"

The lash flicked and the galley-master moved his foot for better
balance. Khefi stooped and his fingers flew out and caught a handful of
the kilt and pulled the galley-master into the oar bank. Zetak the
Phrygian, standing next, struck him twice with the wrist shackles and
crushed the bones of his face, and Khefi took the head in both hands

and wrenched the neck until it snapped loose. The sound went un-heard in the noise of two hundred slaves, grunting together in pushing the blades through the water, with the clanking of their chains in between.

Garvan ripped the oarlock key from the dead man's belt. He turned the rusted lever at his feet, pulling his hand and foot chains out, and went behind the rowers' bench to unlock the waist chains. Excitement flew to every spirit, and men long lost to liberty began to whine from open throats.

A light came from the midships deck trap, and a sailor came down with a lantern. Quick to think of making all appear in order, Garvan thrust the key at Zetak, and crawled to the galley-master's table, lifting the mallets to beat the stroke, and grinning men rowed with him.

The sailor put the lantern on its hook and he might have gone free, but in turning away he showed contempt of slavery by spitting on a slave. But Khefi had been spat upon by many another, and now his hands were free. The sailor halted, seeing the loose chains, and the open locks, and his eyes went to the galley-master's body. Even while his mouth gaped to shout warning, Garvan reached over and beat the mallets left and right on his head, and went back to beating time with no pause in rhythm.

Stavros the Greek, beside Zetak, pulled a knife and marlinspike from the sailor's belt. Khefi put his head out of an oar vent, looking at the land, and turned back, pointing overhead at the deck. His eyes carried warning. The oar banks were crazy in a fight to take the key, and all the blades trailed, and the soldiers might be down at any moment.

Garvan knew the fierce pull of hope. He tore at the lictors' bench and slid it through an oar vent, and wriggled out himself, dropping head down, almost under the keel.

Three years of grime and sweat seemed to peel away in that first clutch of freezing water. He broke surface, feeling the drag of his chains. The galley's stern was dark overhead. The bench floated, and he held on. Zetak swam as a dog toward him. Khefi lay on his back, peaceful as any gull. Stavros paddled, riding with one knee over an oar.

Nothing moved on the water. The galley passed into evening.

Stavros slid the oar through holes in the bench legs and Khefi held onto the blade in front, and Garvan sat on the seat to pilot, and Stavros and Zetak held on behind, and all of them kicked out together.

Currents carried them, and let them go, and carried them again, and they cared nothing. Frozen as they were, and weighed by chains, they splashed the phosphorous, and played as children. But nobody had spoken, because the years of silence on the oar banks had idled their mouths. Garvan remembered the words of his Gallic mother-tongue, but only whispers and a stammer came from his lips. And the others laughed, and whispered and stammered with him.

Stavros drummed on the oar shaft, pointing toward the North Star. Over a wave crest they saw a riding light. Garvan slid into the water, gripping the bench, and taking a breath and going down, held under by the chains. He came up again, and the galley was almost alongside. A sailor reached out with a boat hook to pull the bench in, watched by a group in naval uniform. Garvan tipped the bench so that the hook missed, and perhaps the sailor saw the plank's edge, and let it go for driftwood. He called out that all was well, and Garvan sank again, and came up, watching the lights going away.

"They will undo the seaweed itself to find us," Khefi warned in his strange language, made stranger by a frozen mouth. "I swear not to live if any of you are taken. Let us wander together until the gods are good to us. In that way we shall go free."

"Let it be so," Stavros said. "I am a son of the goddess Artemis, and I feel her smile warm upon me. My life, and your lives, are one."

"I am son of no god," said Zetak. "I spent money on them all, but getting nothing, I'll spend no more. My hand, here, is my pledge."

"Mine too," Garvan said. "I have a sword."

"And I," Khefi said. "Zoroaster keep you strong."

"I have a knife and a marlinspike," Stavros said. "Artemis the huntress will guide them."

"You have great faith," said Zetak.

"Has she not smiled so far?" Stavros inquired. "Are these waters not the messengers of her promise? Be certain!"

Khefi pulled twice on the oar in warning, and then stood to his waist in froth. Garvan felt his feet touch pebbles, and he clasped hands with the others in a circle, laughing at the stars, and dancing, despite the chains, to feel alive and free.

"See how she smiles, my Artemis!" Stavros shouted. "Praise her!" But Khefi squeezed his mouth shut.

They were ashore in a dark land. Firelight reddened the open door of a cottage not far up the beach, and a smell of soup came on the breeze. They went closer, swords ready, careful not to rattle their chains. A woman moved across the light, and Garvan saw her slit ear lobes, mark of a slave bought at public auction. Khefi went boldly to the door, and Garvan followed, to a blaze of sticks, and warmth, and the woman's frightened eyes.

Garvan held out his shackled wrists and laughed at her, pointing to the limp rags of her ear lobes, trying to tell her that she was sister in misery. Footsteps crunched the shale outside, and the woman ran to the door. But Khefi leapt, catching her by the skirt. A man came in under a load of twigs and dropped it beside the fire. Stavros had the knife at the small of his back before he had straightened.

And, hearing the woman speak, Khefi howled like a trodden dog, and swung her about, clutching her in tight embrace. The woman's husband went to his knees, putting his hands above his head, and all three wept, with their arms about each other. Khefi cut his thumb, and smeared the blood on the woman's forehead, on her husband's, and on his own; thus his friends might know they were three of the same people. Then womanlike, the wife brought loaves, and hollowed them, and filled the spaces full with hot meat and vegetables. From a store she brought sheep's milk cheese, and dried figs and grapes, and they ate until the skins of their bellies shone, tight and sore under the chain scars. The man put twigs for their beds and laid hides upon them, and in that time Stavros made a likeness of Artemis in the bread dough, and stood her among leaves picked from the garden. Khefi prayed to Zoroaster, facing the east, with the man and his wife. Zetak watched them, and went outside to pick his own leaf-offering for Artemis, and knelt with Stavros.

Garvan said his nightly prayer to Mithras by habit, and as if Somnus himself had ordered it, he turned away to sleep. But the woman's

husband brought another slave with tools to break their shackles, and
the hammering, cutting through the iron wrist cuffs and anklets,
started fresh wounds. Women came, with leaf poultices and unguents,
and tore their clothes for bandages. But in all the work, in all the
moments, every face was covered, and nobody spoke except Khefi,
to the woman or her husband, Masr'Afoun. For in that way nobody
knew a name or any face.

Garvan went with Masr'Afoun by hidden ways to the harbor, and,
from all the craft pulled up on the sand, he marked one, fast enough
to slip any except a galley, but small, and old, and not worthy of
search.

When the moon had gone, they went out, with gifts of food, kin-
dling for a fire, flint and tinder, and bait and a fishing line. Masr'Afoun
said that a night's sailing would bring them in sight of a flaming
mountain. In the nearby ports of Misenum, Puteoli, Naples, or
Stabia they would find ships ready to sail everywhere in the world, and
many a captain to give them space and food against his price.

Masr'Afoun rested his forehead on his hands, showing his sadness,
and the woman wept. Khefi pleaded with them to leave their slavery
and try their fortune. But the man touched the woman's slit lobes,
and his own, and Khefi's which were unmarked. All free men would
know them for slaves, and therefore they would stay. Better to live so,
under the brand, and go into the grave and become whole in the dust,
he said. Khefi knelt, and kissed the woman's feet, and bowed before
them. The stolen boat went easily into the water, and Garvan steered
south by west, watching the stars.

In the morning, as Masr'Afoun had said, they saw islands in the
mist, and high mountains on the mainland, and one, higher, on the
horizon, covered at its summit by a pink cloud.

They took turns at shinning to the masthead, keeping watch for
naval ships, or for the fishers that nearly always were ready for small
piracy. A naval scout ship's red sail came out of the seaward mist,
and Garvan whistled a warning. He slid down, taking the tiller from
Zetak, and steered inshore. The others lay under the gunwales, hidden.
But with a strong current and a good breeze the scout ship gained.

"Under the net with you," Khefi ordered Stavros and Zetak. "If they push a spear in and you feel the blade, swallow your pain. If they board us, we fight. Towhead, childish in looks, hold the line and go to the prow as if we were elder and younger brother."

"My father would die of shame," Garvan told him. "Childish in looks? I have the thicker beard, dear maiden-cheeks!"

"We Saracens pluck our faces," Khefi grinned. "We do not use the blade except on noisy and impertinent throats. To our duty, now!"

Stavros and Zetak curled under the net, and Garvan sat in the prow. Khefi spilled the basket of bait, and the birds flew as if they circled a fishing boat. A voice from the scout ship commanded him to lie alongside, but he pretended deafness, and the bigger ship's bow might have cut him in two, but he knew the maneuver, and brought his tiller hard over and in time. The red sail came down, whistling in the block and tackle.

"How is this?" he shouted at the officer in the stern. "Do you treat every fisher as an enemy? Are there none to fight that you must pick the innocent and hard-working?"

"Come, no prattle," the officer shouted. "Who are you, which port, by whose commission?"

The scout ship was a tidy craft of new rope and timber and shining metal. Eleven men, Garvan counted, five in the crew, and six soldiers in a group aft, with the officer.

"We are family of a veteran of Sulla's legions," Khefi said. "Our great-great grandfather was given his land and rights in these waters in return for hard services."

"His name," the officer shouted. "Where from?"

Before the officer could say more, Zetak sat up in the middle of the boat, and gathered the net in both his arms. Khefi might have kicked him back, but he stood, taking the net in one hand and throwing it up in a dark cloud. It spread as he threw, stretching all the way over the ship's rail, and settled as if hands were there to peg it, over the heads of the soldiers and the officer.

Zetak shouted a strange and savage cry, and jerked the net's draw-strings taut, bracing himself against the gunwale. The soldiers screamed at each other, fighting to free their arms. But in a couple of easy drags Zetak pulled them all to the rail, and toppled them overboard. Khefi swung the boat about, and let the net trail. Thrashing water showed legs and arms, and sometimes a drowning cry was clear. But when the drawstrings were straight down in the sea, and the net's weight was likely to tip the boat, Zetak let them go.

Khefi went over the ship's rail. The first sailor tried to crush him with a capstan lever. Stavros threw his marlinspike and hit him in the neck, and he dropped. The second sailor came at Khefi with a long knife. Khefi seemed to make a design with the sword point and the sailor's hand came off at the wristbones, clean.

The other two dived overboard, and the handless man followed, bellowing his pain.

"So, here's fortune!" Stavros laughed, holding out his arms. "Artemis, richly you paid me for your shrine!"

"Baal take her!" Khefi said. "Here's your sea horse. We'll chop her lines about, and stain the sail. We'll have the best ship on the seas."

"Out on your dreams!" Zetak shouted. "See, a galley!"

Khefi and Garvan ran for the mainsail. Stavros took the tiller and Zetak hauled on the anchor. The galley, of about four hundred men, made no change in her course, and went on to the northwest into the mist.

"We'll beach her and do our work in peace," Khefi said. "Zetak, you've served your time with net and trident. Never did I see sweeter casting!"

"You do well yourself," Zetak said. "To make plain, I have respect for all here. No man could find himself in better company."

"Death tastes the same with ants or heroes," Khefi said. "I'm not one to die. Make ready to lower sail. Drop anchor!"

They were in shallow water under a cliff. A fisherman's shelter was built inside a cavern with a net drying on poles outside. They ran the ship on the sand, and Khefi went up to the screen of hides, and in.

An old man, white-haired, came out and beckoned them. Khefi sat by a fire, with fish, bread, and a flask of wine untouched until they came. The old man spoke a language nobody knew. Khefi spoke Arabic, Zetak in Phrygian, Stavros in Greek, and Garvan in Gallic. All spoke, but nobody understood until they talked in Latin.

Khefi got up, a giant of pale skin, with eyes the color of milky glass, and pulled out his tongue between thumb and forefinger, and made a cutting motion. His meaning was plain. Sooner than speak the language he hated, he would lose his tongue.

The old man waved him away, and poured more wine.

"I am Uriel, of Agrigento, a town to the south," he said in good Latin. "We are on the northern side of the Bay of Naples. The mountain of fire behind the cloud is called Vesuvius. The isle to the south is Capri. This one ahead is Pithecusa. Where do you go?"

Stavros, with an eye on Khefi, told him by signs that they were escaped from the galley. But Uriel pointed to the bandages on their wrists and ankles. They had no need to tell him.

Khefi looked at them all, and his eyes said that the scars were plain as split lobes. Whatever their story, or their wealth when it came, any Roman would know their status and lay a charge against them. They were prisoners on sight.

Uriel talked as if to himself. Foolish, he said, to come so far, and fail because donkey's ears grew on donkey's heads. Better to use the heads they were given and tarry some days, practicing their Latin speech. If they hid the ship, and rested in the quiet groves on the mountain, sleeping well and eating their fill, he would find a woman wise of herbs with a salve for clearing scars. Such things were always possible for those with patience. Once the scars were gone, they might walk abroad, free and fearless. As they were, they dare not enter the smallest village.

"And why, old one, should we trust you?" Khefi asked. "If you informed, you'd be richer by four rewards."

Uriel smiled, and pointed to a couple of pieces of wood nailed to make a cross, hanging on the wall.

"Charity brings richer gifts than all the gold," he said, and lifted his baggy trousers at the ankle, and they saw the skin whiter than the rest of the leg. And he nodded, and laughed.

"Shackle scars," he said. "I served in the galleys. I was released by fortunate amnesty when Claudius died."

But Khefi gave him the water pot to cleanse his mouth of the Latin, and the old man drank, happily. He led them to a cleft in the rocks where they might hide the ship, and when they had stowed her above the tide line, he showed them a path leading up the mountain. With his gifts of fish, and loaves, and carrying their gear, they gave him farewell, and set off on a long climb. In late evening they built a screen of olive branches in front of a hole in the rock, and set twigs for their beds, and over a fire they cooked the fish, and ate.

"Let us now resolve," Khefi said, looking into the flame. "Who will lead and command?"

"Not I," said Zetak. "Tell me when to fight, and when I am to be in Pergamos, my birthplace. Other things I know not."

"I have a dream for Heliopolis," Stavros said. "Beyond that, nothing."

"You are soon satisfied," Khefi said. "Garvan, your Gallic shore is less than five days away. But you know the coast is thick with galleys. We'll have to get you there behind Iberia, perhaps. What say you?"

"Behind the moon, so long I greet my father," Garvan said. "Are you, now, admiral and general and quaestor and aedile, good maiden-cheeks?"

"I am one to tear an ear out of any head the better to speak sense into it," Khefi said. "Listen then. We shall capture a well-born Roman. We shall hold him or her to ransom. We shall divide the money into four. We shall then take a crew, and sail until we are all once more with our people. Is any against?"

Garvan held up his hand.

"I will not sell any man or woman as an animal," he said.

"Ransom is not sale," Khefi said. "We mean no harm."

"Let Romans pay me for my wasted years," Stavros said. "Yes!"

"Hear the Greek," said Khefi.

"They shall also requite me," Zetak said. "Yes!"

"Hear the Phrygian," said Khefi. "What says the Gaul, of the raw-silk hair and brown eyes, and the look of a milkling satyr?"

"Neither yes nor no," said Garvan. "I am one of four, and filled with fish and sleep. Bring the night into us, good Mithras, god of all, and let our dreams be filled with stars and all the flights of heaven. I will not treat any man as an animal."

"No Roman is human," said Khefi. "Therefore sleep, counting your money."

II

Garvan awoke before the others, and lit a fire. Zetak went out with Uriel's gift, the fish net, and came back not long after with a sheep. Stavros sliced the meat and cooked, and Zetak helped Khefi put an edge on the swords. Khefi talked of capturing a girl rather than a youth, since her parents might be the more willing to save her gentleness. Garvan had little to say for, and much against, and rather than keep silent he left them.

The cave was holed in outcrop high above the Bay of Naples, and he walked on a level, shaded by straw mats on ranks of poles, roofing lemon trees from hungry birds. He counted it little to his credit as a man to be hiding with others, ready to steal anything, much less to steal a girl, for the means of going free. Even so, it was good to draw breath in freedom among the sharp scents of lemon and the odor of leafmold, and luxury yawned in being able to move legs and arms at will. He looked at the shackle scars on his wrists and ankles, and at the flesh about his waist and thighbones calloused by more than three years of chaining to the rowers' bench, and a desire for revenge against Rome, and all its people, was not stronger than a sense of disgust in having to use some well-born Roman as hostage, girl or not.

A good, whole sigh he drew, and looked across the green miles at a fleet of war galleys turning into the harbor. The sails came down as one, and in the same moment all the oars ran out of the vents, and splashed, and dipped, and splashed again.

He grinned, remembering the bite of shackles, and the sting of the lictors' whips, and again he had to kick his feet in the soft earth to assure himself that he lived without imaginings.

Over his shoulder the volcano peaked against blue sky. A thick, fiery stem grew from the tip of the cone, and blossomed in a bronze ball of smoke that drifted off, soft, in white streamers. Earth and rock cooked in a molten liquid poured in a dribble, at times deep orange and sometimes almost pink, over the side of the cone. Lower than the pines on the mountain's fat slopes, olive groves were thick, and lower still the citron trees banked in stone terraces one below the other in wide uneven stairways. Then the clutter of vineyards, and golden cereal patches, and the river's green flanking of pasture, and dark-leaved orchards.

A rich land, and plenteous; one to be loved, he thought. He found a place in his mind for the Romans' boast that no land came near to theirs in beauty. But there was a taunt in daring to think as a Roman. Hours of listening to lictors' boasts could have made him a pawn.

Gaul was as beautiful, as much to be loved, he swore. Until he kissed that earth again, he was nameless among men, bearing a slave's scars he might never lose. And he swore again to carry a burden of hate against Rome and all Romans, their lares and penates, and their lands and territories, their language and manners, and all the peoples in their keep.

Against the cave's darkness he watched Stavros' head of short black curls in profile, arguing with Zetak of the sun-bleached bristles straight as thatch. The two men were almost the same height, but Zetak was broad and squat, and except for scars and weals Stavros might have passed for an athlete. Khefi was the tall one. His shadow fell across them, and in taking the sheep's carcass off the spit, his breadth almost covered them both.

Garvan felt himself at loss. He was shortest and slightest—and worst, he was youngest. Khefi had almost thirty years. Zetak counted twenty-six, and Stavros twenty-three. Garvan could own to seventeen, no more.

Not far away from the harbor the red roofs of a town in flowering gardens brought up the affair of the hostage. While they gnawed the sheep's bones, Khefi decided with the other two to go closer. A careful patrol, the capture of a favorite son, or daughter, and then a fat ransom, and a fourth share each; and that was freedom enriched.

They had begun talking easily among themselves. Arabic, Greek, Phrygian, and Gallic all had a place. But what they spoke had plenty of the Latin metal, at least to Garvan's ear, although he dared not say so.

They walked down the mountainside in the quiet of the vineyards and orchards, almost within a shout of the first houses. Zetak warned of movement in a garden. The four hid in the bushes, and in time, for a gate was unlocked, and a man came out, bareheaded, in a white tunic showing his paunch. A whip swung in his hand.

Khefi sprang, wrapping an arm about the man's neck, flinging him face down. He pressed the arm until the man's eyes bulged. In a whisper he asked if there were not rich men in the area. The man tried to speak, unable to see Khefi's face, or any of the others.

"All men are rich in these precincts," he made effort to say. "These are part of the confines of Pompeii and Herculaneum. Pompeii, to the south, feeds and clothes and builds for the Army and Navy, and the traders have their dealings in all the empire. Herculaneum, a city much favored by Caesar, lies before you. Only Romans may enter by invitation of one living there, or by permission of the centurion at the Gate House. All others must go around the city by land or sea."

"A particular city," Khefi said, putting his knee on the man's neck. "Who is your master?"

"Romans have no master except Caesar," the man said. "My name is Tirius Porrius, living in the Street of the Silver Horses."

"Wealthy, too," Khefi nodded. "Are there wealthier?"

"Many." The headman tried to ease his face, but the knee pressed hard. "Of greater wealth in coins, and in goods, in ships and lands."

"Their names." Khefi pressed the knee impatiently. "The wealthy, with a family. Youths, or maidens. Which family is most blandished by the gods?"

"The house of the Pinarii." Tirius Porrius was not eager to talk, but the knee was an argument. "The maiden Genessa is the only child. The son died in battle. She rules the house. A vestal of Diana, barely seventeen years."

Khefi smiled, content.

"Her name again," he said. "And her father's?"

"Genessa, daughter of Sulla Pinarius."

"You said Pinarii!"

"The family is Pinaria. When there are more than one, we Romans use the plural. We say Pinarii. You are not a Roman?"

"I am better. I am a Saracen. A living Roman is a deathly offense to me. Where is the Pinaria house, or the house of the Pinarii?"

"There is one in the town, and one outside."

"Nearby?"

"A javelin's throw."

"Lead me to the house of the Pinarii. Point to it. Say nothing. Do you know me?"

The man turned down his mouth in a no.

"You never will." Khefi held out the knife in front of his face. "A word from you, and I wrap your entrails around my little finger. Are you ready to walk?"

The man raised his eyebrows in a yes. Khefi's knee was still on his neck.

"Then walk," Khefi told him. "Never stop. Lead on!"

Tirius Porrius led them a short way along a rocky lane, and pointed to a high wall among the pines.

"Here is the house," he said.

Garvan took Khefi by the knife hand.

"This man Porrius," he said. "He goes free?"

"To walk the gardens of his gods," Khefi said. "What, would you let him run and rouse the city?"

"He goes free," Garvan said. "We are not murderers. We are imprisoned men, taken in war. We do not kill the unarmed."

"He is right," Zetak said. "Let him be gone."

"Hold him," Stavros said. "He might have money, too."

Khefi fingered the tunic's cloth.

"Poor quality," he said. "He wears shoes of wood. He is unshaven. Are you rich, Roman?"

"I have enough," Tirius Porrius said. "Kill me if you will. Only my family will suffer."

"He speaks well," Zetak said. "Let him go."

"He'll bring the city guards," Khefi said.

"If he brought the legions, I would tremble," said Garvan. "For the guards, I'll scratch my neck."

"Scratch, then," Khefi said, and looked at Tirius Porrius. "These things you heard, Roman. Take your life as a gift. Go!"

But the man faced them all.

"I take your gift," he said with a hard eye. "I make you one in return. I had meant that you should walk into a nest of swords. Listen well. The daughter is in tutelage to the College of Diana. She is there with her tutors in that garden even now. If you fear Diana, have a care. And if not, go to your doom. Farewell!"

He turned from them, and in no hurry walked off, away from the city.

"A veteran," Zetak said. "He made no flinch. I like them well, these Romans."

"I liked it little what he said of Diana," Stavros said. "Are we come so far in the palm of her hand that now we must be crushed in her fist? What was his meaning?"

"Chatter," said Khefi. "Words will not replace an act. Let us go into the house and see what manner of life they lead. If they are indeed rich, or like yonder Porrius, poor in all except spirit."

"Remember Diana," said Stavros. "If what he says is true, I'll play no part."

"A hair of my head for Diana," Khefi said, picking at his smooth scalp. "Let her strangle with it. Come, one of you. Let's look over the wall and see our money."

The high wall of rocks was set with shrubs along the top. Khefi motioned Garvan to climb up and look into the garden, and bent, taking him by the ankles. Garvan drew himself to the top, and looked through the shrubs, at a garden lost in blossom and set with fountains and statuary.

An elderly woman under a blue parasol sat at a table with sewing. Two younger women, both in pale blue and white vestments, made poses of the dance with a girl in a pink and gold toga. He saw them only for a moment, and lowered himself.

"That's the girl we want," Khefi grinned on the way back. "We hold her, and tell her father to give us ten thousand gold talents."

"A girl isn't worth so much," Garvan said in great astonishment.

"Her father may want to bargain," Khefi said. "Her mother may talk until the poor man feels ten thousand for dear silence is little enough."

Garvan shook his head.

"Girls couldn't have the value of ten, much less ten thousand talents," he said. "What's the use of girls?"

Khefi shrugged, hands behind and shoulders up to his chin, and told the others what had been seen.

"A question," Stavros began. "Remember how the Roman spoke of Diana? How were these women dressed?"

Garvan told him of the younger women in pale blue and white. Stavros held up his palms and fright was in his eyes, and he trembled.

"Mother Diana will forgive her son," he whispered, and turned to Khefi. "Where Diana Artemis puts her foot, take heed. Let us find some other to bind, or we perish!"

Khefi talked with him, and walked a little way with him. But when they came back, Stavros stood with folded arms and closed eyes. Khefi looked at Garvan and Zetak, and shrugged again.

"I am faithful to Zoroaster and the spirits of my fathers," he said. "We believe there is no help except in ourselves. When we do what is to be done with sense and all real effort, then we expect all help. But if we fritter here and frolic there, we expect none."

"My thoughts too," said Zetak. "Let us take the girl."

"Not I," said Stavros. "Find me one of other gods except Diana, and these paws will take her, and this mouth will ask her price."

"Enough of gods!" Khefi shouted. "Must we spend our lives in chatter of gods? For me, there is escape and good money. Who is with me? To escape this blighted land? I die even to breathe this air polluted with the Latin stench!"

Garvan turned his head until his eyes were sidelong.

"Breathe the air?" he repeated. "Who did I hear threatening to cut out his tongue rather than soil it with Latin? Who spoke Latin just now? And whose tongue is still in his head?"

"Yours!" Khefi pointed his finger. "And keep it still. I speak no Latin. I make myself understood to these animals, you follow? That girl you saw. That's our merchandise. We shall take her. Let us go to the terrace behind the garden, and climb in without noise. There might be a troop of guards. They must be watched for. When you stand in reach of the girl, you're a rich man. Remember it. And act!"

They went back along the lane, to a goat track, climbing behind the garden to the lower terrace. Khefi went up to the right with unwilling Stavros, and Zetak went up far to the left. Garvan went in between. But before he reached the top, a hymn in women's voices brought him about. A blue parasol showed among the trees. The girl in the pink toga walked in front, and her long hair spun gold in the sun when she turned, throwing a plait of flowers to the woman with the parasol. Then she was gone, and the hymn was thinner, farther off, among the garden's blossom.

Garvan heard Khefi's whistle, and gave his own finch rill in reply, looking through sunlight cut in white swaths by the straw matting. Khefi's shaven head poked over the terrace stones, and his teeth shone in a grin, and his bandaged wrist pointed down.

The girl with the golden hair brightened a clearing beyond the garden, not more than a hundred paces below. The sun blessed her, shining in the toga's folds that rippled with every move she made in knotting a garland. Someone called her, a high yodel, and she turned and went into the trees almost as a petal floating, and the breeze caught pink furls about her leg, and showed the golden straps of her slipper.

Zetak's chirp might have come from a sparrow. The Phrygian crawled in the dark shade, pointing around the bend of the terrace. The girl and her party had taken another path.

Khefi beckoned to Garvan, and crawled to meet him.

"Go with Zetak," he said. "He'll net the girl. When she is caught, you will carry her back to camp. Zetak will go behind with Stavros to cover you. I come behind all to give warning if any follow us. If we succeed, Stavros will change his god!"

Garvan watched Zetak making trial casts with the net, taking a cumbrous armful, and throwing it to billow and cover its object, and pulling the drawstring to prison it easily, and all done within a blink of an eye.

"He is not the only one to change his god," Garvan said. "I prayed I might not war upon a girl. But Diana is nothing to me. I shall go."

He hoped, nonetheless, that the girl might turn back to the garden, or anywhere except where she might be taken. Zetak clapped him on the shoulder, and they hurried down the terrace to a place above a rock garden where the path turned. The women's voices came nearer in a wailing and a jingling beat of the sistrum, bringing unease to them both. The goddess Diana was known to be a zealous guardian of her children. Stavros, bravest of men, had shrunk from so much as talking about her priestesses, and he was sitting up there, with his fingers in his ears and his eyes tight shut, and praying that his friends might not succeed. But Zetak said that he believed with Khefi. Men wasted time in thinking of the gods.

"Whether one god or any other," he whispered, "why should a man cower? I played gladiator before my time in the galley. With the net and trident I scored more than fifty victories against the best with any weapon. Always I offered a black pigeon to Hera before a fight, and a black goat after. She failed me once when I had greatest need. One of the Emperor's bodyguard called me a Phrygian dolt. Instead of taking him in a corner, I beat him in the palace courtyard. And the Emperor heard of it. I sacrificed a flock of the finest goats in the city. But just the same, I was sent to the galleys. Against Caesar, who is a god?"

"Why not sacrifice to Caesar?" Garvan whispered. "For me, Mithras. But how can I tell? Has he dealt kindly with me?"

"The gods smile when all goes well," Zetak whispered. "When things go wrong, they turn away. I've found it so. From the moment I was chained, I swore against all the gods. The man beside me on the oar prayed to Io, and the fellow next to him had spent a patrimony on Minerva. All around, everyone called on different gods. And everyone dragged his chains. Heh!"

Garvan raised his head among the flowers growing on top of the wall. The women's voices seemed to stay below, in one place, and he turned, a little at a time, looking for movement. First he saw the blue parasol shielding the older woman, only a sling shot to his right. A little nearer the two priestesses, young women with blue paint about their eyes, and red mouths and silver powder in their hair, sang together, weaving ropes of flowers into a wide garland.

And over the ledge a few inches before his eyes a girl's right hand took a flower by its stem, and plucked, and plucked another, and another.

A left hand, small, wearing a ring set with a red stone, clawed its fingers on the rock. Light gleamed in the smoothness of the flesh. A tendril of golden hair tossed by the breeze made a bright arc, and the top of a head came above the stone, and in a heavy breath a girl's face, with lips in a pucker from effort of reaching for a white flower.

Without thinking he broke the stem, and gave it into her fingers.

And instantly he groaned, for Zetak would have seen the movement, and now she must be taken. In those moments he passed through the minutes of freedom, and dread of recapture tore at his spirit, but not with the force of shame at thought of buying liberty with a girl.

Even as his mind gave out its sights and sounds, he felt a dimming of that hate against Rome and all its Romans, and the girl's beauty came in its place. By clear light she told the Roman truth, without a word, or a sound, but only a hand's breadth away, with her eyes, innocent and fearless, and sparkling full of restless life.

He saw them, and smiled into them, thinking of the first glorious moment of hope, though never of this, to stand in a stare, and worship.

Genessa Pinaria was young in her glance, fairer than he had dreamed; not pale or white, but fair of blood in fine skin, with eyes much lighter than the sea or sky, and a maenad's mouth, and gold, bright golden hair unbound, cast golden shadow in her face.

She looked at the given flower as if the gods had spoken, with eyes gone round and an open mouth. But then she remembered the giving hand, and turned only her eyes toward him. But where, at first, he could have sworn them some color between the clouds and the peaceful sea, now they were almost black, and stranger still, full of laughter, and then the lids half closed, and the mouth puckered in another way, as if she had a thought to keep.

Zetak found a hole in the wall for his toe, and stepped up to look over. But the rank growth hid the girl, and he saw only the woman with the parasol.

"Great Zeus!" he whispered. "Here's our chance!"

He got down, and took the net, and ran with little noise around the turn to the garden. The women saw him and broke their song, and the older woman screamed, closing the parasol and running toward him.

Garvan saw the laughter go from the girl's eyes, emptying as a tossed bucket, and fear came in, almost as if she knew and accused him. His mind refused it. He would not be cause of fright in any woman, much less a girl of so much laughter. He saw her fall; but haste to climb the ledge made him lose his grip, and he jumped back on the path. He sprinted for the garden, cursing the weakness in his legs, by no means healed from the years of shackling. The women were screaming, and even as he turned the corner, he heard men shouting in answer not far away.

But the priestesses had thrown themselves at Zetak, and one clung to his back, and the other was so tangled in the net that he had no chance of a cast. And while the three struggled, so the girl stepped about them, cold-nerved as any gladiator, throwing stones at Zetak's head from not a yard away. Already she had bloodied him twice and a third stone hit him above the ear and his knees gave.

Garvan shouted, running toward them. One of the priestesses and the older woman came at him on the instant, teeth bared and fingers crooked. But then at a shout and a rolling of stones on the hillside, they turned, seeing Khefi, a giant in a loincloth, whirling the short sword above his head. The priestesses, with the colors smudged in their faces, ran to the girl and flung their arms in front of her, and the older woman followed. But Khefi reached them, and slapped first one priestess and then the other, knocking them both in the earth. He took the girl by her hair and threw her toward Zetak. The net flew in an easy cast, full over her, and the drawstrings tightened, and she lay screaming, trying to kick.

Shrubs up on the right of the hill waved and parted, and four men in silver helmets and breastplates broke through. The priestesses shrieked, running toward them. Khefi looked first at the men, and then at the girl, and again at Garvan.

"Carry the prize," he told Zetak. "Myself and towhead, here, will attend these louts. They're no fighting men. Only watchmen. Eh, Garvan? Gauls laugh at such, eh?"

"I was to carry her," Garvan said, watching Zetak lift the burden and walk away. "Or do you change plan at any moment?"

"At moments when the rope slips, yes," Khefi laughed. "I know something of young men caught by a pretty face, or a straight toe, or whatever takes a youngster's eye. I saw you up there. She poleaxed you!"

"She?" Garvan said, feeling a blush that might blister his face. "I saw her for a moment——"

"Give your attention here," Khefi warned, placing himself ready for attack. "Don't throw your spear. I can take three at the onset. Wait for the fourth to lift his sword. Then thrust——"

"I used a spear in my cradle, good Khefi," Garvan said. "Let me know if you've seen better!"

The four men, heavily armored in polished steel, came at a run, shields up, short swords held to stab. Garvan ran in, and shifted the spear shaft at a moment when they expected him to throw, slipping it through his palm and turning it until he held it in the manner of a long sword. He pretended to jump, but when their shields went up, he crouched instead and slashed the blade under the fringe of their kilts, cutting the knees of two at the caps, and they fell. He ran in, and made two jabs with the spear point, and both men lay still.

Khefi had the sword arm of one twisted behind his back, and was using him as a shield against the other. But when they saw the other two die, both let their swords fall, and threw their shields spinning, and fell, face down, in surrender. Khefi strapped them about their necks with a belt, and tied their hands above their heads to a lantern bracket in the wall. Garvan watched him, admiring the strength of his hands and arms. But the women were screaming farther down, and men were shouting, a crowd from the sound, and many feet were on the run.

"Come." Khefi took a sword in hand, and piled the shields. "You go first, and I'll go behind. As I planned. And let me say, I never saw a better spearman. But watch your boasting!"

Garvan shrugged at the warning, and ran up the slope, following Zetak's tracks in the growth, and the marks on the wall where he had climbed. In a little he could hear the brushing of leaves in the orangery further on. There was no thought in his mind to kill the Phrygian, but he was sure that the girl must go free, Roman or not.

Her eyes and her laughter touched his heart. The ring's red stone, perhaps her father's gift, seemed to burn between his eyes. He would not buy his freedom with her tears; and foolishly, he could have gone back to the galley's benches to save the bloom of her skin from any scratch.

But Zetak, a gladiator, stronger and taller, was a foeman to be afraid of, and never more than now, sure of the bait that would bring him money and escape. Garvan twirled the spear, and looked about for Khefi, and, seeing no sign of him, ran on.

He saw movement in the grove, and, running closer, he heard the girl's voice, and saw how she struggled in the net that Zetak carried over his shoulders with her head on one side and her legs on the other as a man might carry a goat. Anger came at thought of hurt to her pride. More, he feared she might never laugh for him again.

But then he halted in real anger, for Stavros ran down the path, and helped to lift the burden off Zetak's shoulder. They stood, listening and looking, while Zetak threw sweat from his forehead. The net was still. Stavros pointed toward the sound of swords in clash. Zetak wrapped the net's drawstrings about a branch overhead, and made sure the knot was safe. And both, taking their weapons, ran along the terrace toward the fight.

Garvan felt it against his nature to play the traitor and rob his friends. But there was no rest in other thought. The girl must go free to laugh again, and sing, and pluck flowers. Freedom bought with a girl's tears was less to live for than servitude in a galley. In one was liberty with no escape from disgrace. In the other, pride, and faith that chance of liberty would come.

He ran swift, and leapt at the drawstring, cutting the knot, and opening the net wide.

She stood, lower than his shoulder, looking at him through a loose plait covering her face. The toga was ragged, and she had lost a slipper.

"Go," he whispered. "My friends meant you no harm. They would have taken money for your beauty in ransom."

"But you think me unworthy of a price?" A whisper that matched her mouth for magic reached through the tangled plaits while her busy fingers threaded them. "Am I so evil to look upon? So poor a bargain?"

"Never!" Denial came on a sigh that surprised even himself. "Go, then. I could kill a thousand for enough to buy freedom. But you must not be hurt."

She threw back the mended plaits, and looked at him, and he thought another sun had risen on his life. She smiled, but she made no sound, and he led her by the hand with no word in his head. Yet he wondered if the pressure on his fingers were in a dream, or if she meant a secret trust.

"You are a fugitive slave," she said, pointing at his bandaged ankles.

"No slave, but a free Gaul captured by default," Garvan said. "This is your mark, you Romans."

"This is justice. You were in the wrong."

"The Roman wrong."

"And if you are in the wrong in law you must be punished. That is our discipline."

"Your words rattle as beads on the abacus. Have others no right to laws?"

"The laws of barbarians are customs of a tribe. See, these vines would grow wild and yet give grapes. But they grow with greater harvest when the husbandman has trained them over the trellis. This is the act of law, that we bring to all peoples."

"Men are not vines. They have brains."

"And use them not. Who could deny that our way is better. You know the power of Caesar, and the greatness of our empire? Are there others as great? As rich?"

"Which husbandman trained you?"

"Only my father and the teachers of the College of Diana have trained me," she said. "Should I listen to a slave marked with chains? What would I learn? To be held in a net, a sheep for sale?"

"Then we'd find your worth," Garvan laughed. "And would your bleating impress us with the quality of your fleece?"

"You have rude speech. Roman training would improve you. What is your name?"

"Your name, I know, is Genessa. It is enough. I have no name until I am a man unmarked. Know me as your friend, seeing you with eyes unbelieving."

"Unbelieving? What makes you doubt?"

"That such loveliness could hide so little feeling, and no brains at all. Go back to your dances and your flowers, and there shine."

"I shall pray Mother Diana for your life," she said. "When she finds you for me, I shall keep you. I like you well. Her power stay with you, unruly Gaul!"

"Make an apology to your lady mother," Garvan called after her. "I would lie in the earth and grovel before her foot to know one thought of her forgiveness. She fought as a true mother. She and your tutors showed good Roman blood!"

"But that was not my mother," Genessa laughed up at him. "She is my governess, of Cisalpine Gaul, and a darling. She shall be rewarded. Though nothing will endear you more than that you called her my mother, she will hate you for calling her a Roman. But I will champion you. I have a warm corner for the Gaul!"

She gathered the toga, and jumped down to the path, and ran, and he saw that her heels were pink below white ankles.

III

He wanted to follow her, to play guard all the way back to the garden. But the fight was loud and many were shouting. He ran downhill, to an orchard, where a dozen men in leathern armor struck at Khefi, Stavros, and Zetak, fighting back to back in a triangle. Garvan counted seven bodies as he ran, and another fell to Khefi, and Stavros dropped another.

Garvan shouted the Gallic battle chant, and threw the short sword, hitting a man in the back. Another turned to meet him, and Zetak cut him down. Garvan jabbed the spear at another's face, and when the shield went up, he pulled the haft back, reversing his grip, and lunged, piercing the man under the breastbone. Now the odds were better. Khefi struck down two for a wound in his upper arm. Stavros took one, and Zetak sliced one to his knees, and gave another the dodge and hit him in the neck, and tripped a third, kicking him to silence.

The others ran off.

Stavros put his teeth in Khefi's arm and bit, drawing out the blood. Zetak found leaves, and rolled them in a pulp, and put the poultice on the wound, and Stavros wrapped it with strips torn from branches.

"Lesser men would have been taken," Khefi said. "How well this Pinaria is guarded!"

Stavros finished tying the green withes.

"We were fools to set ourselves against the temple," he said. "We must find a household watched by other gods. Artemis Diana frowns. Let men shudder!"

"We are whole," Zetak smiled, wiping his sword. "Our game bird lies in the net. Diana, I kiss you. You served us well!"

Khefi threw away his sword and chose a better from among the bodies.

"We must cast lots who shall go to her father," he said. "Many have seen us. They will look for us. Garvan, I thought you a hothead given to stretching his wings. But you have a right to speak. You fight as a veteran. How is this?"

"Farmers and fighting men are in my family," Garvan said. "From childhood I learned the plow and shovel with the sword and spear. If I know the plow, should I hold from saying so? The mock-modest are most to be watched, says Mithras. They live in half a lie. Who knows what other things they mock?"

"Here we agree," Zetak said. "The modest ones, and the foot turners and blushers, these are readiest to use a knife in the dark. Gaul, what shall I offer you for the spear? That, and my net, and I'll fight a score and win without a wound!"

"Let him keep the spear," Khefi said, and flexed the muscles of his arm until it moved with comfort. "He's worth six swordsmen. Zetak, bring our catch to the top, and we'll meet you."

Garvan knew the time had come, and his mouth dried against owning to his crime. Khefi could kill him with his hands. The other two were no triflers. Either he must say what he had done, or else play the innocent, not as their friend but as a cheat. Even as he thought of it, he also thought of the girl, and imagined that some part of dishonor would also fall on her.

"I must tell you," he said. "Liking not this business of selling women, I set her free!"

One by one, Stavros tying a sandal, Zetak buckling a belt, Khefi watching a hand come in use, they looked about. Doubt stalked in every face.

Stavros slapped his thigh.

"I knew it!" he laughed at the branches overhead. "Artemis or Diana, call her one or other, right or wrong, she has her way!"

Khefi squatted, rubbing his shaven head with a bony hand. But he was laughing.

"Why must I be deaf against myself?" he asked the sun. "I knew him lost in the moment she hooked a finger at him."

"I would not be freed by holding any girl, even the Gorgon," Garvan said. "Let me see a man, somebody able to give an account of himself. How could I face my father and tell him I take my place by purchase of a girl's body?"

"I'll crawl to a dog's death if he's not right," Zetak said. "Set in that light, we're all bought by a woman. Four for one. This has a taste of maggots."

"Mah!" Khefi sat in the squat, resting his arms on his knees and letting his hands hang. "This is certain. We had the money in our hands, and now we have nothing. If our Gallic friend wants a Roman male instead of a female, let him go down and supply us with one. I have no opinion or any feelings. I want money to buy passage, and gifts of silk for my family. How is the vote?"

"He can't go alone," Zetak said.

"But I will," said Garvan. "Without help."

"Let us keep watch on the way in," Stavros said. "I don't doubt he'll get what he goes for. But how will he get him up here?"

"We got the girl up here," Khefi said. "Let him put his choice in the same place. We'll wait for him where he freed the girl."

"That seems fair," Zetak nodded. "I vote so."

"I too," Stavros said.

Khefi looked up at Garvan, and pointed to the bodies.

"If you want to change your clothes, do so," he said.

"Am I carrion, to nose about the dead?" Garvan demanded. "I am as I am, and the dead are dead. Listen for my call, a finch off the nest, some time this evening. Mithras guard your hopes!"

He left them, going at a run down the path, and then cutting across the terraces, almost in the way Genessa had taken. For moments he halted behind trees, watching, listening. The groves were silent. He ran on, past the Pinarii house, a long flat-roofed villa among pergolas and vines, to a paved road that led past other villas to a main avenue, and a signpost giving the distance to Herculaneum.

A herd of fine cattle tolled bells about their necks; and farm carts heaped with flowers, fruit and vegetables, and trolleys loaded with jars of wine and oil were all going the same way. Garvan walked beside them on the shady side to see without being seen, and because his clothing was poor as the drivers' and herdsmen's. But he also wanted to hear them speak, for a man could be told sooner by his mouth than his dress. He heard a gabble of Greek and Latin in a dialect he could never copy, whereon he decided to speak as himself. He admired the broad, smooth road. A repair gang set large, flat stones together, edge touching edge, without mortar. Over the flat surface they poured a reddish mixture, smoking hot from a kiln built at roadside, and others pounded it flat with iron weights held on long poles. Where the smooth red road turned to enter the city approach, a barrier stopped all traffic. Market carts and animals went along a stone track under guard of the city police. Garvan held back, since all were questioned, and watched drivers of chariots getting down to fit their horses with straw shoes, and to muffle the wheels of their vehicles with straw bands. A notice cut in marble warned all to move in silence that citizens might not be robbed of the peace they had bought as part of their property.

"You won't get in," a policeman told him and others. "Take your chance if you want to. Follow those people in front, and don't stray off the main road. The Praetorians will open your veins if they catch you."

Garvan remembered Tirius Porrius saying that nobody was allowed inside the gates without a citizen's invitation, or by word of the com-

mander of the guard. The wide avenue beyond the barrier gleamed
in patterns of mosaic, and tall columns on each side held rafters bearing flowering creeper and vines. At the end, in a tower of carven
white marble set in the city walls, Praetorian guardsmen in golden
armor, crimson kilts, and crimson-plumed golden helmets stopped all
those going in. Some were allowed inside the bronze door, but others
were sent about. Garvan watched an elderly man turned back, and
hurry beyond his years, pausing to take his breath, and lean against a
column. His gray hairs were combed, and the beard was trimmed, and
his toga was white, and his shoes were tipped and strapped in silver.
He went closer, and saw the man at peace with himself, without anger,
but thoughtful.

"Sir, greeting and good day," he began. "It was in my mind to
enter this city. But if you may not, what should I say?"

The old man smiled a good smile, and even his beard seemed
brighter in the sun.

"Titus Caesar visits the city today," he said. "No stranger may enter
for any reason. Be patient until noon tomorrow. Then you may try.
The city's own guard is less strict than the Praetorians. You are from
northern Gaul, are you not?"

Garvan looked into the old man's gentle, smiling eyes.

"I traveled there as a youth to study at Lutetia and other cities,"
the old man went on in the same tone. "I liked it well. That is how I
guessed at your roots. I am myself from Germania Transrhenana, but
I'm not a Roman citizen."

"I am honored to think we share the same space," Garvan said.
"But I wish I could have set an eye on Caesar."

He could have added that, given any chance, he would have spiked
the tyrant with the spear and so paid many a Gallic debt. But the old
man must have guessed what passed in his mind.

"If they let you in, they'll hold that spear," he said. "If you told
them you were a student traveling between periods, and about to earn
your citizen's toga by army service, they might let you through. If you
said you have a hope of becoming a Praetorian, and that you want to
shout for Caesar, and to glorify Rome, and of all Romans the Praetorians first, why, watch them pace and puff themselves."

"But if you know these things, why are you on this side of the gate?" Garvan asked.

"I have no excuse of youth," the old man said. "They know me as an alien. And they also know that we of the Suevi and Tungri peoples have no reason to hail Caesar or to love the Praetorians. You saw them put me out. The same they have done all my life."

Under the gentle voice Garvan heard the thunder of spirit long held in dominion by cruelty.

"Have they done in Transrhenana what they did in Gaul?" Garvan asked, watching the Praetorians at the gate passing some in, and sending others away. "Did they take women and children as slaves, and slaughter the males? Did they destroy the cities and burn the scholars and teachers in their schools?"

"More," the old man said. "They brought slaves of other countries and built Roman cities above the ruins of ours. And they told all the world to see how the land shone now that barbarians were gone. These things, and more."

"As," Garvan went on, "burning down the temples and burying the priests alive? And cutting the hands off artists and workmen in the arts and putting them to draw the plow in place of cattle?"

"This, too." The old man turned to Garvan in a look of power, and yet not stern. "They burned the libraries. They sought to banish all knowledge. Many acts of war and bloodletting lie at our door, but as one of the Tungri, I say in certainty, that never did we set hands upon the scholar."

"Someday our time must come," Garvan said. "There are many of us."

"Is it safe to say so?" the old man smiled, throwing off the toga in the noonday heat. "How know you I am not a spy, ready to call the quaestors?"

"I could not believe it," Garvan said in a frown. "You said as much as I."

"Spies are always at elbow." The old man held out a coin taken from his belt. "The happiest smile, the most agreeable manners, the smoothest tongue belongs to the spy. Watch your words, boy. Food is costly in the city, therefore take this money."

"I was taught never to take money for nothing," Garvan said, and put the coin in his headband, and caught his spear at the neck. "But if I am challenged, I shall use it to prove I am no beggar. If all goes well, I shall look for you. My name is Garvan."

"And mine is Ultor," the old man said. "You shall find me at the house of Petrus Borbo, in the Street of the Happy Tortoise. What gods have you in their keeping?"

"One," Garvan said. "His name is Mithras."

Ultor nodded, but his smile held no welcome.

"I know it well," he said, and made a sign. "Peace be with you!"

"Light cherish you," Garvan said, raising his hand. "Light fall in your path and around you!"

He stepped out, wondering at Ultor's manner, scholarly and yet martial, although there was nothing of the taskmaster in him even when he spoke of tragedy among his people. There was sorrow, and wrath, but in balance and without hate. He tried to guess how enemies of Rome could travel without guard, clothed and fed, and with money in gold to spare for strangers. He found no answer, and turned his mind to matters nearer himself, and walked with the crowd toward the bronze gate. Smoke billowed blue from the top of the tower, and cut away as if no fire were there, and ruffled again, short and long, in signals.

A crowd of people, most from farms, in clothing with the smell of the bazaar scarcely out of them, were being turned away from the city gate. Many of the men and women were in tears, some clutched at their hair, and others beat their breasts. One man might have torn his new toga, but his wife pulled at his hands.

"Would you waste more money in Caesar's honor, poor fool?" she screamed. "If he misses your voice among the thousands, be sure he'll send a special chariot for you!"

A dozen people waited to be questioned under the shadow of the archway. One by one, or as a family, they went in to a seated Praetorian officer. Some passed through, but most came hurriedly out, covering their faces. Many, it was plain, felt disgrace not to be citizens of Rome, and if they were citizens, they were shamed in having none in the city to vouch for their probity.

The man beside Garvan was a citizen, flaunting his white toga with
the purple edging for all to see, and every other moment he wrapped
it in a different way, and flung and swirled as if he held the honor as
an itch. He looked at Garvan's patched rags and bare feet, and at the
strip of sheepskin tied about his head.

"You, fellow, you're a stranger here?" he asked in a loud voice,
bringing heads to turn. "From whence?"

"From the south," Garvan said as loud. "I am a student from
Crotone."

"Ha," said the flaunter. "Then we should speak together of philosophy. Know you the school of Anaxagoras?"

"Indeed," said Garvan. "His, and other systems I was taught."

"Then tell me," said the flaunter. "What is your opinion of the
greater intelligence?"

"Who is greater than Caesar?" Garvan said, knowing little enough,
except that all was being heard by the Praetorian officer. "Are these
things of interest to you?"

"As a citizen of Rome, all things are of interest since all things belong to us," the flaunter said, knowing too that he was heard. "Come
in with me, and I will be your brother for this day, and we will stroll
the Forum and talk on these high matters."

A guardsman sent the elderly couple in front to the officer, and
turned to the flaunter.

"Who signs for you in this city?" he asked.

"I am from Paestum," said the flaunter as if he were ready to stand
in the Senate. "I drove eighty miles to greet Caesar!"

"Drive eighty back," the guardsman said, cold and straight. "The
city is full."

"This is not proper to be done to me, a citizen," the flaunter shouted.
"I will see the aediles!"

"They meet the Lord Caesar," the guardsman said. "Go!"

"No lowly one speaks so to me!" the flaunter shouted again. "Let
me speak to the officer. The Senator of Campania is my friend!"

The Praetorian officer pointed at him with a gold stick, sitting back
in his chair with his golden shin boots up on a stool, restful.

"The fine for conduct unbecoming a citizen is multiplied one hundredfold on imperial holidays," he said quietly, with a smile. "Are you so wealthy that you can afford to obstruct a guardsman in the performance of his duty?"

The flaunter said no more, but suddenly his toga looked too big for him, and he turned about, and pushed his way through the crowd.

The Praetorian officer with only a few more years looked at Garvan head to toe, and at the spear. Garvan meantime looked at figures worked on golden armor, at the badge on the helmet, and the pleats of the kilt, and vowed he would take a set back to his father as a gift. The officer shifted the sword hilt, and cleared his throat.

"Well," he said good-humoredly. "I saved you a lot of talk about the Greeks, at least. What have you to say to me?"

"I heard that Titus Caesar was to pass through the city," Garvan said clearly. "I wanted to hail him after my own manner, and to glorify Rome as my father taught me. But more, to watch the Praetorian Guard, and how they carry themselves. I long dreamed of wearing the red plume before my father."

"The dream augurs well," the officer smiled. "You have the height. What friend have you in the city?"

"None," said Garvan.

"You are mistaken," the officer said. "Go, talk to the petty officer here."

He signed to a Praetorian with less gold about him.

"Let him enter the city," he ordered. "And speak with him of service with us. He has the stamp of the eagles upon him."

A second Praetorian came from the guardroom, and the petty officer spoke with him in a whisper. The two came close to Garvan. The second Praetorian was exactly like the first in height and bearing, but he wore more gold about his shoulders, though far less than the officer.

"Listen here," he said in a low voice. "This is how we stand. The company goes to guard Caesar at Capri tomorrow. Will you promise to get back here before nightfall? Enroll tonight and come with us."

"Tonight?" Garvan stared. "As soon? But am I fit?"

The second Praetorian pinched Garvan's biceps and pulled a face at their size.

"Fit, by Gracchus!" he laughed. "No trouble with you, I'll wager. Will you come to us, boy? We'll see you get the fat of all that's going. Praetorian treatment, in short. And Capri, that's milk and honey, if you like. You'll serve with free men, of great honor in battle, and no small merit in time of peace. Well?"

Garvan sent a prayer of thanks that bandages covered his scars. "First I would see Caesar," he said.

"With this company you'll see him every day," the petty officer grinned.

"Leave it too long at your age, and your school or the city council might sling you at the Army or the Navy," the first Praetorian warned. "Make it today and come to us. Look around you, it's a man's life. You could come in the arena this afternoon and see the sports. Free. You'd be nearer the fights than Caesar himself."

"Why do you press me?" Garvan asked. "Is Rome in peril that she needs me so much?"

The first Praetorian frowned at the second, and for a moment the two looked as though they might swell out of their breastplates. But then they nodded at one another.

"No," said the first, looking at him with one eye shut. "But I see you are not the wet wood we had thought. There is money for enlistment, and this you knew. If we let you in, what share is ours? A half?"

"Too much," said Garvan. "How would my father listen? He would want the half. My mother would like a peplum of linen to wear on feast days. I would want a coin or two. When a man has money, there are many wants."

"Spoken like an old 'un," said the petty officer mildly. "Very well. A tenth part. Not a sesterce less. Such is the bargain."

"How long have I in the city?" Garvan asked, as if it were little matter.

"Till the sun hits the gnomon for the second hour." The petty officer pointed at the sundial on the guardroom wall. "That'll give you plenty of time to see the procession and get back here. Then you can follow the company to the arena."

"Good," said Garvan. "But tell me this. Why was I let in where citizens were turned away?"

"Citizens come as stones in a load of gravel," said the petty officer. "But Praetorian timber is hard come by, and rarely got. Do you find the tall trees every day? Citizens are leaves on the streets. Praetorians are Caesar's bodyguard, rare men every one. Remember this, and take pride. There are few of us!"

The petty officer put his hands on his breastplate as if he would feel his rarity, and the other mouthed his chin strap as a bridled horse tastes the bit. Both looked distantly away to the empire's farthest marches, but with no tremor, for all was safely in their keeping.

"My father will have great joy in knowing his son part of such splendid company," said Garvan. "The officer was kind to me and I would know his name."

"Aristarchus Cornelius, Ensign of the Legion of Vespasianus," the petty officer said. "Fortune has it we're without our centurion, or we'd enroll you now and save time. But the countryside crawls with jail breakers and runaways, and he's out directing the search."

"Do Praetorians search for runaways?" Garvan asked. "I'd thought you held for sterner work?"

"No work is sterner than when Caesar gives command," the petty officer laughed. "His good friend, the Tribune, almost lost a daughter this morning. By the rods, when the culprits are taken they'll suffer!"

"How, lose a daughter?" Garvan felt his skin go cold. "Are the roads unsafe?"

"Even in their own house," the first Praetorian said, holding up a finger. "The Pinarii, the Tribune's own family. Think of this. Attacked in their own garden!"

"Yet the girl spoke without fear when she came through," the petty officer said. "A true daughter of her father. And Caesar's favorite. So the signals go out to other legions to scrape the land foot by foot. They'll be caught. How they'll welcome death!"

"And I'd thought all Romans well guarded," Garvan said sadly. "Caesar's favorite, in her own garden!"

"Now the family has us to guard them," the petty officer said. "Before, they used those cutthroat dogs from the temple. Are you by chance a Dianist?"

Garvan shook his head.

"Good!" the petty officer laughed. "We are loyal to Mars. He shows us greater favor. And this reminds me. The candles burned to him are bought from me. You'll want a pair tonight. Give me the money, and it's done."

"And for special offerings, and use of his shrine, you'll come to me," the first Praetorian said. "Pay us now, and all will be prepared for you."

Garvan took the gold coin from his headband, and spun it. Two hands reached for it, but he took it back.

"Until the second hour," he smiled. "Fortune touch your steel!"

He left them in empty looks and hands outstretched, and walked out of the archway's shadow, through the gate, and into the city of Herculaneum and the smell of blossom growing by the mile.

But he stood in cold amazement, at once admiring and hating, in rage and yet at peace, for now he knew the secret of Genessa's air of grace.

And her beauty hung from a ribbon in his mind as seal to great magnificence.

IV

A wide avenue, surfaced in black and white mosaic, was bordered in red along the gutters, with pavements of white marble on both sides shaded by glass roofs on columns bound about with floral garlands. Flagpoles wrapped in purple cloth held golden shields bossed with Caesar's head, and a golden eagle spread its wings on top of each, pinning a golden festoon. Crimson, and blue, and purple and cloth-of-gold canopies, one after another, swung on poles wreathed in gold and set in regular spaces high above the roof tops, each heaped with blossoms to shower Caesar's passing beneath.

The avenue turned left and right. The main way went on, down shallow steps flanked by urns in high flame with scented herbs, into the wide space of the Forum drawn about a fountain of bronze nymphs playing in spray that made the marble paving shine. Temples to Jove, and Mars, and Venus, and Apollo and Diana, each with a shrine of

the deity in a garden, all burned offerings among choirs of priests and
priestesses along one side. At the end the law courts' golden doors
stood half open under a flower-banked colonnade. On the left flags
and flowers dressed the exchanges and banks and the public gardens,
all crowded with people. Men and women strolled in white and purple
or wholly in shades of purple, and parasols twirled bright colors on a
thousand shoulders, and on every head a wreath of Roman myrtle
gleamed pale gold, and flew a tail of purple ribbons.

Garvan felt his spirit become a weakling.

Here was outward sign of power that ordered all things from Africa
to the isles of Albion, from Iberia to Thrace, and in every territory
between. A dream of destroying the monster had livened his hours
of slavery. It seemed simple enough to collect all Rome's enemies into
one army, and march. The nations of the Keltae, and the Thracians,
Boetians, Greeks, Persians, Arabians, to a man would join the battle
flags against Rome, or so he had thought.

But among all the color and proof of wealth, and listening to the
happy noise of a crowd at festival, he had a doubt. He wondered if
Ultor were not also doubtful of conquest and so, perhaps, careless of
revenge. Something about the man's eyes had seemed unsure, or wist-
ful. And suddenly, in all the splendor, he felt disgrace for his rags.
But in fury he told himself he would not feel envy, and lip-serve the
monster in its elegance, remembering the bideless grief of millions that
had helped to make it so.

"Take your fill, lad, take your fill!" A half-naked man with a red
beard, and a head of red curls crowned with vine leaves, carried a
goatskin with the neck held out toward him. "The wine of Falernius,
Rome's best, and free to all in honor of Caesar. A gift of the noble
citizens of this great city of Hercules. Kneel, and take your fill!"

"I'm not a citizen," Garvan said, and might have passed on.

"Neither am I," Redbeard said. "Is that good reason to deny yourself free wine? Kneel, and let me pour. Not for Caesar. For us!"

"And who are we?" Garvan asked, standing.

"Who could we be, but us?" Redbeard still smiled, perhaps for the
benefit of any watcher. "We, who haven't a rag to our backs or a shoe
to foot. Kneel and drink!"

Garvan knelt and made a funnel of his hands, and a stream of wine filled his mouth.

"That's it," Redbeard said. "Don't mistake me for one of these citified puppets. I'm too well dressed. Drink some more!"

"Enough." Garvan wiped his mouth, and stood. "How do you, a stranger and no citizen, get work from the Council?"

"I wanted work, and I looked for it, and I got it," Redbeard said. "I knew on a festival day they'd want wine carriers, so I dipped vine leaves in red ochre for a fillet, and I went along to the City Hall, and I stood straddle-legged before the city fathers, and I laughed at them. I got the job!"

"But how did you get in the city?" Garvan asked.

"Climbed the wall, of course." Redbeard opened his gray eyes. "What's amiss? You think I'd let those Praetorians pick my bones? You've got to use your head. See mine. With the vine leaves I made a Silenus out of myself. So tonight, I eat. Here, put some more wine in you. Liven up, lad, liven up!"

"I want no more of chains," Garvan laughed. "Let the Romans be lively."

"These?" Redbeard looked at the crowd, smiling still, but his mouth was fixed. "Porcine brutes. All they're good for. Leathering stone and showing off their finery."

Garvan heard Ultor's warning about the spy, his manner, and his tongue.

"Their soldiers scored the victories," he said unwillingly. "Their merchants took the spoils. Why shouldn't their families enjoy the profits?"

Redbeard looked at him as if, smiling, he could kill.

"They took my family for profits, too," he said, shifting the wine bag. "I'm looking for a wife and five children. A boy and four girls. I, also, will enjoy profits when I find them. And so will their owners. I've sacrificed at every altar in every city I've been in. Here, wet your hands in wine. And pray for me. Pray for us!"

He splashed the wine on Garvan's hands, and pinched the neck tight again. He threw up his red head, shouting a long-drawn sound that could have been a cry of wine servers, but Garvan heard the tremor and he saw the man's eyes, and knew that he gave the prayer call of his god.

"So-ho!" Redbeard ended his shout, and faced the crowd. "Another brave 'un satisfied. Farewell, good youth. Call me Tadmon if we meet again. Remember, through the Forum, along toward the sea, and hard by the statue of Hercules, there you'll find the peace of Vesta, and her temple of the common hearth."

He put his head close.

"Sanctuary, if anything should befall," he whispered. "No man knows when one of these brave citizens might take it well to challenge you."

"Challenge me?" Garvan asked. "For what?"

"The look in your face," Tadmon grinned. "Romans hate those in rags with eyes that look above their height. Be heedful, and remember. Vesta has a sanctuary for us. Save us!"

"Wait!" Garvan took him by the sling of the wine bag. "How do you tell I am one with you? How should you know I am not a spy, or one friendly to Rome?"

Tadmon laughed, deep and content.

"I watched when you came in," he said. "I saw your limbs spring hard as if you'd struck a hundred blows. I knew. D'you think I'd have let you drink otherwise? See, I make a bully's brawl of invitation. But no Roman drinks of this. I, give a Roman a drink? Of less than his own blood? Watch!"

He went calling among the crowd. A citizen broke from talking to another, and knelt, carefully folding his toga with the purple stripe, holding a hand cupped under his lower lip. Tadmon tipped the bag, but the spout was held too high and the drinker caught it, impatiently pulling it down, and waiting for the wine to pour. But Tadmon's fist was tight about the neck and nothing came through.

"Very well, fool!" the drinker shouted. "Let the wine come out to me!"

"Aha!" said Tadmon, open-eyed and -mouthed. "So that's what you want?"

He took his fist away, and instead of a drinkable stream, a pale gush poured over the Roman's head, wetting him through. He lost balance and sat in the gutter. His friend came to help him, and Tad-mon jumped here and there to give a hand, but the bag gushed wine without pause, and the more Tadmon jumped, the further the wine splashed, and Tadmon jumped like a landed fish, trying to come at the victim first this way, and then that. He wet and rewet him in the gutter, and soaked his friend head to toe, and sopped any within reach, until a woman took a splash and screamed, high above the laughter, for the city police.

Tadmon squeezed the neck again, and turned to the two cursing wet-legs, putting his hand to his head in tragic apology and appealing to the crowd whether or not he were innocent. And the crowd was his friend, for the vine leaves and free wine were marks of festival. Two city police ran up, and took the scene in a dry look at each person near the puddle of wine. Tadmon stood, looking down at his toes each curling in a different way, and sang a little, though out of tune.

The wet-legs argued, unheard in the noise, pulling at their clothes. The woman and her husband shouted, and the rest of the crowd catcalled. With no other word the policemen marched the wet-legs off, still shouting, and Tadmon eased the bag on his shoulder and looked about until he caught Garvan's eye.

"They're much stricter with citizens than with us," he said behind his hand. "Citizens are all supposed to know better, and behave them-selves. I'll have the jails full of them by tonight. Farewell!"

Loud cheering came from the end of the Forum, and the crowd around the sides hurried to the barriers. A body of cavalry trotted out of the street on the right of the courthouse, and behind, men in the purple filled the seats of a line of golden wagons. After them Prae-torian musicians, forty in a rank, and each rank playing a different instrument, with tall copper horns openmouthed in rear. Behind them a regiment of infantry in blue and red, and a crowd of girls in white, all dancing with half-hoops of flowers.

"Hail, the Senators!" the crowd shouted. "Senators, hail!"

Drums beat, and all the instruments were raised on a clash of cym-bals. The band halted beside the fountain, and the horns blew a re-frain in harmony, and the doves flew off the courthouse roof, spraying the Forum with their shadows.

Pipes and flutes, and the silver and copper played together in time to the drums, and even a lazy crowd had to tap their toes, and soon their heads and shoulders all moved together as if they marched.

Now seemed a good time, when all the people were in one place and other streets were empty, to go through the city, and make sure of a way of escape. Climbing the city wall was easy by himself, but with a hostage to prod, some easier way must be found. So far, look as he might, he had seen nobody worthy of capture. Thinking further, he was not certain what sort of victim he was looking for, except that plenty of money must come with him. All the men he saw were clothed in silks and brocades, and shod in gold- or silver-figured leather. There were few young men, perhaps because most were away with the Army or Navy. Young women passed by the hundreds, all of them beautiful with paint and jewels, though none compared with his memory of Genessa.

He was hungry and thirsty to see her again, and perhaps it was his sharp look on every side that brought a woman, not old, but with a face that might never have been young, to smile at him and tip the strip of sheepskin over his eyes. She wore two colors of orange, and a yellow peplum over braided hair, and her eyes were lined in black paint and her mouth was large and shining red.

"In for the day, sprig?" she laughed. "Come, when will you bathe and attire yourself? You'll be late for the fairings."

"Not I," said Garvan, not unpleased. "These are my only clothes. When I reach the sea I'll swim. And what fairings are there?"

"The day's, of course." She stared. "Is this how you appear for Caesar?"

"As I am," said Garvan. "Would he expect more?"

"I know you wealthy ones," she laughed again, and waved a hand. "Rags and undressed hides to fool the thief, eh? Why, some of these in the silk, they'd like to make you think they had a finger in the Treasury. But most are meager-found and wanting for a copper coin. Well I know it. Tell me where you go?"

"Anywhere," Garvan said, looking up at the sun. "Where my shadow falls, there am I."

"But your house," she coaxed, coming closer. "You have many

rooms, and stuffed clothespresses, and a moneybag with loose strings? Where, and I shall walk with you?"

"Better choose one fatter padded," he said. "You'll walk with a pauper if you walk with me."

"That's my custom," she said. "I am public nurse at the baths. But on days like these I pine for better company. See, there's Servius Mammius, poor as watered soup. And mean as any vinegared fish."

A tall and pale young man, wearing a gold fillet bound with purple a little over one eye, trailed a robe of heavy purple silk, threadbare and patched and sewn again. He passed, talking to another, pushing among the crowd as if he had no care for anybody.

"See his rags," she grimaced, lifting her skirts in contempt. "Worn that all may see it's his republican grandsire's, so far back is he made a citizen. That blear-eye with him is Rufus Ferra, a nonesuch, spending his father's fortune at the dice and wine. But no coin for another."

"You know many of these people," Garvan said with an eye on the short man. "Which, think you, is richest of them all?"

"That one with health, and clean skin, and good feet," she said. "Those things cannot be bought. You are bandaged. Have you been fighting?"

"One here and there," he said. "It is nothing. And I must leave you."

"Not so," she laughed. "Come, I'll take you to the bath. And there borrow a toga for you, and a pair of shoes."

"If I had time, it would be a happy turn," he said, watching Rufus Ferra's head, distant in the crowd. "You have spoken well to me. I hope we meet again."

"But what is this, I'm noed?" she demanded. "A ragged one, in a sweat from the fields, and giving me a no? Come, pay me for my time or I'll swear you in for a salty rogue!"

She took him by the collar, and swung him against the crowd, and he knew himself held by one not unused to heavy work.

"How's this?" he whispered. "What must I pay for?"

"Time, that all men waste except with me," she spat. "Give me your purse, fondling, or I'll swear you in for a cheat!"

"I have none, hussy," he said, and broke her grip. "Stand away!"

"Help!" she screamed, raising hands to the skies. "Help me! A bond-man! A fugitive!"

People came about them, all in a laugh. Garvan took her by the waist, and danced her in small circles, and the crowd began to dance all around them in a joining of hands, and others were singing and stamping their feet.

"Listen well," Garvan said, pretending an endearment in her ear. "I am recruit of Praetorians on license. Shall we go together to the gatehouse, and there tell our tale?"

She looked at him in quick fear, and her hands fell loose.

"Go, off with you," she said. "I want no trouble. But remember, when coins come easy, you owe a few to me, Pharia, in the bathhouse. Back to your mother, sprig!"

Garvan took his chance, and broke the chain of hands, pushing through with no thought except to be distant. The wealthy one he could have followed had gone. He worked through to the back of the crowd, and chose a street to the left, toward the side of the Forum with the public gardens and the offices.

He had to make way slowly, for the crowd was in no hurry.

A blind man, ragged and dusty of foot and covered in ashes, had no trouble, but strode a fine, firm pace, and, hearing the tapping of his shepherd's crook, people drew aside, and gave him clear way. Garvan got closer, until he walked behind, and after some distance, in an open space he tried to pass. He felt his arm pulled, and looked down, seeing himself caught with the curl of the shepherd's crook.

"Hurrying, eh, hurrying?" The blind man laughed aloud. "I got your scent. Ah, a dog's nose. Caught your draft. You're not of this city. You're no Roman, either. A foreigner, in haste? Who are you?"

Garvan pulled his arm from the crook, and stood away.

"What's it to you?" he asked. "How do I smell different from a Roman?"

"Ah, difference of sausage to good solid meat," the blind man said. "No Roman would let a blind man guide him. Too much pride. And not enough sense. There's fear in your voice, youngster. That's got to come out. I'm Afra, the weaver."

"Light shine——" Garvan began, and stopped, for a prayer of light for a blind man seemed silly.

"Go on, go on," Afra laughed. "I know the Mithradites. They deal well, believing well. 'Light shine on you and around you.' Isn't that it? You don't worship in this city, though. And you don't live here. Did you come in by sea? Which port? Puteoli? Stabia? Misenum? Cumae? I know them all. Which one?"

"Not a dog's nose, but a busy snout," Garvan said, worried that the man's voice might carry to some sharp ear. "Why should you know my business?"

"I have no worries," Afra said. "I could bear others. Yours, perhaps? Where do you live? Who are your parents? What do you do? I smell the sea. And wounds. Fear. And doubt. You fidget. I hear you swallow. Should I distrust you? Could you face the quaestors? Or the lictors? Should I call the city guards? Answer me!"

Garvan looked at the blind, laughing face.

"I answer nothing on demand," he said. "I am not a Roman. That, yes."

"Good," Afra said unexpectedly. "I am not. Neither have I ever seen Rome. Romans I saw once, as a child. They killed my mother. That I saw. They killed my sisters. I saw that, too. I was bound, and I could do nothing. But I spat on one of them. Also a Roman. And he put out my eyes. How did you get here? Of which people are you, boy?"

"Of the Keltae," Garvan said, daring to judge his man. "I am of Armorican Gaul. I escaped the galleys. My name is Garvan, and I greet you with an open hand."

Afra nodded.

"Garvan, this hand, too, is open," he said. "Two things. Walk as Romans do. Slow. And practice to cure that limp. Your left stride is shorter than your right. Did you know? The chain on the right ankle was a few links longer, yes? And if a galley officer were to question you, what would you say to him?"

"I'd kill him," Garvan said.

Afra shook his head, and wood ash flew.

"To such an answer, there is only parry and thrust," he smiled. "Tell

him you work a treadmill on property of Caesar's. That's all. Are you
hungry?"

The word brought the taste of food into his mouth.

"Come with me." Afra took his arm, running his fingers over the
cloth. "You need clothes, and shoes. We'll get you some. And the midday meal is ready."

"I want no gifts," Garvan said, taking his arm away. "I shall do well
as I am."

"Eating is not a gift, but a right," Afra said. "Every creature born
must eat. Is Garvan different?"

"I was taught to earn my way," Garvan said, unwilling to appear
churlish. "Work and eat——"

"One of my own kind," Afra said. "Then be my guest. You won't
deny me that? A blind man? Be my eyes!"

"That I will," Garvan said, relenting. "Say where, and I'll lead you."

"To the cookshop of Chote, the Carthaginian," Afra said. "How
this sun brings hunger!"

He tapped his way into a busy crowd among stalls heaped with
toys on sticks in the likeness of Caesar and the gods and public men,
which peddlers carried off by the armful to ply the crowds. Bakers sold
cakes and nougats next to tinsmiths hammering models of trumpets,
and swords and spears. Carpenters made toy wagons and chariots in
the fumes of glue, and the painters brushed gold paint. Among the
dust and shouting Afra passed easily, calling names and hailing friends
long before they saw him. Garvan felt suspicion, wondering how a
blind man could tell his friends from others. But the secret was only
that he knew their voices, and when they reached the cookshop, Afra
paused, and pointed toward a long-drawn sound between a whistle
and a scream.

"You listen to Chote the cook," he said, cupping his ear. "Chote
came of a family of tumblers. His trick was to hang by his tongue from
a rod held by his father. He never fell, except when a Roman cut him
free. Nose and ears followed when he kicked. And his arms were
shortened when they were lashed to his feet. Perhaps for a week.
However that may be, he's a marvel as a cook. But he cooks only for
the doomed. A great part of appetite is in the eye. Blind men, myself

for example, have little taste and no choice. Knowing this, he cooks to please us. Savory messes are happiness for me and my kind. What misfortune have you that he might cosset?"

"A horse's appetite," Garvan said.

"Chote!" Afra called. "Come, screech-mouth. Set a table. Nobility waits!"

"Have you, then, a rank?" Garvan asked.

"Not I, but you," Afra laughed. "Are you not of noble blood among the Gauls? I hear it in your talk. Some learn Latin from their fellows. Others learn it from scholars. Scholars leave their mark in the tongue of those they teach. And who employs the scholar except the nobleman? Here is Chote!"

Chote was thin and tall, and his breath came loud as a cat's purr. His arms were short, barely to his waist, and his hands were a baby's, with a star tattooed on the back of each. He was dark, with long black hair and his eyes were soft as a milch cow's, except that they smiled. And, on seeing them, his ruined face was never seen.

Afra held out a little finger, and Chote also, and they linked the fingers.

Chote tapped his fingers on Afra's forehead, and Afra tapped his fingers on Chote's right-hand shoulder.

"Thus we speak," said Afra, when Chote had gone. "Come, he has places for us."

The front of the shop was trellised, with vines growing thick for shade. Blind and deformed men and women sat against the walls, eating and drinking. Inside the shop men and women crowded the floor. Garvan felt himself unwilling to eat. The smell of the rags, and the bodies beneath, reminded him of the galleys. But Afra walked on, to a lower level, darker, with a few tables and no people. The potmen greeted him by name, with respect, and he returned their greeting, also by name. Chote stood at the counter, smiling. Behind him many fires glowed red, and the ovens showed heat through the bricks.

Here the smell was rich with the heavy steam of soups.

"My family live at the farm in southern Campania," Afra said when they sat at a scrubbed table. "I live here, near the work. Few beyond this city could afford our prices. Have you heard the name of Lydia of Thyatira, sometime of Samaria?"

"The name is not known to me," said Garvan. "I am well traveled, but with little acquaintance."

"The lady employs me in her service," Afra said. "I am weaver of rare stuffs. A place is made for you if work's what you want? Shelter of the best, good money, good food, and a trade for your fingers."

"For the second time, I am offered those things in the same day," Garvan said in discomfort. "This is well meant, and good. But as my fathers before me, I'll never weave more than a tale for my children."

"As I thought," Afra said, and smiled. "What is your purpose in Herculaneum, nobleman of Armorican Gaul?"

"To trap a fat Roman and set him to ransom," Garvan said, daring again. "With my share, buy passage to my father's house, where I belong."

Afra sat against the wall, and laughed the silent laugh.

"And having trapped your Roman," he began, "what then? Where would you go for money? And having got it, could you spend it?"

"These things I would consider," Garvan said.

"You'd be an old man at the end," said Afra. "Old, and in the copper mines many a year. Or long dead, after long in the dying. This is no scheme for one of noble birth. You mixed too long with others not your kind. You might take a rich man off the highway and rob him of what he has. But ransom? For a Roman, in his own country?"

"Somebody must pay us for the years," Garvan said, remembering Khefi, and Zetak, and Stavros. "There should be some way of taking light profit."

"There's no profit except in work," Afra said. "And you mention 'us'? There are more of you?"

"I speak of myself only." Garvan frowned at his carelessness. "My years were taken."

"And mine, and the light that was mine," Afra said. "But Rome repays me now. Where else in all the world are men able to work in peace? And save? And have property of their own?"

"But why, then, do you walk in rags, with ashes in your hair?" Garvan asked. "Is this the dress of one made happy by his lot?"

Afra poured wine from a flask brought by a potman.

"Think," he said. "I am blind, and that means darkness. I use no guide because my nature resists guidance as unicorns resist the bridle. Therefore, I wear rags and I throw ashes in my hair. To those who see, I am a poor fellow and dirty. They give me passage, allowing me courtesies that are rightly Caesar's. Why? They fear to touch me, thinking me unclean. But I, of all men, am most given to the bath. My rags are laundered day by day. And ashes? What is cleaner, or easier to wash away? And the result? Those with eyes become blind of their conceit. I'm helped in what I do and where I want to go. In public places I have room and air, where those with sight are lost for breath. When the theater is full, and patricians are turned away, I have a seat and space on either side. Should I dress myself in gold, and wear perfume in my hair, and be as other men, pushed and thrown, and part of a mob? Or wear rags, and rival Caesar?"

Garvan watched, and gratefully, the many dishes set on the table by the potmen. A chicken, in sauce with a bouquet that made his mouth run, and vegetables at prime were put before them in hollow trenchers of butter pastry, and while he ate, he wondered what he would say to Khefi and Stavros and Zetak. That he must keep his word to them was not in question. But how was another matter. Even so, he felt no regret at having freed the girl. Thought of her, of her eyes, and her mouth, and the pressure of her hand, brought him to stop eating, though not for long.

"Are you familiar with the city?" he began. "The families, and people of rank and wealth?"

"None more," Afra said, cracking the carcass. "I weave for everyone. Even for Caesar. And his father before him."

"Do you, then, know the Pinarii family?" Garvan asked.

Afra put a chicken leg in his mouth, and drew out the bone.

"I know them all, from the father down to the last slave," he said. "Speak soft. The city broods over that name today. Caesar himself has ordered a search of the countryside, twig and stone. The mother and daughter were attacked this morning. For Herculaneum, that is something not to be borne."

"Not the mother," Garvan said. "The daughter and her tutors."

But then he frowned, and bit into a drumstick.

"As I thought," Afra laughed. "You were one of the miscreants."

"We meant no harm," Garvan said. "We wanted ransom."

Afra nodded, and picked up another bone.

"See how desperation makes the best of us a fool," he said. "Sulla Pinarius, her father, would give you nothing. He is Senator and Tribune, and head of the Pinarii family. That family, with the family of Potitii, are jointly guardians of this city from the time when Hercules set the first stone. Do you think he'd waste a word with robbers for any reason? Do you never think in the shoes of another man?"

"Wouldn't he pay to save his daughter?" Garvan asked. "What father is that?"

"A Roman," Afra said. "He'd spend to the last drop of blood not to see her suffer. But not a coin to satisfy a robber. She wouldn't accept such a bargain. She'd kill herself. I've woven for her. A girl from the fountain of all goodness. She is greatly loved. And greatly hated."

"Why is this?" Garvan asked.

"She has ten times what many another woman lacks once," Afra said. "Beauty, and brains, and temperament. The last not less important than the first."

Garvan felt his heart lifted, and although it might have been the wine, he wanted to sing. The more he thought, the more his memories of her came sharp, until he could almost have closed his eyes and imagined her looking at him among the flowers on the wall.

"We should go," Afra said. "There's a pipe in the yard outside if you want to bathe your head. I think we ought to go there right away. In your case, it's the only thing to be done."

"Go where?" Garvan asked.

"To the Pinarii pavilion," Afra said.

"Why should we go to this pavilion?" Garvan demanded, leaning across the table. "I have no place there."

"But you have," Afra said, looking at him with closed eyes. "You will stand before Sulla Pinarius. You will tell him that you tried to take his daughter for money."

Garvan looked at the blind, lined face, pale even in the light of the kitchen fires. It was hard to tell if he was serious or not.

"Are you also mad?" he whispered. "He'd kill me!"

"You would have killed his daughter for money, you or your friends," Afra said. "If he killed, it would be in payment of a crime. Are you afraid to face his anger?"

"No," Garvan said, but without any sure tone.

"Does the well-born Gaul speak lies as other men?" Afra laughed silently. "Or is he one of honor? Can he, indeed, plot to take a girl, and sell her father his own flesh, and yet think himself a hero?"

"I think only in shame," Garvan said. "But what is it to you?"

"The blind, seeing nothing to tempt them, are seldom wicked," Afra said. "The well born with the gift of sight should never be. How could you become a robber? How could you, of name, of position, so twist your father's trust? Have you no wish to purge yourself? Or is the baser Gaul open to challenge?"

"I am true-born," Garvan said in warning.

"Then come with me." Afra stood, and knocked on the floor with his crook. "Chote, count our dishes, and know two honest men, well met, distended by your art, and in a word, sated!"

V

Garvan argued with himself, walking in hot sunshine beside Afra, on the yea and nay of allowing a blind man to talk him into doing something absurd. He was not afraid of what was to happen, though he had no doubt that every step took him nearer to death. It might stand in his favor that he had set Genessa free, but repenting his crime did not absolve him. The act of opening the net was only more proof that a crime had been committed. Yet beneath it all there was joy in thought of seeing her again.

Afra said nothing in the empty streets, but, coming nearer to the sound of the crowd, he began tapping his crook harder on the pavement and shaking his head so that the ash flew.

"A mighty city, this, of Herculaneum," he said at last. "The only city I feel any comfort in. There are strict traffic laws, you notice? Drivers may use only main streets at certain hours. The avenues and public places are for walkers only. So I'm very comfortable. Sulla Pinarius's forebears made that law. He sits at the head of the city fathers, and of course, he is responsible for the upkeep of the temple of Hercules and for the god's tomb in the fire on the mountain. They say a Pinarius and a Potitius carried the god's corpse up there. But that was many a long day ago. However, you believe in Mithras, don't you? Hercules has no interest for you?"

"I know nothing of him, except that he was a giant given to muscle," said Garvan. "I was also told by various mouths that he performed twelve miraculous labors. But that of cleaning out the Augean Stables I do not believe for one reason. No man, much less a king, would keep his cattle in such a way, and neither would men employed by a king allow so many animals to rot in filth. Because of this, I have no trust in the story. And if one is false, all the others may be. So, I disbelieve them."

Afra laid his finger over his mouth.

"Wise men hold such words," he said. "This is the city of Hercules, named and founded by the god. Remember it. Worshipers are all around you. Doesn't Mithras ask you to consider how you should think, and what you ought to say?"

"Keep the light about you," Garvan quoted from memory. "See your errors before you make them. I know the scripture. But errors are difficult to see from the front."

"You sound much more as if you worshiped Dionysius," Afra said. "I did, in my youth. Then I started taking a brace of white hens to Demeter. But it did me little good. I went to Rhea, and Urania, and Cybele. I spent all I had on birds and animals. The gods are very greedy. I even wasted my time with Mars. There, it's all a question of how your life falls out. To these eyes, all gods look the same. A happy mind I found in none of them."

"But you laugh often," Garvan said. "You appear a happy man."

"Half," Afra said, tapping harder. "Whether it's the years, or another faith, count me halfway happy. And we are more than halfway to the pavilion, on the right hand. Now we shall walk the processional route, and Caesar shall follow us, though without our ease. Here!"

They were on a corner, farther down from the Forum, and behind a

crowd lining a wide avenue. Afra started toward the thickest part,
tapping his stick and lifting his laughing face. People gave way, and
a path opened that might have taken a dozen soldiers all their time to
clear. Afra went through without thanks or any word, but as if he had
the right. Out in front of the crowd, walking along the empty avenue,
passing the sentries, Garvan felt himself an impostor. But Afra laughed,
and pulled his sleeve, holding him to the road.

"If they think you're blind too, what matter?" he said. "In this city,
the blind and crippled are always sure of kindness because of the kind
hearts of the women. Herculaneum is known as the city of women.
Women govern it. Sulla Pinarius may be a senator and a tribune,
an important man. But in the city's affairs, his wife and daughter have
far more to say than he. And the College of Diana, and the priestesses
and vestals of her temple? They have second voice only to Caesar!"

"It makes no difference," Garvan said, knowing himself looked at
by thousands along the route, and despising his unkempt garb among
so many groomed for the festival. "It isn't proper for one with eye-
sight to pass himself off as a blind man."

"Oh?" Afra held up his hand in surprise. "This from a nobleman,
thief, and body stealer? Not proper? We may creep into the city on
some pretext, and accept the citizens' hospitality, and take advantage
of a blind man, and eat and drink our fill, and talk largely of this and
that, knowing ourselves to be a criminal, and friend of criminals, and
giving off the odors of the galley. But something, some small thing,
isn't proper?"

"The things you say are half wrong, and therefore worse than a
lie," Garvan whispered, hoping that no sentry might hear. "Rome is an
enemy. I believe all things are good to do against her, and any Roman!"

"We are in accord," said Afra. "But let's have order, and some
decency about it. Because we deal with criminals must we all be criminals? If others think meanly, must we be mean? Can't a good man
deal in a good way and still defeat the less good or no-good? Because
if he can't, why isn't everybody here cutting everybody else's throat
and running off with everybody else's daughter? But they're not, are
they?"

Garvan saw very well that they were not. The avenue went down for about a mile to a slight rise. On either side covered stands were crowded with people, all carrying green branches to lift in acclaim. Behind, on rostrums of planks, and thick in every tree, and on all the roof tops, lesser men and their families crowded.

The voices, in talk and laughter, sounded like the seas in storm. Garvan thought of the galley, wondering if he might be sent back to the rowers' bench. It seemed strange to think that except for Khefi he might be dead or maimed and at work on the oar bank, and could have been working now, as he walked the avenue. Nothing would have happened down there among the rowers but only hours of sitting, and when the wind dropped and sails were furled, hours of working the oars, and feeling the whip, and then sleep on wet decks, huddled for warmth.

He asked himself again how he could allow himself to risk being sent back, even less of dying. There was also the matter of keeping his word to Khefi, Stavros, and Zetak. They had kept faith with him. But in this way, walking like a fool to stand like a fool in front of Sulla Pinarius, he could expect only to be treated like a fool. And the three up at the cave would wait a long time, and then think him dead. Perhaps they might even grieve for him as a comrade, of courage, and one to sing about when the wine was in them, and the fire warmed, and memory stirred the pot.

The notion gave the comfort of a bed of nettles.

If he had thought for a moment he might have bargained with Afra to go back to the terraces and warn the three up there of his desire to confess to the girl's father, and so take proper leave of them. But when he told Afra, the blind face laughed long at the sun.

"Your years have taught you little," Afra said. "How would you escape the legions?"

"I walked in by the highway and saw nothing," Garvan said.

"Do you suppose these Romans, spending their lives fighting the crafty, would march nakedly along highways?" Afra demanded. "A slave hunt is no pleasant thing. Now look to the right. Do you see two tiers of gold seats, with scarlet carpet to the gate, and the roof and pillars hung with purple and gold?"

Garvan saw the pavilion, farther up. All the stands and pavilions were poled and strung in house colors, in yellow and gold, or green and gold, or red and gold, all with some stripe of purple to show the rank of the family. But only the purple decorated the Pinarii pavilion, the imperial purple without any paler shade. Flags, and banners of honor flew from the lower poles. In the enclosure chariots were drawn up about a statue of Hercules with his club and lion pelt, wearing a floral garland about his neck.

The pavilion's golden chairs were empty, but under an arcade in the courtyard perhaps fifty people sat, and servants brought dishes and flasks among them.

Afra stopped at the blossom-wreathed hurdles keeping the crowd from the pavilion gate.

"See among them if you notice one, white-haired, a little tall, wearing the purple," he said.

Most of the people Garvan could see wore the purple, both men and women, and at least twenty of the men were tall. But one woman caught his eye and when she turned and he saw her face, his breath was gone, and he could have run and knelt at her feet.

"I see no man I might point to," he said. "But I see a woman in the purple, and crowned, and she must be mother of Genessa."

"Genessa," Afra repeated. "He calls her Genessa!"

"That is her name, and the only true reason I'm here," Garvan said. "Now go in to them. Tell Sulla Pinarius I am Garvan, son of Orberix, Prince of Armorican Gaul, and why we are come, and so finish your work!"

But Afra turned his open mouth to the sentry's face, breathing his laughter.

"Tell the Lady Lydia of Samaria that I am Afra the weaver, half-son of a carpenter," he said, easy, without haste, and turned again. "A servant will lead you to Sulla Pinarius and the Lady Thalia, his wife. Are you so used to slavery that all men are become your slaves? Must everybody run because you say so? On the other hand, must you take everybody's word? Let the blind lead you? Go, weave your tales, though not this time to children!"

Garvan watched Afra tap his way toward the pavilion. Eight sentries, in the red and black uniforms of the city police, stood near. At any other time he might have jumped the fence and run. He was ready, at any rate, to fight twice that number. But these men were all older, taller, of better bearing than any others he had seen, and he suspected they might be ex-Praetorians turned house guards, and man for man a match for any fighter with any weapon.

He had been led into a trap, he told himself, by softheartedness. In being gentle to a blind man he had let himself be taken like a sheep to the butcher. Appealing to the claims of his birth and a sense of chivalry, and, at the last, shaming him into playing small gallant, Afra had cast a net and drawn the strings as expertly as Zetak, but with a tithe of the effort.

He looked about, in disgust at himself, but in admiration of all else. A little of Rome, where some ruled and many slaved, was on display, and here he stood, sworn enemy, making easy gift of another victim.

The pavilions were flower-banked in rear as in front, and all the colonnades were filled with Romans and their women. In the Pinarii courtyard four ranks of slaves in Pinarii house colors of pale blue, gray, and purple waited with baskets of blossoms on their backs. Behind, stables were busy with the horses of the guests, and to one side drivers polished the chariots or rubbed harness.

A manservant, one of rank from the richness of his dress and the staff of office, came toward him, and motioned toward the colonnade.

Garvan looked about, and breathed long, once, the fresh, free air, and immediately followed on. He walked in the colonnade's shade, smelling the scents that came from vases filled with blooms. Some of the guests looked at him and turned away, but he knew they looked again after he had passed. His feet were silent in deep fur, and then on Arab mats. The manservant stopped at a doorway, and struck a gong, and bowed almost to the floor, and went in with the staff held across his chest, and knelt.

"If it please Your Excellency," he intoned. "Garvan, son of Orberix, is here."

He lowered his eyes as if a signal had been given, and walked out, backwards, bent over in a bow, and at the doorway nodded to Garvan.

And Garvan, flinging aside any thought of bending his head, walked in three or four paces and stood, uncertain.

The room was high, and large, windowed on to the colonnade, and paneled in dull gold, with Caesar's profile in a wreath of precious stones over a shrine where incense burned. A dozen or more Dianic priestesses in pale blue and white robes knelt on either side of the shrine's white columns.

In front, on two chairs, an elderly man in the imperial purple toga sat with the woman Garvan had already guessed was Genessa's mother. The priestesses held their hands on their knees, and looked with closed eyes, and he felt as if he were being watched by the eyeballs of statues in a stare of things that once had life.

"I am Sulla Pinarius," the man said, in a high, distant voice. "You have something to tell me."

"I am Garvan, a Gaul of Armorica, and a prisoner from my father's house," Garvan said. "I am here to make known to you that I was one of those ready to capture your daughter."

"Who were those with you?" Sulla Pinarius asked.

"It is enough that I was one," Garvan said.

"The lictors would find out for me," Sulla Pinarius said in the same voice. "They have many means."

Garvan shook the sleeves from his wrists, showing the scars crusted and half healed. The woman's quick frown he saw, and also the move of her hand toward her husband's lying on the chair arm.

"Lictors have practiced their means on this body," Garvan said. "There is pain left, but, at the end, death. Send for the lictors."

"It stands well that you speak so," Sulla Pinarius said. "What says my wife?"

"How could they enter the garden and kill our servants?" she asked in a whisper. "What condition of the land is this? Had I been there, would I have had to fight to keep our daughter? Is my home to be in danger? Must I think of these things before going out to enjoy our garden? These are the times of our grandsires, when none were sure of safety. I'd thought us better guarded, better behaved. And the others are free? We're not safe, any of us!"

Sulla Pinarius took her hand, and pressed, and let it lay.

"See how you frighten women," he said. "This is honor indeed for a man. I had thought Gauls to be warriors. I served many years with the legions in every part of Gaul. Therefore I know what I say. How does a Gaul become a dealer in women? Is this not a low business?"

"If your daughter had been offered, would you have thought it low?" Garvan asked.

"Romans do not deal in Romans," Sulla Pinarius said.

He was paler, and his fingers trembled, touching his wife's hand.

"This is why I am here," Garvan said, feeling the deep shame of one forced to open a dirty thought. "Gauls have no commerce in people. They neither buy slaves nor sell them. They have no slaves."

"What is done with the captured in battle?" Sulla Pinarius asked.

"None are captured," Garvan said.

"They are killed?" Sulla Pinarius suggested.

Garvan nodded.

Sulla Pinarius touched a small bell hung in the curve of the chair arm.

"The officer of the guard," he told the servant, and stood, turning to the shrine. "It is our custom to bring one who has wronged the household before the lares and penates, and there, allow him to seek forgiveness of the gods. You were not brought a prisoner for trial. You came here freely. Freely, then, do you make a plea for forgiveness? Not of the mother, or of the father. But of the gods, who protected the daughter brought up in their keeping, and saved her with help of Diana. Praise, Great Mother. Know my thanks!"

Garvan looked at the shrine, a small replica of a temple with flowers and herbs and bowls of uncooked food and spices on the offertory table. He imagined Genessa kneeling, morning and night from infancy, confiding the safety of her parents and herself and all in the house to kindly guardians. A thought of the child with her hands clasped and showing the pink heels of small feet, praying for all things good and peace over all, made him feel some of her father's cold rage that any might seek to violate her trust.

Shame fell with greater weight.

"I have no belief in these gods," he said. "They make nothing in my mind. Should I ask forgiveness of disbelief? Let me say to you that I

would as soon have harmed your daughter as my own mother. Let
forgiveness come from any that hear me!"

"So be it," Sulla Pinarius said. "You believe nothing except what
you can see, and you appeal to nothing except what you know is
tender. And what more than a woman's heart? If this was your object,
you fail. I am no woman. Neither do I pretend respect for barbarians.
You are a Gaul, and so shall you be treated. Captain Tabis Netto, take
this criminal in your keeping. Hold him at Caesar's pleasure!"

Garvan heard the guards come in, and felt his arms gripped. He had
time for a bow toward the Lady Thalia, and then he was pulled almost off his feet, and turned, and marched out among an escort of
six men.

But he saw the eyes of Genessa's mother close as if with sorrow,
and at the same time all the priestesses opened their eyes, and stared,
and he saw them, black.

"Caesar's pleasure." Tabis Netto, the officer of the guard, spoke
against his chin strap, quietly, for the benefit of his men as they
marched. "This is an imperial prisoner. No ordinary fellow. No chains
or locks. Unsheathed swords, day and night, until Caesar speaks. And
no sitting down. No lying down. No eating, or sleeping. No washing,
or drinking. No shelter and no fire. One imperial prisoner, and four
drawn swords. And it's pay in gold coins till Caesar speaks. Those are
the orders. Pray the gods this Gaul has good legs. And for a long season,
may the Emperor lose his voice!"

Tabis Netto halted the escort a short distance behind the rails along
the processional route, in a corner to the side of the pavilion, where
the guards had built a shelter for their capes and sleeping rugs and
cook pots. Four guardsmen, all veterans, stood close about Garvan with
drawn swords and slung shields.

Cheering came louder, and fathers in the crowds lifted children to
their shoulders. Runners in the imperial purple padded by, shouting
a warning that the procession was near. Officers in crimson and gold
rode in pairs on either side, looking to see that sentries were in their
places. Bands could be heard, one tune over another, coming nearer.
The crowds pressed against the barriers, and all the pavilions filled.
Garvan watched Genessa's mother stand for a moment against the

rails with a woman of deep complexion, wearing a saffron robe and a headdress of pale green, and looking, whether to the left or the right, with the straight gaze of a man. They talked together, without smiling, paying little heed to anyone else.

Garvan might willingly have given his life to see Genessa once more, but there was no hope in him for the joy. He knew how it would be to die, and he swore to die well. It mattered little enough, he thought. Pain, and then death, as he had seen others die, and nothing more. But in the pain and up to death's grasp, he swore to keep her memory in his mind and so pass, in a smile.

From the moment of seeing her laughing among the wild flowers a change of thought had been at work in him, changing hate, which he knew he ought to feel, into a foolish and lax enjoyment of all he could see and hear of the Roman way and the Roman style. All, the color and music, seemed so much to belong to her, but her absence made him curious.

"Why is it that Lady Genessa is not with her parents?" he asked Tabis Netto.

The Captain looked at him, and the scar across his face became dark. His fist came swift to Garvan's mouth.

"No words," he said. "Enjoy Caesar's pleasure in decent silence!"

Garvan saw nothing of the weaver, Afra. He had no grudge against the man. But he wondered how anyone could interfere in such a manner with another's life, especially after breaking bread and eating salt at the same table.

Outriders in purple and gold, on black horses, came in ranks stretching across the avenue. They clattered by, for Caesar made nothing of the local laws and his cavalry went shod, without the straw shoes. After them a legion from Greece in blue kilts and silver armor. More cavalry, in red, bearing standards captured from the enemy in Palestine— so the criers told the crowd—and a seven-branched candlestick from the temple in Jerusalem, and then another legion, in gray and green, from the lands of Germania. Carts full of rich plunder came next, and then another band, of reed pipes and many drums, and behind, chained in scores, naked men and women, all with stains of dried blood spread black on their bodies from fresh-slit ear lobes. Some among the older men and women fell. Then soldiers ran in and chopped them free of their chains, and pulled the bodies to the side of the avenue for the city guards to drag away. But they walked on, men and women, looking, and seeing nothing in a shining stare from every face, as if they knew, and knowing, disbelieved.

"Jews," Tabis Netto said. "Not worth the shipping room. They have the twist of dying when they want to."

"Food for the games, my captain," one of the guardsmen said.

Tabis Netto shook his head.

"They die in silence," he said. "It doesn't make good sport."

Garvan heard a Gallic tune and the words came to him on Gallic pipes, and he saw the ranks behind the pipers, and prayed to find himself dreaming. But in companies steady as the Praetorians true Gauls marched past in uniforms of black kilts and golden armor with the Roman eagles carried high among their spears.

He wondered for the safety of his mother and father, and his brothers and sisters. But most, he wondered how any Gaul could march behind the eagles.

A hundred trumpets sounded out a brazen scream. Men in the Praetorian uniform, in phalanx, carried the standards of the Imperial Army, Caesar's own, and behind them the Praetorian eagles. People in all the pavilions left their chairs to crowd against the rails. The slaves with the baskets of flowers ran out, each kneeling in front of a guest.

Horsemen in gold trappings and white plumes, riding white horses with golden caparisons trailing the ground, rode by with Caesar's flags. Equerries carried the furniture of his office; the gold swords and scepters of each province, the lances and javelins, the bows and the arrows, and the imperial body armor piece by piece, each held on a purple cushion, and behind each a sweating face.

Now the crowds began to chant, seeing the marching heralds, in white, carrying their scrolls and wands; and behind, the provincial embassies, and foreign princes waving from little gold houses on the backs of elephants.

And in a gold chariot drawn by two cream stallions, a general, bareheaded, in gold armor, held the reins; and behind him a man

leaned on one arm, with a fold of his purple toga hanging over a
wheel, and his eyes were lined and tired, but he smiled.

The people pressed, a crowd no longer, but each one a Roman,
and every right hand stretched out toward the Roman of all Romans,
and Romans shouted the Roman greeting, waiting, and shouting in
unison so that voices came in a roar, clipped, with silence in between.

"A-ve Cae-sar!" The syllables cut plain in mighty chant. "A-ve Caesar!"

Garvan looked at the kindly face, watched an ordinary hand waving and catching at the flowers' lively rain, and instantly he thought
that here was nobody to point at in a crowd, but one even as the rest.
A man, no more.

He thought of the oar benches, and the lictors, and the Jews walking ahead, and of Masr'Afoun and the tears of his wife, and Tadmon
the wine carrier, and he looked at the one man of all men able to
give them ease with a word.

But in a few steps Caesar passed, still smiling, waving, and shouting
a greeting to the Pinarii.

Garvan let him go, looking instead at a dancing chorus of girls, all
in pale blue chlamys, with lily wreaths in their hair, carrying a garland,
some with pipe and sistrum and others with the lyre, singing a temple
ode. The sharp, ranting tune was sung by the crowd until the bands
and all the cheering were lost.

But one among them all took Garvan's mind and made it hers; and
he knew why she had been absent from the pavilion.

Genessa came close to the rails, throwing out her arms in greeting
to her father's guests, and blowing kisses to her mother, and to the
woman in the saffron robe, and making a curtsy to her father's smile
and wave. She wore the pale blue chlamys, and the lily wreath, and
the silver sandals, and she carried a white rose garland. In dress she
was no different from the others.

But side by side with the fragile sculpture of her legs and arms and
a body that the chlamys hid but failed to hide, Aphrodite might
have taken second place and never another look.

The voices came clear, from strong throats; and Genessa passed,
dancing, with the chorus all around her.

And she saw him among the guards, and stopped an arm's reach away, and her mouth closed on a sung note.

Her eyes, which he had thought between the sea and sky in color, or darker when she laughed, looked green, or perhaps the garland's leaves lent light. But while he stared, trying to decide, she vaulted the rail and ran toward the pavilion, and the Dianic chorus went on without her. The four sentries stood too close for him to move his head. He could only watch priests and priestesses about their gods on shoulder-borne palanquins; Jove, and Mars, and Mercury, and Dea Dia, and Horus went by, all in hymns.

But then Tabis Netto pulled him to face a group, with Genessa in front, smiling, holding her mother's hand. Sulla Pinarius, with the woman in saffron, walked behind, with others of his guests.

Genessa stopped in front of him, and looked at her mother.

"This is the Gaul," she said.

"But are you certain?" her mother asked in a frightened voice, frowning, and turning a bracelet on her wrist. "He said there were others."

"There were," Genessa said. "I saw them. But this is he who broke the net and took me by the hand."

"Then if he, as you say, freed you, why didn't he say so?" her father asked. "I don't understand it. Speak, Gaul!"

"If there was a crime, it was thoughtlessness," Garvan said, trying not to look at Genessa. "I told you the reason. But the blind man made me see that there was no other way than to tell you, and clear my conscience."

"Conscience?" Lady Thalia's smile started in her eyes. "Where did you learn such a word?"

"From my father," Garvan said. "Our god is Mithras. His other self is Conscience, the master."

"A youth speaking so," Sulla Pinarius laughed to the woman in saffron. "He must have a word with you!"

"But isn't he to be set free?" Genessa demanded. "He did nothing to harm me. He followed as I told you, and broke the net, and said the things I've told you."

"A moment." Sulla Pinarius held up his hand. "Listen to me, Gaul.

My daughter's plea is just. But answer me one question. If your object was capture of a Roman citizen, and you gained what you sought, why did you release her without ransom? For what reason?"

Garvan looked at the maenad's mouth, laughing now, and he looked away, at the gray eyes of the woman in saffron. He was unsure, but she seemed to be nodding at him to say what was in his mind.

"Two reasons," he said. "I would not buy liberty with a girl."

"Good." Her father nodded. "And the second?"

"Her beauty," Garvan said.

The Lady Thalia shook her head, turning, smiling to her husband.

"Release him," she said, shrugging. "Let him be bathed and fed. And let the child go back to her place in the procession!"

Genessa threw herself at her father, with her feet off the ground, hanging about his neck.

"And he shall join the house and be with us," she wheedled. "I prayed Mother Diana he might be found. She answered me. Yes? Yes, Papa. Say yes!"

"Very well," Sulla Pinarius said, and signed to Tabis Netto. "Release him!"

"Genessa," her mother said. "Back to your place!"

Genessa curtsied, and turned her fingers in a wave, and laughed at Garvan, and danced away.

VI

Seles, the major-domo, took him back to the Pinarii house in Sulla
Pinarius's own chariot. The houses were rich with mosaic fronts and
bas-reliefs of the gods in marble, and designs in bronze, silver, and
gold, and flowers bloomed outside all the doorways. Sulla Pinarius's
house took the corner of the Street of the White Peonies, and the
Square of the Singing Muses. In the middle of the square a statue of
Apollo, banked with wreaths, showed smoke stains from the day's
sacrifices, and a crowd knelt at prayer. Downhill, beyond the roof tops,
sunlight shone in the blue of Naples Bay, and glinted in ships' rigging
filling the harbor.

"The Apolloites kept us awake with their songs all last night," Seles
said, leading the way into the house. "The master doesn't like it, but
there's nothing he can do. They're very strong. He's up for re-elec-
tion in a couple of months or so. He's got to be careful. Let me explain

the house, my lord. Some of the rooms are still being painted, so we're rather crowded with all the extra guests."

They entered the street doorway to a square, walled and floored in white marble, with a marble bath full of lotus under a smaller square in the roof open to the sky. A gallery that Seles said led to the bedrooms ran all the way around the top story. On the first floor columns and a silver rail allowed strollers on the terrace to lean over and talk to those on the ground floor. Left and right four rooms, each furnished with a couch, two chairs, and lampstands, but without a front wall, could be shut off by a carved lattice screen on rollers.

"This is the atrium," Seles said, clapping his hands. "These open rooms are used for the siesta. And for guests. You'll sleep here, tonight. This will be Your Lordship's slave, Corbi."

Seles pointed to an old man, laughing, bobbing his head, showing none of the marks of slavery except in his downcast eyes.

"I'll have no slave," Garvan said. "I'll pay a servant."

"As the master's guest, you will be served by Corbi," Seles said, and made an end of it. "Outside is the garden. To that side, the women's bath, and tiring rooms. That part of the house is for the women. At this end, the dining room. Next, the withdrawing room. Next, the common room, and here the reception. You will use this side of the house, Lord Garvan."

"But I am not a lord," Garvan said.

"So the Lady Thalia instructed me," Seles said, bowing. "And so it must be, Lord Garvan. I am Seles, major-domo, and slave. I have no wish but my master's. In his word is my life."

Under the quiet voice Garvan thought he heard a sneer. It would have been simple to knock the man down. But Seles could only obey orders. There was still that menial sneer for one of no rank and confessing it, by appearance dirty, barefoot, and ragged, and having nothing in the way of arms or armor, animal or servant, bale, sack, or bag.

"I haven't a piece of linen to my name," he said, as if he spoke to a bird perched on the camellia tree in the garden. "I'm fresh from the galleys. I know the way slaves talk. I shan't trouble to speak to Sulla Pinarius. But if your attitude toward me doesn't change, and instantly, I'll run you down to the harbor and drop you in, and hold you under till I'm sure you won't look, or talk in this fashion to me again. You understand me?"

Seles bowed, a little high of color in the cheeks.

"As you will, Lord Garvan," he said. "I abase myself in apology. Should I bring the whip?"

Garvan snorted a laugh.

"Doesn't do any good," he said. "You've had a taste too many, that's plain. Who last whipped you?"

"The Lady Genessa," Seles said in the same flat voice. "I had the unhappy duty of putting her spaniels into the stables by order of the master. She whipped me, and the master heard me crying, and he ordered the animals brought back. He said they made less noise than I."

"You cried when a girl whipped you?" Garvan frowned at him. "You, a man?"

"The Lady Genessa wanted her puppies in her room," Seles said. "Her cries produced nothing. My cries produced the puppies."

Garvan nodded, seeing a little more.

"You may burn the whip, for me," he smiled. "Now, perhaps you could tell me. How am I to dress? After bathing, what's there to put on?"

"It is ready, my lord," Seles said, and motioned to Corbi. "Be good enough to follow your servant to the bath. He will lead you back here. You will find everything you require, by the master's orders."

Garvan followed Corbi's bare feet into the garden, along a corridor to the hot room of a steam bath. While his body warmed, he thought about the day, and marveled at the turn of fortune. He swore at first chance to find the Temple of Mithras, and offer the best he could buy in thanks for deliverance. It occurred to him that for one without a single coin except one borrowed he was promising too much. But he hoped the god would hear and understand.

Heat rising from the hot bricks underfoot, and from the hollow walls, soaked him in perspiration. The grime of three years began to roll out of his pores. His unhealed scars burned with soreness, and in trying to forget them he stretched flat on the slab, thinking of the times during the early days and nights in the galley when his prayers had been for a washed body and fresh linen and plain air.

But languor dropped away at thought of Khefi, Stavros, and Zetak waiting for him. They would go back from their vigil to sleep in the cave, that hole dug in the terrace, with olive twigs for beds, and a fire on the stones for warmth, and perhaps a rabbit, or a stolen kid or a sheep for supper. His first duty should have been to get back there, and warn them of the search and to tell them what had happened to him. If he owed it to his conscience to confess to Sulla Pinarius, then certainly he must owe more to the three men on the hilltop, for without their efforts and joint risks he could not have enjoyed the privilege of confession.

And here he was, forgetful, sweating like a hog in comfort, and about to enjoy the sweets of luxury in the company of Caesar's own friends.

He went into the steam room, and scalded himself for as long as he could stand it, and went out, to lie on the rubbing slab. A Numidian, even taller than Khefi, brought a bowl of soap and poured it over him, and started to rub him with straw gloves in a manner to strip him of his hide. But when he thought himself flayed, the Numidian started to slap, and every time his palms struck, Garvan kept his mouth shut against a yelp. If this were the Roman way, then a Gaul must accept it. The slapping stopped when he was certain he must strike back in self-defense, and then he was picked up, bodily, and carried a few paces through the steam, and dropped into a bath floating with ice.

He found himself crouched in the deep end, stunned with cold, and swallowing water. He came to the top, and crawled up the steps, and sat, spitting his lungs clear and retching for breath.

"The towel, Lord Garvan," Seles's voice murmured above his head.

The major-domo bowed toward a square sheet held out by Corbi.

Garvan stood, and wrapped himself, and Corbi dried his head, and then his feet.

"Corbi will lead to Your Lordship's room, and I will attend when Your Lordship is dressed," Seles said. "I hope Your Lordship enjoyed the bath?"

"His Lordship did not," Garvan chattered. "Is this a Roman bath, this torture?"

Seles looked at the Numidian and back, in mock surprise.

"But I was told these were the habits of the Gauls," he said softly.
"Strict and powerful, and hot and cold, and nothing in between. Was
this not so, Lord?"

Garvan watched him, trying to see in the man's eye any hint of
laughter. There was none. The Numidian stood with folded arms, staring at the slab.

"A Roman bath next time," Garvan said slowly. "But not till I'm
healed of this one. We haven't known each other long, Seles. But I
begin to know more."

Seles bowed, low.

"It is well, Lord," he said. "Much to learn, too little time, so says the
book. Take what you would know, and learn it, and be wise in that.
Only fools go to puddles. Wise men find the river."

"This is the scripture of Mithras!" Garvan laughed. "Are you his
follower?"

Seles smiled.

"I know a little of all gods," he said. "Would Your Lordship see the
god himself? Please!"

Garvan forgot his frozen body, and wrapped himself, and followed
Seles down the corridor, and into the atrium, and up a stairway to a
small room beside the stairhead.

But he halted, and knelt, looking in sorrow at the peaceful figure
with folded arms, and a face, resting on the fingers of one hand,
turned ever to the right in tranquil thought, and the body always in
repose, one foot crossed over the other.

The statue, in red marble, was mere support for a makeshift table.

"How could this happen?" he demanded. "The god, himself, a
table leg? How does this house sustain itself?"

Seles put his hands in his sleeves, and bowed.

"This one the Romans call Atys," he said. "A Phrygian shepherd,
beloved by Cybele."

"This is Mithras," Garvan whispered, covering his eyes. "I will not
look upon him so disgraced!"

"The Lady Genessa found him in the market, and bought him,"
Seles said, closing the door. "When Phocis the Greek has finished

painting in the room upstairs, the table will be taken off and the god will be restored. Let us be moderate, say the priests——"

"We will use angry words as treasure, spending little," Garvan quoted. "How do you know these things?"

"I was a scholar of Tripoli in my youth," Seles said, and smiled. "I am more than forty years in the service of Sulla Pinarius, the master."

"Forty years?" Garvan whispered. "In slavery forty years? You never ran for freedom, or tried to break a chain?"

"Should I?" Seles held out both hands. "For forty years I have lived a life that only the wealthiest in Rome could afford. I have mixed day by day with the greatest in the world, even with Caesar. My food, my wine, my bed is the same as my master's. He bows to Caesar. I bow to Caesar and to him. Which is the slave?"

Garvan nodded, looking at Corbi, standing outside the room and bowing toward a dressing stand hung with clothing fresh from the pressing iron.

"There is no disgrace in willing service," he quoted again. "We must speak more, Seles. These are my clothes? And when I'm dressed, what then?"

"Then you are to go to the arena, Lord," Seles said. "I am to take you. And we should be there soon. It is late."

"The arena?" Garvan turned to the dressing stand, pretending to make a choice, but seeing nothing. "Why is this?"

"To be the Lady Genessa's guest, Lord," Seles said. "You will meet at the imperial loge. By order of Sulla Pinarius, and the wish of Caesar."

"Mithras, watch over me," Garvan prayed. "Here's trouble, by the scent of it!"

Seles brought him by chariot to the arena's gate, and left him with a word to the officer of the guard. Garvan smiled to himself, walking along the arena's main floor toward the imperial loge. All the way from the entrance, Praetorian sentries flourished their swords in salute to him, and each time he thought of the petty officers waiting to share his enlistment bounty. Seles had shown wisdom in advising him to wear a dark blue toga with gold edging, dress of all important foreign guests, and red silk bandages Corbi had tied over his wrists and ankles hid the galley scars, and set off the blue.

A captain of Praetorians took his name, and went behind the velvet curtains. The deep roar of the crowd reverberated among the stone floors and pillars. Among the smells of cooked food, and a mass of people, and the arena's fresh earth, Garvan sniffed that of cats, large as cattle, black, and tawny, and striped. He had never seen them close to, but on one voyage to the Alexandrine coast the galley had taken aboard three cages for passage to the arena at Rome. He had never forgotten their smell, or the screams of those dragged from the oar benches to feed them, and the lictors and the galley-master had told of their size, and fury, and of the terrors of their claws and teeth.

The officer came back, smiling, and saluted, and sentries held aside the curtain for them to enter. A great stone circle cut in shallow tiers of steps and crowded with people was set about a ring of red earth. Dozens of men were clearing away hurdles in the shape of an oval, and others raked the ground flat from chariot ruts and hoof tracks. Rows of cushioned chairs sloped down to a line of a dozen couches at the balcony rail, about forty feet above the games floor. Each couch was taken by a man or woman, and in the middle, under a canopy, Caesar lay with his hands behind his head, talking to Sulla Pinarius and the woman in saffron and green on one side, and the Lady Thalia on the other. Genessa, in pale blue, sat on the balcony in front of them.

Sulla Pinarius stood, bowing to Caesar, and Genessa jumped down, running up the carpeted stairs, ignoring the many turning around to watch her.

"Garvan!" she greeted him, and gave him her hand. "You've missed the chariot races, that's all. Come, meet the Lord Caesar, first. Did you find all you required at home? I'm sorry we couldn't be there, but I had to dress and get here, and Mama, of course, had to attend Papa. Titus Caesar's a darling. Don't be the least bit shy. His only hate is shy people. He's so shy himself!"

"Most exalted Caesar, I have the honor to present Garvan, first-born son of Orberix, Prince of Armorican Gaul," the officer called out. "Guest of the Senator Sulla Pinarius, and admitted to the imperial presence by order of the colonel of the bodyguard!"

Caesar turned his head, laughing at a whispered remark of Genessa's, and looked at Garvan.

"I have great interest in the son of my friend, Orberix," he said in a deep voice. "Let us first see the games, and afterwards we shall speak. Genessa, keep him company. Since he was so anxious to be free of you, keep him close prisoner for revenge!"

Genessa curtsied, and took Garvan's arm, turning to the woman in saffron and green.

"The Lady Lydia of Samaria," she whispered. "Our dearest friend. We shall dine together tonight."

Gray eyes looked direct as a man's into Garvan's, and smiled.

"Afra told me of your meeting," she said. "He's anxious to talk with you. He feels you may bear him ill-will, and he meant none."

Trumpets sounded in the arena, and the crowd settled for the next event. The Lady Lydia turned toward Caesar, and Garvan found himself pulled down on velvet cushions.

"Our driver won the chariot race," Genessa whispered, sitting close to him at the foot of her mother's couch. "It was marvelous. I wagered five talents with Caesar. Our man came in half a lap in front. These are the fights. I've got another five talents on the swords over everything."

"This means you wager on all the swordsmen against any other weapon?" Garvan asked in surprise. "Do you know so much?"

Genessa put her head on one side.

"If you know better, would you double the stake?" she inquired.

"I haven't any money," Garvan said. "But I'll wager my head I'll beat any swordsman with a spear or javelin, and he can name his price!"

Genessa cried out loud, and the sound echoed, and the crowd jeered, and then laughed. But she ran to Caesar's couch, telling him of the bet.

"A hundred talents, and other prizes, if you beat the champion swordsman!" She came back, breathless, laughing. "Otherwise, your head. My father said you were joking. I said you weren't. Were you? I can't stand people who say things and don't mean them!"

Garvan wished he had kept his mouth shut. It was one thing to talk, but a wager of his head was a serious matter.

"Did you invite me here to see my blood?" he asked.

She looked her surprise.

"If you were not confident, why did you speak?" she asked. "Or are you given only to words?"

"I have confidence enough," said Garvan. "But how do you, a maiden, speak in this manner, more fitting to a matron?"

"Of Gaul, perhaps," she laughed. "But now you sit with Romans, dear Garvan. And we are something more. Here are your friends!"

The doors at the end had opened, and a band of trumpeters came in front of a cohort of mounted and marching men, swordsmen, lancers, net-and-trident fighters, fist-fighters, wrestlers, giants, and other monsters scarcely human, some crawling, others sliding, some without legs, others with three arms, or two heads, and some with legs or arms three times the size of their bodies.

In dress, bearing, and drill the gladiators showed the veteran stamp, and even separated by a wall and at distance, they brought a chill that made the loudest shouters stop their cries until, almost by signal, the crowd leapt up, shouting and waving.

"Now, are you settled to fight?" Genessa asked. "Or shall I cancel the wager?"

Garvan wanted to say a few words that could have startled her, but Sulla Pinarius was smiling at him, and he had to smile in return.

"Let the wager stand," he said. "I have little to lose."

A man in purple silk came along the aisle, and bowed to Caesar, and sat on the other side of Genessa.

"Julian Potitius," Genessa smiled, taking his hand. "Here is Garvan, a Gaul of Armorica. He, you remember I told you about."

Julian nodded in a smile that might have been a sneer. He was tall, broken-nosed, and pale, and his hair fell out of the gold wreath.

"Greeting," he said without warmth. "Genessa, my mother wishes to talk with you. Why did you leave us?"

"I sit with my guest," Genessa said. "When the games are done, then I shall visit your mother. Be silent, dear Julian. They begin!"

The trumpets sounded, and the pairs faced each other, and on Caesar's wave the ringmaster dropped a flag.

Instantly the blades cut, and the lances flashed, and the pairs of champions circled. Battle shouts echoed, and the crowd roared out at a falling body gushing blood, and a second, one shout overlaying another.

Garvan watched swift play by a pair of blades below the balcony. Two men, helmeted so that both faces were hidden, advanced an inch, retreated two, took blows on their shields, jabbed, cut, and one, seeing a gap, raised his arm to strike, but the other brought his sword down on his shoulder, and the arm fell off easy as cutting a loaf. The man turned to look at his arm, and his hand still holding the sword. Perhaps some thought was in him to use his left hand, for he dropped his shield. But even as he bent, the blood held in by a fold of leather jerkin splashed out, and he fell.

Most fights were won. A net-and-trident man had tripped the swordsman fighting him. The net closed on the struggling man, and the barbed trident was held up, poised, ready to spear him. The ringmaster looked up for Caesar's sign, holding up his flag.

Garvan looked about, at Caesar's couch.

But Titus was speaking to the woman in the saffron robe, a serious talk, from their faces, and the Lady Thalia listened.

Caesar heard the crowd call out, and turned his head to look at the arena. He saw the ringmaster's flag upheld, and impatiently he turned his thumb down in a signal of death, and realized too late that to please the crowd he should have turned it up in reward for a good fight.

But the ringmaster had copied the death signal with a thumb turned down, and the trident stabbed the netted body. Caesar frowned, holding up his thumb, though by that time the swordsman was kicking away his last breath. Caesar shrugged at the error, and half smiled, and went back to his talk.

"Silly man," Genessa said, watching the swordsman's body dragging a furrow in the earth. "He must have been too close in his offerings to the gods. They don't like meanness."

"How is it that you watch these things?" Garvan asked her. "What do you find in this carnage? Is it anything good to see?"

"Blood and pain displease me," Genessa said. "But I like it because I'm safe. It doesn't hurt me. And if you can't talk about the games, and whom you liked or whom you hated, how can you talk to anybody?"

"That talk deceived me," said Julian. "I should now be vice-consul in Mauritania. Instead, I fought here, and took a gash. Five months of bandage and possets. Beware her tongue!"

"You groan too well," Genessa laughed, patting his hand. "We grew almost together, but now we are grown apart. When I was a baby, he fetched my dolls, and stood guard over us, fighting legions for our sakes. Now he's scratched, and how he makes complaint!"

A young Praetorian officer stood beside Garvan, and invited him to follow. Immediately Garvan recognized the ensign at the Gate House. He got up, answering the waves of people sitting about with a wave of his own. But Caesar and the others were still talking, although the woman in saffron smiled, he thought, to give him courage. Genessa walked beside him to the velvet curtain.

"Aristarchus will show you the armory," she said, looking at the officer. "Choose a good weapon, and make certain of your man. I shall be waiting here with your victor's laurel."

Garvan frowned at her.

"You appear to know as much of this as any shock-head in the gallery," he said. "What if I don't come back?"

Genessa laughed, swinging her hair all around her waist.

"You will," she said. "I know. I prayed well today. I know when Mother Diana is not in proper temper. Aristarchus, bring him back. I say so!"

The officer bowed, and dropped the curtain, and started down the causeway, through an arch, to the arena level. Gladiators lay on the floor letting crones bind their wounds. Others, luckier, stood by, drinking. Garvan refused armor, but he went into the weapons store, and took an armorer's advice on a spear with a handle of polished bamboo weighted at the end with lead, and a broad-leaf blade sharpened to cut a hair.

"You're fighting the swordsman first, and the trident man after," the old armorer whispered. "Listen to me. The swordsman's a slasher. Lead him in, and try for the armpit. The trident man's the best for years. Keep busy on your feet. Never let him stand to make a cast. That's all!"

Garvan nodded, grateful for expert advice. Aristarchus gave him a sponge to suck water from, and took the blue toga, and held out his hand.

"I have a strange feeling of having met you before, though that were not possible," he smiled. "I expect to see you again. I lit a candle before Mars just now in your honor. Force and courage!"

Garvan grinned his thanks and shook hands, trotting out to the arena in time to hear his name called. The swordsman stood beside the ringmaster, armored, with his visor down, ready. Garvan, in a blue himation reaching to the knee and tied at the waist, felt cold. Caesar still talked to the Pinarii and the woman in saffron and green. Genessa leaned on the balcony, smiling down at him.

The trumpets sounded, the ringmaster dropped the flag, and the swordsman came in, hunched behind the shield, pointing the blade, edging inch by inch. Garvan stepped in, and flung the spear into the man's left foot, pinning him. The man halted, in pain or surprise, and Garvan leapt, pulling the spear out by its weighted end, and turned again, plunging the blade into the toes of the other foot. The man fell, and Garvan caught the sword hand, breaking the grip over his knee, and setting the sword point at the visor slit so that a push could have sent the blade through the skull.

But the ringmaster held up the flag as a sign that the contest was over.

The net-and-trident man was out before the attendants had taken the swordsman away.

"No easy spearman's tricks this time, Gaul!" the fighter sneered, making casts with the long net as easily as if he were swinging a fish-line. "A wager with Caesar? Let's see you work!"

Garvan gave him no chance. He leapt in as if to throw, and stepped aside, and when the net flew, he cut it with a slash. He knelt, making the easiest of targets. But instead of spearing, he split the net with an overhead slash. He stood, inviting a cast, and when it came, he slashed the net again.

"Fight me!" the trident man screamed in rage. "You fight string, you Gallic misbreed!"

Garvan kept his temper, and his training. He had long been taught that most men made the mistake of fighting the trident instead of the net. He slashed twice more, and the entire net was a long flail of ragged string. He jumped in, feigning to throw, and when the trident lunged to pin him, he drew the spear's blade over the man's knuckles, almost taking the fingers off.

Again the ringmaster held up the flag for Caesar's decision. But Garvan shook his head, and raised the spear in salute.

Titus Caesar looked down upon him, and in a slow movement turned his thumb to death.

The crowd shouted, a strange, loud sound.

Again Garvan shook his head, and offered a hand to the trident man, ready to leave the arena. But Genessa waved her toga fold, from her expression, displeased to point of horror.

"Lord Caesar desires the kill," the ringmaster shouted. "You can't win wagers with wounds!"

"I said I'd beat them," Garvan told him. "Why should I kill them?"

The ringmaster looked blank. The trident fighter knelt, nursing his hand, and waiting. The crowd was afoot, shouting, throwing all they could find into the arena. Some, nearer, were laughing, but most that Garvan could see were angry, perhaps, at being cheated of blood.

"The people who wagered on you can't get their money," the ringmaster explained. "Caesar has given the order. You must kill!"

"Why should I kill beyond a battle?" said Garvan, and turned, without a look for Genessa or anybody else, and trotted back to the arena doorway to puzzled looks from the competitors, and a silence.

"You're going to need that," Aristarchus said, when the armorer tried to take the spear. "You disobeyed Caesar's wish, and I am ordered to escort you to the next event. You should have killed, and you refused. By custom, you'll fight again. Shall we go one and one, or must I call for others to take you?"

"We shall go one and one," said Garvan. "No man carries me to fight. But why should Caesar, a man of kindly heart as I have seen, desire so much death?"

"Kindliness has little dealing with custom," Aristarchus said. "And what is death? Farewell, nothing more. We say it every day."

Garvan heard his name called in the arena, and while the crowd shouted, men shut and barred the entrance gates, and the gladiators climbed ladders to the upper level.

"Come," Aristarchus said. "They are ready."

"And who is it I fight?" Garvan asked, following into a tunnel.

"Lions, and others with claws," said Aristarchus. "By the cageful, and three days without a meal. Can't you hear them? Those in the color of sand are called lions. The striped are tigers. The black are leopards. Between all, there is little choice. They spring, they tear out the belly with their hinds, and eat."

"A friend I had," said Garvan. "With talk of such small comfort."

Aristarchus shook him by the shoulder.

"I'll burn a second candle to Mars," he grinned. "That, and Genessa's prayers should save you. Or some of you. Courage!"

A feral stench became plain along the tunnel. They came to a stair going up, but Aristarchus turned to the left, and a guard opened an iron door. The howls fell to rumbles that echoed against the walls.

A torch flared on the stairway, and a linkman helped a swathed figure by the hand.

"Garvan!" The clear voice cut the din. "How could you be so foolish? They admired your play but you lost favor. How could you disobey Caesar? Will you survive?"

"By the spear or not at all," Garvan told her, face to face. "How is this? Have you nothing of a woman's heart? You speak with the grace of a slaughterer."

By torchlight he saw her eyes fill, flashing.

"I speak of things I know," she said. "Why am I here if I have no heart? Must I be weak?"

"Better this than one speaking of steel and blood," Garvan said, softer. "Tell your Lord Caesar I wagered to win, not to kill."

Aristarchus touched him on the shoulder.

"Come," he said. "You should be out there. Caesar waits!"

"A fig, and less, for any Caesar!" Garvan shouted. "I'll kill the largest cat and call it Caesar!"

"Watch your speech!" Aristarchus commanded. "My friendliness has limits. Come!"

Garvan felt his hand grasped again, as he had dreamed, as if in trust.

"Try to kill!" she whispered. "Try. And come back to me!"

He followed Aristarchus, and the iron door slammed behind them. The way grew light, leading out to the arena. On both sides cages were full of snarling shadows, and fangs longer than a finger shone white behind the iron cages.

"The Egyptian legions have practiced lion-killing," Aristarchus said, halting at the gateway into the arena. "They say you can fight them best by getting under them and stabbing upwards. As they leap, run in——"

Garvan watched the men above the cages getting ready to haul at the ropes to open the doors.

"If you're not quick, you'll be taking your own advice," he said, and smiled. "I'll do my best. My thanks!"

Aristarchus pushed the hilt of a small dagger into his hand.

"If you should be taken, and the teeth bite slow," he whispered, "better to die as a man than as meat for cats!"

Garvan pushed the dagger into the tie ends at his waist, and walked out into the arena.

The crowd shouted to see him. Some of the nearer faces made motions of spitting at him, and most of them had their thumbs turned down. But in a blast of trumpets the doors on the other side of the arena swung up, and some dozens of naked men and women were herded out by guards, and driven to the middle of the ring, and the guards ran back, and the cage doors slammed.

The bony figures clung together, and some knelt, praying. An old man raised his arms to exhort them, and the men formed a ring on the outside in pitiful defense of the women.

Garvan walked through the soft earth to them, feeling like a small boy left out of a game. But the look in their eyes he had seen before, in the procession of Jews, staring and shining, and in some way, despite their helplessness, with no sign of fear. His heart was caught to see the tears of the older women, and the desperation of the young men begat a wish to give them any chance of defending themselves. He went close to the circle, and looked at quiet appeal in the old man's praying hands and the movement of his lips.

Without any word Garvan pushed into the front rank of men, and took out the dagger, giving it into the hand of a young man holding a woman and trying to soothe her through a mouthful of broken teeth that might have been smashed with a sword hilt. But relief glowed in his eyes to hold the steel, and the ecstasy of his thanks came in a high note, and every voice joined in. He turned to the woman, and kissed her close, and while they kissed, she groaned and went to her knees. The man pulled out the dagger, and thrust the blade into himself, and fell across the woman.

Garvan turned about, seeing another man heave the body free of the dagger. A sound of chanting came from the group, but trumpets sounded loud from the balcony, and the crowd shouted louder than all. The animal cages screeched open, and two lions ran out, opening their maws as if they yawned. But their howls brought his scalp to tighten. More lions ran out, and a couple began to fight.

Garvan walked to a place not far from the loge, and saw that Caesar and his party were standing, looking over toward the group of Jews. He turned, and saw the oldest man stab himself and fall among the mass of bodies running blood.

The animals took scent, and ran, leaping, and tearing among the mound. Other cages opened, and leopards bounded in long, unbelievable leaps, ripping among the heap of bodies forepaw and hind. Tigers sprang, howling, and joined the bloody mass.

But the crowd was cheated of seeing the living Jews pawed and eaten. They screamed, all the massed thousands of them, and again they threw what they could into the arena until the air was thick with missiles.

Garvan waited his chance. The animals had all of them taken plenty, and the ends of limbs, and bones, were strewn in bloodied earth. He went nearer, where two lions licked themselves, content. They saw him, and growled, but they were lazy. They stood, and one

ran at him. He stepped aside and jabbed the spear into its ribs, and it
fell. Another lion sat back on its haunches, but before it was off the
ground, he slit its throat. A tiger took little notice of him until he was
almost in jabbing distance, but then it left its meal and leapt, snarling.
Garvan saw the shadow overhead, and thrust, and blood splashed
down upon him. But a hind paw ripped his left shoulder and the arm
swung, useless. Some of the animals were fighting together. He saw
the dagger lying in the earth, with three lions nearby. It seemed to
matter little that he killed or not, for the blood that oozed from his
arm threatened to weaken him until he died.

With closed eyes he raised the spear, facing the East, home of
Mithras and source of light, and by chance, the position of the imperial loge. He offered a death prayer to his parents, and his family, to
his people and to the common stock, and to Mithras, father and master
and giver of life and light.

And having taken good leave of all, he ran in and picked up the
dagger and pushed it in his belt. Two lions made a move. He stabbed
one in the neck, and thrust one through the heart. A third was clawed
in the death throes of the first. A lion's forepaw ripped the flesh from
the outside of his right leg. He jabbed down, barely able to get away.
Weakness clouded his sight. The crowd howled, and he raised his
head, howling at all of them. He ran in with the spear, jabbing, thrust-
ing. He saw nothing through blood, but only the open mouths, and
the teeth. His strength was going, slowly, as if strings were being
bound tighter about his limbs. The smell of blood and torn flesh, and
the stench of animals filled his mind and brought a rage, and madness,
and every time the spear struck he screamed his hate for Rome and all
Romans.

He was taken by the spear arm in sure grip, and other arms lifted
him up. He saw Aristarchus laughing, and the guardsmen holding him
were cheering. An attendant poured a bucket of liquid that might
have been hot metal over his shoulder, and another bucket splashed
down his wounded leg. Pain thudded, making him catch at sense. In
a swift, clear glance he saw the archers were killing the remaining animals, and sweepers were clearing the earth.

"It's thumbs up," Aristarchus told him, and took the dagger from his belt. "When you saluted Caesar in the middle of the fight, you took the crowd with you. And when I saw you give that dagger to the Jews, I thought I was finished. My name is on it. Say nothing, for my sake. Now you go to the house of the Lady Lydia of Samaria."

"How is this?" Garvan tried to question him. "I am guest of Sulla Pinarius."

"Genessa has been taken home," Aristarchus said. "She left her wits, poor thing. She wanted Caesar to stop the fight. So her father was ordered to take her away. And by invitation of the Lady Lydia, you will go to her house in company of Caesar's own physician."

"I would give anything to go to the house of the Pinarii." Garvan felt his head raised, and a cup was put to his mouth. "Is there some reason why I could not see Genessa?"

"A good enough reason," Aristarchus laughed. "Now sleep, good warrior. That, too, by Caesar's order!"

VII

Garvan opened his eyes in a small room of bare white walls, and a latticed doorway that led to a red-tiled and vine-grown terrace above the perfect blue of the sea. He felt sleepy, and rested, but his joints were sore.

Shoulder and spine on the left-hand side were set in hard plaster, and his right hip and leg were held in a plaster boot. His head was bandaged, and both hands. But a fly crawled on his nose and showed him his real weakness. There was not the strength in him to raise breath to puff it away.

A sound of wood on wood, with a scrape in between, rhythmic and ceaseless, made him want to turn his head. But a trial move and quick pain put him back.

"He wakes!" a voice whispered nearby. "Tell the Lady Lydia. Bring the cold jug. Here, help me!"

He was raised at the shoulders by a woman on each side. They were dark, with black hair and faces nobody would ever remember, and they wore saffron-colored tunics. But held there, he saw the loom, cause of the rhythmic sound, and Afra, the blind one, placed threads and pushed the bar, adding to a width of crimson material shot with blue and gold.

One of the nurses held a glass. He drank, tasting lime and honey. A woman came in from the terrace, and stood at the foot of the bed, smiling at him with gray eyes that had the look of a man's, hard and direct, and yet not. She wore a toga of saffron, and a pale green headdress, both of silk.

"I am Lydia of Thyatiras," she said. "Do you remember me? You came here by Caesar's permission and with his interest. You'll stay here until you are well. Is the pain gone?"

"It is nothing," Garvan said. "How long have I been here?"

"Two months less a day." She smiled at his surprise. "You were kept in sleep by Caesar's physician. The wounds were poisoned. Is there anything I might add to your comfort? An actor to tell you tales? A musician? Or one with the news?"

"Where is Genessa Pinaria? How could I speak with her?"

Lady Lydia's smile showed a dimple.

"She will be here this evening as she has since you came," she said. "She attends school for her examination, with many studies, poor girl. Is there anything you want?"

"Health," Garvan said. "Strength. Sound limbs again. And words enough to thank you."

She reached over, laying a hand on the plaster foot.

"You'll have them all, never fear," she laughed. "I shall see you tonight."

She went out, and stood talking to Afra for a few moments, and joined another woman carrying an armful of bales. As if he had been waiting for her to go, Afra set the loom aside, and tapped his way over to the balcony outside the room.

"So, Lord Garvan, you remember me?" He rested his chin on the crook, and widened his mouth. "Here was fortune in a meeting. See how you fare!"

"Better with a fare-well," Garvan said. "Go away!"

"Precious treatment for a blind one," Afra nodded. "To think I paid for the meal!"

"I'll pay for poison," Garvan whispered. "Fling yourself off the roof!"

"Here's fine return," Afra laughed. "Here do I make certain of your introduction to the Pinarii household by the only proper means open to you as a nobleman. As a man of any substance, could you walk about the city and know yourself less a creature than any cutpurse? Could you look the most debased mortal in the face? Could you speak an honest word? When has the nobleman been a woman stealer?"

"Hole the river!" Garvan said.

"Could I know you'd take stupid wagers at the games?" Afra inquired. "Was I to know you had less brains than the Lady Genessa?"

"Guard your mouth," Garvan said.

"We often speak together," Afra smiled. "She calls down contempt upon herself, not I. So again, had you not made wagers in things that are small concern of yours, how could you be lying here? You, a man of attainment, smiled upon by Caesar——"

"Thread yourself in the loom," Garvan said. "Go. Let me sleep!"

"That I will," Afra nodded. "But soften your words to me. Was it not the lowly weaver who brought you, by Caesar's own friends, before the Eagle himself?"

"These things, yes," Garvan said, and unwillingly. "But I grieve for the friends I forgot. What of them?"

"I know the turnkeys at the prison." Afra tapped his stick. "Tell me the names of those you seek. If they live, I shall tell you."

"If they live!" Garvan groaned. "What must they have said of me?"

"Small moment, any word of theirs," Afra said. "Be intent upon yourself. Sleep!"

He woke up with a hand over his eyes, cool, soft.

"You're not to move," Genessa whispered, close to his ear. "You're not to talk too long. I shall go to the temple and take doves for Mother Diana. See how she answered me!"

"Take also white flowers and put them before the altar of Mithras," he said. "When I am well, I'll take six white bulls for offering."

"There is no temple to Mithras here," Genessa said.

"But I saw him in the small room in your house," Garvan said. "He, under a table!"

"This is not Mithras, but Atys, a shepherd, beloved of Cybele," said Genessa. "She threw him into madness, and he became a tree of fir——"

"This is the speech of an idle girl," Garvan said. "He is Mithras. He who thinks well, and thinking well, speaks the better. Is he yet a table leg?"

She laughed down at him.

"Seles told me of your anger," she said. "Be content. He is in friendly company. And if you please, he shall have white flowers this night."

"Say also these words for me," Garvan said. "That his son gives thanks for survival. And prays also that his parents know the godly smile."

"This, too," said Genessa. "But you must be admitted to Diana. Julian shall take you, and you shall study."

"Never," said Garvan. "Mithras is all. Could other gods have strengthened me to fight the lions?"

"Did I not pray all that time?" Genessa smiled, and moved. "Enough. You shall sleep. When you are strong, you'll come back to us. The bones must grow where the claws broke them. This was my fault, and I must repay you. I have sworn it. Please, Garvan, remember this!"

"I shall remember," Garvan said. "But how was it your fault I was brought here?"

Genessa sat on the bed, taking his hand.

"I begged Caesar to stop the fights," she said. "Because of the people, he would not, and I screamed at him. So Papa took me away; he wouldn't hear of your coming to us after that. So my mother got Lydia to offer her house, and Caesar permitted it. That was only because you saluted him, even among the animals. Oh, Garvan, that was brave!"

Garvan grinned up at her, and he wished he could touch her hand. Some weakness in him seemed to take strength from her presence. He flicked his eyelids to bring her head down. The golden hair touched his face, and he smelled the balms and perfume of her toilet.

"You sniff as a dog," she whispered, laughing.

"As a dog, I'd follow at your heel," he said. "As a dog, I'd take the throat out of any with a thought to touch you. Listen close. My three companions, those who might have taken you? What way is there to find if they lie in prison? If they are, is there a way to bring them better food, or better quarters? Could we find a lawyer to defend them? They are not evil men. This I swear!"

"Julian might know these things," she said. "He controls the Curia, where justice is done. I shall ask. Sleep again. I protect you with my prayers. Garvan, think of me!"

He thought of her, and of other things. A first duty must be to send a message to his parents. Grief came that they might be dead. But grief, the scripture said, was a greed for more than was given. And, thinking of things given, he remembered he must return the gold coin to his friend, Ultor.

The Lady Lydia came as a shadow, looking at him. Behind her the moon lightened the white stones of the terrace, looping scarlet in the folds of her toga.

"Give me the names of your friends," she said. "Genessa told me of your thought. I go to the prison every day. If they are held, I'll find them."

She laughed at his surprise.

"There are many held in the prison here, either by appeal to Caesar, or in his pleasure," she said. "Where did you learn about conscience?"

"From the priests of Mithras," Garvan said. "I know little enough."

"There are others to teach." She put the cover over the stand lamp, and the room was dark except for a wick beside the bed. "Let Afra be your friend. He has no sight, and sometimes his tongue is cruel. As sight is sometimes cruel, showing us things we had rather not see. Be kind to him. And God hold you this night."

"Which one is this?" Garvan asked.

He heard her laughing.

"There is only one God," she said. "The God of gods and men, and every being, and every thing. He has no name."

"This is Mithras," Garvan said instantly. "So he says. 'I accept all things because all things are acceptable.' That is his teaching. 'Life is a short journey, thus choose your burdens wisely, and walk with ease.'"

"Let it be so," she said, and smoothed the sheet to his neck. "The God of all says, 'Put your burden on Me, and you shall walk at rest.'"

"But this gives us little to do," Garvan said. "How is this done?"

"By faith," she said. "You had faith in yourself and in the spear? Why? Discover why, and put the same quality into the God of no Name, and Maker of all things."

"And Caesar?" Garvan asked. "How might he think of this? Was not Caesar born of the gods?"

"Of the same God," said Lydia. "With a mother. As other men." Garvan nodded.

"So I thought," he said. "Looking at him, I saw a man. Not a god. How is it the Romans worship him? Do they not see clearly?"

"They worship themselves," Lydia laughed, outright. "How else, except by choosing one among themselves, could they worship? Can a city, or a country, or an empire be worshiped? They make themselves an image. And any fool with a hammer can smash an image. Any fool with a knife can murder Caesar. What are these to worship?"

"Then how is it that you are friends with Caesar?" Garvan asked. "Believing these things, how do you smile upon him?"

"As a woman upon a man," she said. "As one in commerce with one who buys. And he is a good man, well natured."

"Yet he watches Jews torn by lions?" Garvan said. "And condemned me, also? Is this a well-natured man? And are you well natured to sit and watch?"

She turned toward the doorway as if she might not reply.

"I was invited," she said loudly, as if she forced herself to hear the words. "That is a command. Others rely upon my help. If I were taken for disobeying Caesar, many would suffer. Therefore I went. I was able at least to add my plea for Genessa's sake against Caesar's anger, and to implore that you be brought to my house. If only for these things, I am grateful. Sleep in peace."

He slept peacefully enough, and woke, and slept, and woke again, and counted time by his visitors and the noise of the city's life. The day nurses came at sunrise to bathe him and give him goat's milk and honey. He never knew their names, for neither of them could speak, and when everything was done, they went away, sitting outside to sew or knit, and coming, running, when he rang. The Lady Lydia said she had brought them long ago as slaves from Carthage, captured as children and marketed with their tongues slit to render them mute. They loved her, looking up as dogs when she put a hand upon their heads.

The physician came at six o'clock. He wore the white toga with the purple edge, always in fold from the hands of careful women, and he carried the smell of his calling, a little of cloves and mint and anis, and the edges of his fingernails were always white. Sometimes he lifted Garvan's eyelids, or looked down his throat, and sometimes he put his nose to the plaster as if he were smelling. But he said little enough, and his order was that Garvan should not talk until he gained more in strength, and neither should he accept visitors. The Lady Lydia saw to it that the orders were obeyed, and even Afra had to work in silence.

After the physician the barber, Fetio, a retired sailor making a business of sharpened steel and haircutters, and nimble fingers trained in the art of plaiting hair by practice with twine and rope. Despite the warning Fetio talked under his breath for twenty minutes without pause, giving the news, the gossip, and the rumors of the day. Garvan half-listened to begin with, but as the days passed he opened his ears. The barber spoke the common language of Rome and not the more refined speech of the Pinarii world. It was plain that he and his friends had a different point of view, and small fear in telling it. He spoke of the hard lot of the working people, and of a common resolve to elect as senator one ready to speak only for them in the Forum. It was no new thing to Garvan that men could vote. But it was a new thought, and strange, that men could be elected for a special cause, and a special good, and not for the cause and good of all.

Fetio left at the moment the blacksmiths' hammers started work in the harbor, and then Afra came. Servants carried the big loom out of its shelter under the pergola, and the weaving began the moment Afra sat down, and it stopped only when he took his midday meal, and during the afternoon space for a glass of wine and a biscuit. Garvan never forgot the fingers picking threads and feeding the loom almost with the fluttering lightness of playing moths. Sometimes a thread broke, and then the fingers went to it, and tied, never making an error, and the loom went on again. The material, of a special silk, shone red at one angle to the sun, and blue at another, with gold threads in between. Genessa was to wear it after the ceremony for vestals entering the service of Diana. Each night she measured the day's work, and with the passage of days she was able to wrap more and more about herself. And the more she wrapped, and the more the folds, the more it seemed to Garvan that she clothed herself in his thoughts of her.

When Afra had been working for a while, the bazaar opened. From the edge of the terrace Garvan was able to watch the traders decking their stalls with flowers, fruits and vegetables, meat, and cheeses, and cereals, and every sort of fish.

At times priests and priestesses and their followers sang through the streets with their gods carried in procession. Believers stood on the roof tops to throw flowers, and toss coins into squares of cloth held ready. Sometimes a fleet came in from a consulate. Then the harbor gongs rang, and all the flags were flown, and people ran to buy flowers, waiting in the streets to cheer weatherworn troops, and their captains and generals, admirals and consuls, but mostly, it seemed to Garvan, to watch the plunder, and note its quality, and be first in the market with a price. The slaves were always looked at, and pulled and squeezed to tell the tone of their flesh. Women were sometimes bought for their looks, but the men were paid for by weight of muscle. And while the coins were counted, ear lobes were slit, and blood ran. The skin-and-bones and sickly, or those pining and dead of spirit, were often chopped down as they stood, and left for the dogs.

But when it was told that children were among the slaves, then the Lady Lydia went in the street with her headman, Yosef, a thick-bodied, black-bearded Assyrian, and bought all she could, though often she could make no bid because the children were promised. Garvan asked her what she did with her purchases, and she told him they were sent to good homes to be brought up and schooled. But once, in asking what became of those promised to others, her eyes grew wide and filled with tears, and then she went out.

That and a talk about Fetio were the causes of his first quarrel with Genessa.

Always in the evening when she came to see him they spoke in defiance of the doctor, but in whispers, that the night nurses might not hear. Garvan asked her, one night, about Fetio the barber and his friends, and of their desire for a senator to speak for their cause above any others.

"Some are covetous," Genessa said. "These would like a man to speak in the Forum, and make laws giving the rich man's property to the poor."

"Fetio said nothing of that," said Garvan. "He said there was enough for all men. But because of the laws, it was hard for all men to have enough. What laws are these?"

"At home we always speak of laws and policies and those wanting this and that," Genessa sighed. "An election is on us, and my father works day and night to keep his chair. His name is on every building. And as fast as his men paint it, others paint over it. Remarks that bring a blush. And my father is not a wicked man. He is good, and just. But others make him a criminal."

"But is it true what Fetio says, that some Romans are hungry?" Garvan asked. "Fetio is fat enough. Nobody starves here."

"Herculaneum is only one city," Genessa said. "I feel that many Romans are hungry in the land of Italia."

"What land is this?" Garvan asked, surprised. "Is Rome not a land?"

"Rome is a power, and a city," Genessa said. "The land is called Italia, from the Oscan word 'vitalia' which means an ox. We won the land from the Oscans and Greeks. Perhaps the Oscan people worshiped Europa. You remember that Zeus fell in love with Europa, and to be near her changed himself into an ox? And when she sat on his back, he swam with her to Crete and made her his wife? He, as the ox, gave the land its name, perhaps."

"I never saw an ox swim more than a few paddles," Garvan said. "Let us say a mile, or if it's not an ordinary ox, even a few miles. But not to Crete. I've sailed there."

"This was Zeus, a god," Genessa said. "It is in the great books."

"The books are absurd," said Garvan.

"That is not for a barbarian Gaul to say," Genessa said, looking over the terrace.

"I believe in other ways," Garvan said, looking at the ceiling. "Barbarians though they may be, Gauls do not elect senators especially for barbers and their kind. Neither do they use slaves, and sell children, and murder helpless people in the arena——"

"We do none of those things for ourselves but because our fathers did them and so made a custom much liked by the vulgar." Genessa stood with her fists clenched and her teeth showing. "Only the worst among us favor it. The slaves? Are they not property? Should a man not have servants of his own, won in war? Can the servant not enjoy his life far better in a settled Roman household than rotting in some cave in his homeland?"

"Did I rot in a cave?" Garvan demanded. "Let me inform you, there are other cities wealthy as Rome. Other lands as fruitful as this Italia——"

"Nonsense!" Genessa flung a fold of her toga over her shoulder and around her arm. "You speak without knowing. I waste time talking to you!"

"I'll guard against it." Garvan got the bell rope in his teeth and pulled. "Go home to your settled household, Roman. Let a barbarian know peace in his cave."

"But this house is guarded by Romans!" Genessa laughed. "You gain health in Roman hospitality with Caesar's own physician as your watchdog!"

"The Lady Lydia is not a Roman," Garvan said. "She is of Thyatira, and Samaria, and Athens, as much a barbarian as I. She keeps no slaves, even as my mother. And Caesar's physician is a citizen by right. He is a Greek. And which Greek was ever Roman by choice?"

"Wallow in your barbarism!" Genessa spat, and spat again, for good measure, out, onto the terrace. "Should I trouble with offal flies?"

"Only if they make you scratch," said Garvan. "Go. Employ yourself!"

Genessa looked at him with eyes red-bright in the brazier's coals,

and swung away, and through the door, leaving her perfume where
she had been.

"You rang, Lord?" the nurse asked from the doorway. "A drink? A
little wine? Or a steeping of myrrh for sleep?"

"None of these," Garvan said. "But if the Lady Lydia is not asleep,
I'd like to speak to her."

The Lady Lydia got up early, he knew, because he often heard her
voice before the day nurses came in the morning. Afra told him about
her business of woven cloths and silks, which began in her father's
time in Samaria and now was over all the empire, and of the fleets of
ships and the hundreds of horses and wagons she owned wherever
there were ports or cities. Lydia made the purple for Caesar's robes.
She made the gold cloth, and capes, and badges for all imperial occa-
sions. She dressed most of fashionable Rome and all its consulates beyond the seas. In wealth she was Croesus, and in power it was
whispered that she was closest to the ear of Caesar, and it was certain
she knew most of the Senate by their given names. With all that no
man had come into her life, and never tongue wagged with hint of
one. Yet, Afra told him, the thousands of men in her employ would
have gone into death or worse at her slightest word, not for fear, or in
any coercion, but from love of her.

She came when he was almost asleep. He heard the sound of her
many keys. She wore the scarlet toga, glorious in the brazier's light,
and her eyes were gentler, and they smiled almost with tears. But they
were dry.

She sat on the bed, and took his hand. He told her of the talks with
Fetio, and with Afra, and of the night's quarrel with Genessa, and all
he thought of Rome and Gaul, and of slaves and their treatment. But
she stopped him, smiling.

"All these things are good to think about," she said gently. "But
having thought about them, take them out of your mind as you void
chewed food from your mouth. The goodness is got. So swallow, and
take other. These things are thought about by many in every part. We
pray together for their ending."

"You pray for the ending of slavery?" Garvan asked. "What use in
such prayer?"

"You remember the God of no Name we spoke about?" She turned to the brazier, putting fresh pieces over the burned, and her face was hidden. "He says to all believers that if they ask, it shall be given. If they seek, they shall find. And if they knock, the door shall be opened."

"All believers?" Garvan said. "Believers in which god? This One, of no Name?"

"He," she said. "Believe, and it will surely come to pass."

Garvan thought of the temples to Mithras, and of the priests. He remembered his mother and father and the prayers they had taught him. It was strange to find this strong woman turning her back upon Mithras and believing in some other God, of no Name. He felt sorry for her, but, as with believers in Diana, there seemed no way of giving help.

"How is it," he asked, "believing as you do, and with all these other believers praying as you say they do, that there are still slaves, and children taken from their parents, and men and women killed?"

"It is because we must work in love, and there is not yet enough," she said. "We must weave our threads as weavers, patiently. When the threads are strong enough, the cloth is whole. We pray in love, for love."

"And what is love?" Garvan asked. "Isn't it weakness in men for women, and in parents for their children?"

Lydia shook her head. "It is a command," she said. "The God of no Name says that we must love one another. All of us. And we must love our enemies. If we are struck on one side of the face, we must offer the other."

"You believe this?" Garvan said, shocked. "You? That I must love the men who shackled me and used the whip against me?"

"Even they," Lydia said. "They of all men are most in need of love. And all the others you hate and want to kill, you must love them even as yourself."

Garvan tried to hold laughter, thinking of himself having desire other than to halve the head of any lictor he had ever met.

"This word love I have heard only from my mother," he said. "And in stories of traffic among the gods."

"For one about to sleep, you walk in thorns," she sighed. "Who knows the universe of this word? For me, love means the denial of myself, and where I once was, a hunger to serve others. Even the worst of men and women. They more than any."

"If you enjoy a meal, much more will you enjoy one shared," Garvan quoted. "Give much, that others may have enough to give to you. Here, perhaps, the Lord Mithras joins the God of no Name."

Lydia folded the toga over her head. He was surprised to see that she was laughing.

"You and your Mithras!" she said. "Sleep well. Till sunrise!"

VIII

He awoke before dawn to a new barber, an old man, not given to talk, and so quick in his movements that he finished shaving and trimming before Garvan was able to ask a question. And when the nurses had changed his bed linen, and before the servants came in to carry the bed onto the terrace, the headman, Yosef, came in with Seles, the Pinarii major-domo.

"Lord Garvan, greetings!" Seles held his staff across his chest, and bowed. "I was commanded to bring you this, with no greeting."

He held out a tablet wrapped in one of Genessa's kerchiefs.

"My devoted thanks," Garvan said.

He unwrapped the silk. The clay was painted in a white glaze, and something more than a student's hand had drawn a posy of lilies, emblem of Diana's fairest thoughts, with a message cut by stilus telling of the writer's sorrow for angry words and of her desire to be at peace before she went to the shrine with her morning prayers.

But no name.

"I have little schooling in the Roman script," he told Yosef. "But I must reply to a maiden of degree. If I had money, I would send her the finest perfume, in keeping with her age, and order my name cut in the vessel. That is our fashion in Gaul."

"You have a great sum in wagers won at the games, Lord Garvan," Yosef said. "You have also Caesar's gifts, and your name is vouched for at the counting houses. May I bring the perfumer, and a stonecutter?"

"At once," said Garvan. "Before I leap down to them!"

When bells rang at the terrace door, Yosef bowed beside an Arab bearded to the waist and with jewels and ribbons plaited in his hair. Behind, an older man, bent on a stick, with white hair stained at the ends with henna, prodded a string of boys carrying heavy trays on their heads. The Arab pulled his robes about him, and squatted by the bedside, putting the first tray of phials across his knees.

"She is a maiden, more beautiful than all the oceanids and dryads," Garvan said. "Orpheus dreams no rarer melody than her smile. Now, bring out a perfume that says these things to me!"

The Arab held up his finger, over one tray, and the next, and the next, and in the fourth tray he picked up a long-necked phial of glass overlaid in many colors. With care he took out the stopper, and first motioned to one of the maids, and then made a sign for Garvan to close his eyes.

In that darkness he smelled Genessa's presence.

He opened his eyes again, finding the Arab holding the phial in one hand, and the maid's wrist in the other.

"Only the warmth of woman's flesh gives savor to a perfume," he said. "Would my lord choose from the store of my colleague?"

He made way for the stonecutter, an Egyptian, speaking in a voice that was almost in lace with age, of imperial service since the earliest days of Caligula. All the trays of crystal bottles and those carved from rare stones and the alabastrons were unpacked, and set out, and

Garvan chose an alabastron, pure white, as long as his forearm, with a neck of chrysoprase, and a gold stopper.

"Cut my name in the gold," he ordered. "Prepare the box for the Lady Genessa. Give me also a crystal bottle, and the Arab shall fill it with a perfume proper to my mother. Know that doves answer her call, and come to her shoulder."

The Arab touched his breast and forehead, and started a search of his trays.

"Added to that," Garvan told the jeweler, "a fitting brooch for each of my sisters. The eldest is twelve, the next ten, and the baby, eight. Pack them safe together, with the crystal of perfume, for a journey to Gaul. Now the Lady Lydia——"

"The Lady wears neither perfume nor jewels," Yosef said, looking across the bay. "For gifts she prefers clothing, and loaves, wine, and fishes for the poor."

The Arab sat cross-legged among his trays, waiting. The stonecutter held the bottles and brooches in a silken wrap. In the shade of the pergola the boys watched Afra pick and kick, and pick and kick. Down in the harbor seamen shouted a capstan chant, and the blacksmiths' hammers struck clear notes among a nearer coo of doves in the garden.

Afra stopped weaving, and the silence was tenfold. He took his crook, and stood, turning his blind face toward them.

"Loaves, wine and fishes!" he laughed. "She, the richest of all the women in the empire, will accept such paltry gifts? This artist of the loom, kept in life by wealthy patrons? She will not accept the work of artists in other walks? No jewels. No perfumes. No paintings. No sculpture. No marbling. No carpeting. No furnishing. Men of those arts might die and she'd spill no tear. Yet, if these same men were hungry, see her run to feed them!"

"Go hence!" Yosef shouted at him. "Do your work, and earn a prince's wealth. Should you burrow in the affairs of your betters?"

"Keep silence, pot carrier!" Afra said. "When you stand in the street to be bought like a dog, you'll have time to think of these things!"

He tapped his way to the terrace gate, and went down the stairs.

Garvan pretended he had taken little notice. The tradesmen packed and left, watching the carriers to see they kept their hands out of the trays. Yosef showed himself ready to talk by busying himself at the bedside, and glancing here, and there, and then at Garvan.

"You may go," Garvan said.

"Afra speaks, seeing nothing, knowing less," Yosef began.

"Go," Garvan said. "I am master of no man's speech. Neither am I a box for another's words. When my name is cut in the gold, take the alabastron to the Lady Genessa. Enough!"

Yosef bowed, and went away.

Garvan felt sorry to have been harsh, for Yosef was plainly devoted to his mistress. But there was danger of becoming spattered in the gossip of servants, and in any event, he decided, the Lady Lydia was well able to manage all things within her domain.

Trumpets sounded, and people ran in the street, and cheering came nearer. A herald came out on the terrace striking a gold wand on the ground.

"O, you, hearing me, know this!" he shouted. "His Exalted Excellence, Senator, plenipotentiary of the Lord Caesar, Tribune and august guardian of this city, Sulla Pinarius, with all honor, he comes!"

Staff officers in flashing breastplates came into the sun, and stood in two ranks with drawn swords.

The Lady Lydia came between them, and curtsied low, facing the doorway.

Sulla Pinarius, in a purple robe, and wearing a golden wreath on his white head, came into the sunshine and took the Lady Lydia's hand, and led her toward Garvan's bed. He waved a scroll of parchment carrying a seal, and his eyes shone gray, and he smiled Genessa's smile.

"Hail now, good Roman!" he greeted Garvan. "You look rather better than when I last saw you. How shall it feel, think you, to receive the Lord Caesar's affectionate greeting, and the blessing of your royal father's hand, and your mother's tears, all in the same moment?"

He rested his hand on Garvan's head.

"This I do by the Lord Caesar's command," he said, and took a long-necked phial from a pouch. "This, from your lady mother. Also by command of the Lord Caesar. And here, by the Lord Caesar's wish, I read you news of your father. Let all be silent!"

"Pray silence!" the herald shouted, and struck the wand on the ground. "Here speaks the Lord Caesar!"

The herald opened the scroll at arm's length that Sulla Pinarius might read.

"Hear, then," Sulla Pinarius began, placing his forefinger on the written words. " 'I, Titus Flavius Sabinus Vespasianus, Pontifex Maximus, to Sulla Pinarius, Senator, Tribune, and loyal friend, greeting. Let these things be made known to Garvan, Prince of Gaul, in your keeping at the city of Herculaneum, at the house of Lydia of Samaria. That by my will, his father, Orberix, is crowned King of Northern Armorica, joining all between the Seine and the Loire, north to the coast, and flying his flag at our city of Parisii, lately known as Lutetia. My General of the Legions of Gaul reports that when, by my command, he gave news of the Prince Garvan's release, the royal mother was taken prostrate away. With the family, all is well though, since his going, two children are born, a boy, named with my praenomen, Titus, and a girl, Keldar. I caused inquiry to be made into the facts of the Prince's capture. Troops of the Iberian Legion raided into Marcomanni lands, and the Prince Garvan, then being at his father's summer villa, was captured with his servants. The servants died, and the royal youth, without those to speak for him, was first set to work at road clearing, and then, being angry in his conduct, was sent to the galleys.' "

Sulla Pinarius paused.

"Were these things so?" he inquired.

Garvan nodded, unwilling to speak. All his thoughts were for his mother, and the new boy and girl, and his father, made king of lands far greater than those he had ruled as prince.

" 'No record is made of him after that time,' " Sulla Pinarius read on. " 'The King, Orberix, knows these things, and proper sums in quittance have been paid into his treasury for his own and the prince's use. This is my wish, that between Rome on the one hand, and Orberix and his brother kings of the Keltae on the other, there shall be a state of peace. To this end, I have commanded that a Gallic legion be formed, under Gallic officers, and Orberix shall be its colonel, and Garvan, his son, a captain. One company of the legion shall be sent to

Rome as part of my bodyguard. To this company Prince Garvan shall be joined. The remainder shall serve on the borders of their country, and also in other parts of the empire, at command. Let the Prince Garvan, when he is in health, come to me here at Capri. I wish him well. I send him from the hand of his father, a blessing, and from his mother, this phial of her joyous tears. Let him drink, thinking on her. Let him also remember Titus, his friend. Signed, under this writing by A. Balsae, the scribe. Titus Flavius, Caesar.' "

Garvan put the phial into Lydia's hand, and she put it in the small armoire at the bedside. He tried to tell Sulla Pinarius what he might say in thanks to Caesar.

"Why, when stenographers are here?" the Senator laughed, and snapped fingers at the herald. "The Lord Prince would address Caesar!"

The herald brought a man in blue uniform, with a pocketful of quills above his heart, and carrying a small desk. He knelt before it, and took a square of wax out of the space under the lid, and chose a stilus from those in his side pocket, and waited.

"Garvan, son of Orberix, King of Keltae Northern Armorica, to his overlord and emperor, most excellent Caesar, Titus, surnamed Flavius Sabinus Vespasianus, Pontifex Maximus, ruler, loyal greetings on the knee," Sulla Pinarius dictated. "My heart is full. The gifts by your imperial hand given unto mine by the loyal Sulla Pinarius, Senator, bring once more to my eyes the peace of my father's house made safe by Caesar's thought and the vigilance of his consuls. For the gift of captaincy of Gallic legionaries, I send my thanks and promise of loyal service and a life devoted to the further glory of the Eagles. These things I swear by my father's blessing and my mother's tears, both sent by the imperial hand, and taken at the hand of the said Sulla Pinarius. When Caesar's own physician makes orders to that end, I shall without delay sue for audience at the imperial villa on Capri."

Garvan watched the scribe finish the shorthand almost before Sulla Pinarius had finished speaking.

"Lord Sulla," he said. "My thanks for your kindness. But one matter takes my mind. Has my father sworn loyalty to Caesar?"

Sulla Pinarius held up the parchment.

"You heard what I read?" he queried. "Should I read it again?"

"My father's father and his father before him, all swore everlasting enmity to Rome," Garvan began.

"In Nero's time, perhaps," said Sulla Pinarius. "Ten years ago, or even five, things were very different. But nations tend to settle down, you know. We've just pacified Judea. Britain is almost settled. All of Gaul is at peace. Naturally your father has sworn loyalty. Why should there be doubt?"

"How could I sign that letter?" Garvan pointed to the scribe. "Could I swear those things without my father's permission?"

Lady Lydia smoothed her toga, and settled back in her chair.

"Ah, men," she sighed. "Always words and more words. If the tear phial comes from your lady mother, could she have sent it by other than a proper way?"

"Enough," Garvan said gratefully, and at rest. "I will sign."

But Sulla Pinarius frowned.

"Is this so, that you feel no loyalty to Rome?" he asked with his head on one side and a cold eye. "For all these gifts, and news gathered by Romans and sent by special couriers, yet you doubt at heart? Are you worthy to serve the Lord Caesar?"

"But Lord Sulla, from the other side, is he not the worthier?" Lydia asked, gently enough. "Should he profess loyalty with a doubt? Does speech alone make a man loyal? How many gather Caesar's spittle?"

Sulla Pinarius's face lost some of its lines.

"True, Lydia," he said. "These questions, I suppose, are excusable. Be it so. But I've no liking for it. Rome deserves better thought."

"You spoke of Rome's gifts to me," Garvan said. "A place in the kingdom, and in the Army, and my father's blessing and my mother's love. But these and other things I had before, though not from Rome. They were mine by right of birth."

"They were Rome's to give you by right of conquest." Sulla Pinarius stood, and all his officers with him. "Lose the dreams of boyhood, Garvan. Become a man, and see that Rome and Gaul are one by common wish of Caesar, and the Gallic kings and their people. Rather than fight, they work. And their forces are joined to Rome's. Now we are one, and Caesar rules."

He held out his right hand in salute.

"Ave Caesar!" he smiled. "May it always be so between us!"

And in quick thought, flashing brighter than all the swords and breastplates, and despite a denial of conquest, Garvan imagined he saw Genessa's eyes, and in them, he thought, was goodness, and seal enough for loyalty.

He raised his right arm.

"Ave Caesar!" he smiled in return. "I serve!"

Sulla Pinarius brought his hands together, and all the doves flew, and he laughed up at them.

"That's how it must be!" he laughed. "Now, a glass of wine, and I must go. Garvan, we shall be friendly. Where there are doubts, tell me. Genessa told me of certain matters last night. She was distressed. But you know many things unknown to her. Say nothing to shake her confidence. She'll learn, but gently. That is my wish. Since her brother died and scarred my heart, I've treated her more as a son. She knows Rome well. In government, and in the way of policy, she is pre-eminent, young though she is. Guard your talk with her, I beg you. I want nothing to upset her, even less her mother."

"Be certain of my discretion," Garvan said. "But where is the use of knowing policy, if the ills creating the need for it are unknown?"

"If the aediles send notice that you break a law by having a choked drain in your house, must you know all its contents and every stink before you act?" Sulla Pinarius inquired. "Is it not enough to know you make a nuisance? And what is any policy except an attempt to clean a drain?"

"I wish Genessa might come to Athens with me this year," Lydia said. "She'd learn much more than locked inside the temple."

"She'll serve her time to Diana." Sulla Pinarius spoke good-naturedly, but Garvan sensed a taste of vinegar. "I thought you'd said enough on that head, Lydia?"

"I'll never say enough." Lydia spoke with equal good humor, but with the same smack of vinegar. "She's going to be spoiled. There's the tragedy!"

"Lydia." Sulla Pinarius put down his glass. "If you persist, I must leave your house. For the last time, Genessa will enter the temple after the feast of Diana. Garvan, my thoughts for your health. I shall sacrifice doves for your safekeeping, and I shall drink with you when we meet under my own roof. Until then!"

He got up, almost as an afterthought offering his arm to Lydia. She smiled at him with the gray eyes, and her head was lowered as if she made to see through him. But she took his arm, and walked with him to the doorway.

The officers followed them, and Yosef came with a team of servants to clear away. In shortest time Garvan found himself alone, in the sunlight, listening to the hammers on anvils, and a distant bee, and a man singing at the wine stall.

Afra appeared at his side, coming from the stairway behind the bed. He paused for a moment, and then went on, toward the loom.

"See what she attempts to do," he said, as if to himself. "A word too many, and we'll all perish. All, every one of us!"

"How is this?" Garvan asked in astonishment. "By whose order will she perish?"

"Caesar's," Afra said. "He has a way with enemies."

"Lydia, an enemy of Caesar's?" Garvan laughed. "You talk a fool's indecency!"

Afra turned his blind face.

"Noble Prince," he said, feigning a meek voice. "Bear with me but a little longer. I say to you, be patient. I am a very young man. I have seen nothing of life. Forgive my foolishness."

"What makes an enemy of Caesar?" Garvan asked. "Is she not best of citizens? Working from first light to last? Ever at hand to help? Where is the enemy?"

But Afra turned to the loom, and started weaving, picking and kicking, and neither would he answer nor make a sign that he heard.

Garvan's thoughts were busy with the tear phial resting in the armoire, and the news of his home, and the changes come about, and most of all, with Genessa, and her term as vestal. He wondered how long she might have to be shut in the temple, and what she would do, and why Lydia's feeling was so strong against it. The evening seemed far away when Genessa might come, and he could ask her, and then speak with Lydia.

He waited patiently, but only the scribe came with the letter to Caesar written in many colors, and Caesar's titles in gold beaten into the parchment. Garvan signed it, finding himself ashamed of his scrawl. But the scribe dusted sand over the ink, and bowed himself away, with no change in his face.

The physician came soon after. He, silent man, took a lever and a knife, and cut the plaster from the leg, and from the shoulder. Garvan lay helpless, feeling naked as a trussed fowl. The wounds were healed. But there was no strength in the leg or the arm, and the physician said he must have one to massage and stretch the muscles.

Lydia came after the physician had gone. She was gentle as ever, but her thoughts seemed elsewhere. Garvan had no chance to question her, for Afra came in and talked loudly of work yet to be done and what should be started after. Lydia dealt shortly with him, and came back to the bedside.

"The tear phial," she began. "I have a room set apart for prayer. Tell Yosef when you have need of it."

"You will not be harmed by Mithras," Garvan said. "I will use it as a shrine."

She looked at him as if she had something more to say, and smiled.

"You'll soon be going to the Pinarii," she said. "You'll be much more comfortable there. I've often been sorry I couldn't spare more time with you. But you'll have Genessa and her friends to talk to. And the physician said it might be well to take lessons in weaving to loosen the tendons in the leg and arm. So Afra will come over for an hour or so every day to teach you. And so, in any event we shall keep our friendship."

Garvan caught her hand, and looked up at her.

"If I knew how to thank you," he said. "If I could show how grateful I am!"

She bent lower.

"Save Genessa!" she whispered. "Help her. Help her poor mother. Help me!"

He saw the tears start in her eyes. But they heard the bells of the terrace gate, and Yosef came in, and behind him were Khefi, and Stavros and Zetak. Lydia put a hand on Garvan's shoulder to hold words, and she went, taking the nurses, and shutting the inner door. Garvan tried to sit up, but weakness held him flat. He could only look at each in turn, and shake their hands, and laugh, miming words in pretence of the galley stammer. They were dressed in new camel-cloth tunics, and they were shaved and bathed and happy with health, though paler and heavier.

"We've been sitting in there like fattening geese," Khefi said. "We are free of prison till our trial, and we have the best of good food and clean cubicles. I love the day you let that girl go!"

"How is this?" Garvan asked. "Weren't you thrown in prison because I didn't give you warning?"

"Do we complain?" Khefi stared. "We live like captive kings. Two meals a day, both hot. Clean straw every night. A barber every other day. And it's free!"

Stavros laughed.

"We thought you'd be gone for a day or two, that afternoon you went away," he said. "We went back to the cave and finished off the mutton. And we slept."

"Next thing we knew, the ropes were around us and the Praetorians had their swords at our throats," Zetak said. "Dogs scented our tracks."

Khefi pulled a face.

"We'll be lucky to be sent back to the galleys," he said. "Our only hope is the lawyer you got us."

"I?" Garvan laughed. "How was this?"

"Through the blind man, Afra," Zetak said. "He's looked after us like a father. He took us to have our meals with Chote. We eat and sup the best, day after day."

"Chote, the Carthaginian?" Garvan said. "And does Afra or the Lady Lydia pay for this?"

Khefi looked as stupid as the other two.

"Afra told us you were paying for everything," he said. "That's partly why you see us here. To thank you. And for our clothes, and the money in our pouches. And the lawyer."

"In this I am happy," Garvan said, straightening his face. "Afra's a very strange man. What does the lawyer say?"

"We must be well behaved," Stavros said. "He said you'd speak for us."

"What did he think I might say?" Garvan asked.

"That we were men of good character," Khefi said.

Zetak laughed so that his hair shook.

"Afra told us you were a prince of Gaul," he said. "That made it as meat for any buffoon. We didn't know if you could open your mouth without putting yourself in reach of the executioner. What a joke if we all died together!"

"A question," Garvan said. "Has any man spoken of the girl we tried to capture?"

"We were asked, but we said nothing except to Afra," Zetak said.

"What name had this questioner?" Garvan asked.

"One, an aedile, Julian Potitius," said Khefi. "A sly, morose fellow. With my thumbnail I could split him down."

"Ultor says we'll go free if we say the right words and nothing more," Stavros said, as if he feared they might not. "The jailers said he's never lost a case when there was any doubt."

"You said Ultor?" Garvan remembered his friend, and the loan of the gold coin. "Is he gray of beard and hair, and of the Tungri peoples?"

"A fatherly one, from the north somewhere," Khefi nodded. "They don't like him at the courts here. He wins too many cases for non-citizens. He's also the Lady Lydia's lawyer. He visits from Rome now and again. You know him?"

"Stavros." Garvan pointed to the bedside. "Look in the armoire here. There's a gold coin of Nero's reign. Take it, and when next you see Ultor, tell him that I will do all he requires, in gratitude for his kindness to one he thought was a nameless youth."

Khefi got up, pointing at the sundial.

"We'll have to gallop," he warned the others. "There's just time to get back to prison and report ourselves. Garvan, we won't come again unless we have news. Jailbirds are followed. My hand, and my thanks. What of this Julian Potitius?"

Garvan thought for a moment, looking at Khefi's milky-glass eyes that looked back, wide, at him.

"A scorpion," he said. "One I shall watch."

Khefi nodded.

"As I thought," he smiled. "So shall we watch, and listen. Gain in health!"

"We have to show our faces to the guard eight times a day, or we might stay further," Stavros said. "It's a good way off. Diana keep you close, boy!"

"I've started at her temple too," Zetak said, watching the others go. "After what she did for us, I thought it fair. She saved us, didn't she?"

"And the Lord Mithras?" Garvan asked. "Didn't he do much more than she? He saved me, and through me, all of you!"

Zetak watched Stavros trotting across the terrace after Khefi, and his eyes said he wanted to stay and talk, but he dare not.

"Looked at like that, there's no doubt about it," he nodded. "A man gets mixed up. Tell you what we do. I'll buy a dove for you at the Dianic shrine, and you do the same for me with Mithras. We can't lose, can we?"

Garvan shook his head, grinning.

"It's like knowing the dice before they fall," he said. "Be of good spirit!"

He watched Zetak's burly legs plod over the terrace, feeling that he was missing some great adventure, even the wearing of a new camel-cloth tunic, or the taste of two hot meals a day from Chote's kitchen, or the feel of clean straw in a prison cubicle.

But then he heard a voice he loved, and while his eyes turned toward the balcony door, a flower was thrown into the air, high, and landing on the bed.

"Guess who?" a voice called.

"The ugliest creature in Rome," he said. "Or let me say, in all Italia."

"You say ugly?"

"With cross-eyes and stilt legs. Ugly enough. And a shrew's tongue."

A pause and the pigeons settled and folded white wings.

"Did you get my message?"—softly, a whisper, from the doorway's shadow—"Did somebody read it for you?"

"I was able to. It was indifferently done."

"I'm glad you liked it. I love painting."

"You painted the flowers? You haven't that control of the brush——"

"I've brought you another. To thank you for the alabastron——"

"Let me see!"

"No. Not now. You wouldn't like it. I'll go away——"

"Come and sit down. Why wouldn't I like this new painting?"

"It's a portrait of the ugliest creature in Rome being very happy with a wonderful gift of perfume——"

"Let me see it. At once!"

"But imagine! A portrait of cross-eyes and stilt legs?"

"I love to see your eyes when you lose your temper. They're more beautiful even than when you smile."

Another pause; and a long sigh.

"Well, when we deal with barbarians, as Papa says, I suppose we have to make allowances. As I do, dear Garvan. Or I'd smite you with the weaving bar, you recalcitrant Gaul!"

Genessa came out into the sun. Her hair was bound in two plaits with golden ribbon. She wore the pale blue and white chlamys, full about her shoulders and falling in silken folds from a gold waist belt to just below the knees, and golden sandals with jeweled toes were laced to the ankle. She held her hands behind, and he saw she carried a package.

"You look terribly pale," she began. "And you are thinner than linen. I can't tell you how glad I am you're coming to us. It's a nuisance coming over here day after day!"

"Then why do you trouble?" Garvan asked. "Isn't there better to do with your time?"

"Plenty," said Genessa. "But we are taught to take the trouble to perform our duty. That is our discipline."

"You make it sound a penance," said Garvan. "I'd rather you kept away!"

Genessa put her hands on her hips in a gesture of impatience.

"The moment we speak, we begin to argue," she said. "Is this an augury for friendship? I can talk and talk to Julian and never, never quarrel. He's much better behaved, of course."

"A lap dog," Garvan said. "A bark when he's given a piece of sugar."

"He is Aedile of the city, and chief justice in the province," Genessa said. "My father likes him well. But then, we were walked together by our nurses. Dear Julian!"

Garvan yawned, looking away at the harbor.

"I shall be sorry to leave this house," he said. "I'm almost tempted to ask the Lady Lydia to let me stay."

"Impossible!" Genessa came and sat on the bed. "Our house is much more for living. People don't work there. You'll be much happier."

"I doubt it," Garvan said with great indifference. "Why, if I don't want to go? Why shouldn't I stay?"

"Caesar has ordered it so," Genessa said, direct. "You're coming to us to study. Papa said he would take you in charge until you're well. He thinks you come too far under the eye of our Lydia. And here are my thanks to you!"

She gave him the package, bound in silk, with flowers and myrtle tied in the binding. He cut the knot, and forthwith shouted his delight. Genessa had painted herself, mouth open and eyes wide, and hair flying for joy, and the message said that here was the effect of a gift in terms that even an uneducated Gaul might understand.

He told her of the tear-phial treasure, and brought her smiles by placing the portrait next to it. But Lydia was in his mind, and he asked why her father was distrustful of her.

Genessa looked out toward the sea.

"She doesn't believe as we do," she said quietly, and even sadly. "You notice the house has no lares or penates? She makes no sacrifice or offering even to Vesta, goddess of the hearth. She is an infidel. And Papa says that such a woman, of great wealth and influence, is a danger."

"Then why does he talk to her, or allow his family to mix with her?" Garvan asked. "Isn't it foolish to think in one way and act in another?"

"My mother loves her, and so do I," Genessa said, and smiled. "He can't go against us. And he can't prove what wrong she does. He has nothing against her, except that she's an influence. Especially with the poor. She feeds them and gives them clothes——"

"Is that wrong?" Garvan asked.

Genessa sighed as if she were uncertain.

"I can't believe it is," she said. "But my father says she's interfering in politics. All the slaves worship her. When she speaks in public, even the temples are empty. And there isn't a servant in any house."

"Lydia speaks in public?" Garvan tried to imagine it, with memory of a gentle voice. "And what does she say?"

"Oh——" Genessa straightened the chlamys's folds, frowning as if she were speaking of something distasteful. "My father says it's unhealthy. He forbids any mention. They start up like rats in a nest, he says, destroying the social fabric little by little. He hates them. Not another word, now——"

"'They' and 'them'?" Garvan laughed. "What are the names of these terrors."

"I wish I hadn't started," Genessa said impatiently. "I've stayed here wasting time for too long. I must go."

"These rats in the nest," Garvan took her hand. "Shall I ask Afra who they are? He knows everything——"

"No!" Her eyes were hard, almost ugly in warning. "Say nothing to him. Have no speech with anyone. Garvan, you must promise me!"

"How are we placed that we tremble at a name?" he laughed. "You speak of rats, and destruction of the social fabric. I've seen nothing of this, and yet I've lived here——"

A movement from the doorway made him pause, raising his head, ready to send any servant away.

But instead, he stared.

Three priestesses, elderly women, in resplendent blue, white, and gold robes, stood beyond the doorway, and they looked with the same black stare with no blink. Genessa turned, and terror came into her face, and she crouched, and Garvan heard the whispers, as if she prayed.

She ran, and knelt before the eldest woman, and stood again, running out and down the stairway.

All three kept their eyes upon him until the sound of Genessa's flight was gone, and without a sign they followed, but their steps were silent.

And Garvan was surprised to find himself in a shiver, even though he knew the bronze table top too hot from the sun to rest his hand upon.

IX

As though the household knew of the visit, all was still that afternoon and night, and all next day. Garvan practiced exercises, and
listened to a player reciting, and tired of it. He told Yosef of Lydia's
offer of the private room, and said he would be glad to go there.

That evening four footmen lifted the bed to carry him to the
women's side. It was the first time he had been into the main part of
the house, and, passing down the staircase, he was surprised at the
bareness compared with the splendor of the Pinarii mansion, and the
absence of any color, or picture, or sculpture. Remembering Afra's
complaint, and Genessa's warning, he wondered that a woman so
beautiful in herself could live in a house less comfortable to the eye
than many a servitor's hut.

The rooms were large, and open to the air. There was no glass in
any window, and no marbling or mosaic on the floors, but straw mats

over stone. Limewash glared on the walls, and the furniture was all
of black wood in the Grecian style, plain, without cushions, and there
were no couches or deep chairs, but only straight backs and small
seats.

They went through the atrium, piled with merchandise, out into
a space that should have been a garden, crowded with women sitting at
looms under flares, and along a colonnade filled with girls picking
silk and wool. At the end women stood to their knees in a long stone
bath washing wool, and others were busy at dye vats gleaming under
the torches in circles of color.

Yosef opened a small door leading to a flight of steps. Two of the
footmen linked hands and Garvan was lifted to sit in the chair of
their wrists and forearms. They climbed the stairs to a dark landing
and squeezed through a passage to a door with a lantern alight over it.

Yosef turned the lock, and the servants put Garvan in a chair and
they all bowed, and left him.

The room was small, little more than a place to hang garments. A
clay lamp in the shape of a fish hung from the ceiling and lit the lime-
washed walls and a floor tiled in red. A small cupboard of dark wood
with a red velvet knee-rest was set in the middle of the wall under a
square frame hidden by a red silk curtain. A bronze pannier holding a
loaf of bread and a small wine flask stood on the floor to one side,
and on the other a shepherd's crook lay its silver curl against the frame.
On the cupboard's top, in a silver dish, incense burned with more
delicate aroma than any he had known, and fine smoke darkened the
curtain's gold fringe.

In that small place was silence seeming to quiver. Here was a shrine,
though for what purpose he was beset to think. None of the Roman
gods could have any place, since the Lady Lydia had spoken enough
against them. But it was hardly possible that any could raise a prayer
for a God of no Name. He wanted to look behind the curtain, but
then it came to him that the frame might hold a portrait. Many peoples made prayers to their forebears. Perhaps Lydia, a Samarian, held
such a belief. If that were so, then he would commit a gross crime
in opening the curtain without her permission, besides bringing upon
himself the curses of all her kinsmen. He left the curtain alone.

He drew the tear phial from his breast pocket, holding the slender shape as if his mother's spirit lay in his keeping. He remembered her, but over distance, as he might know her voice if she called from far away. Hair, in thick plaits bound under a lace coif, he saw, and her smile when she gave him a swanskin cap on the last birthday they had all been together. He remembered her in the garden, and her impatience with insects that made holes in the leaves and spread balls of froth about the flowers. And remembering, he broke the seal, and drank her tears caught beneath her eyes for thought of him. Yet he tasted no salt but only a liquid easier to the mouth than rain water, drops, soon gone, as if she first had wept and then, knowing him safe, had the sooner smiled.

Lydia came in, wearing a scarlet toga, and knelt in front of the curtained frame, and made a sign between her head and breast, and stood, looking at him.

"Did you find the peace you sought?" she asked. "I was sorry you were kept waiting, but the room was in use nearly all day."

"It served me well," Garvan said. "I shall say a prayer for you when next I enter a temple to Mithras."

"Let it be so," she said. "Let me ask something more. Say nothing, I beg of you, to Genessa of my worry for her. I should have said nothing. Diana is powerful on earth. She has many servants."

"More than the God of no Name?" Garvan asked.

"We believe in His power, in all places," Lydia said.

"So Mithras says," Garvan said. "I am with everyone who calls on me."

"All things work together for good," Lydia nodded. "You Mithradites have strong faith."

"And what do they call the followers of this God of no Name?" Garvan dared to ask.

"We are the children of the King," Lydia smiled. "We are the Anointed, His sons and daughters."

"These things are strange to me," Garvan said.

"You shall hear only what you wish." Lydia put her hands together, facing the curtained frame. "One other thing. Let none know you were in this room, or that we spoke of these things."

"I am a Gaul," Garvan said. "I am your guest. In both, you shall know that I am careful of your confidence. Is the God of no Name frightened that His children shall talk, and thus be known?"

Lydia turned her laughter upon him.

"He is not, and neither are His children," she said. "But to some, even a knowledge of our work, or acquaintance with us, is enough to bring down their wrath. Therefore we speak care that innocents may not suffer."

"One question," Garvan said. "What is behind the curtain? What does it hide?"

"It does not hide," Lydia smiled. "But what it covers is not for our common eyes, except when we enter into common prayer. Then we uncover what is hidden."

She knelt again, making the sign between her head and breast. Garvan watched her tidy the lampwick, and gather the ash of incense, and bring the bread pannier nearer, and push the wine flask a mite away, and she appeared to draw strength from each article she touched, and love for the modest pieces seemed to light her finger tips.

She opened the door and went out to the passage, clapping her hands. The servants came in, and took Garvan up, and through the women still at work, back to the terrace.

He found a message from Genessa by Seles, with her usual flowers. Adding to her greeting, she said that he would leave the house of Lydia during the afternoon of the day following, but that her examinations would keep her from him until the evening and she trusted that his Gallic patience would be equal to the strain, or if not, he might call upon Mithras of the crossed feet. And if no help from there, he would be glad to know that Diana's flame had burned with great clarity at sound of his name, and doves sacrificed in his honor had passed unscathed through the fire. She knew that he must, one day, come to Diana, and sent her prayers with sorest knees.

Seles and liveried Pinarii grooms waited next day with a palanquin drawn by four black ponies in scarlet harness. Lydia waited for him in the street, and she helped to settle him among the cushions. The grooms chirruped the ponies into a walk that made the harness jingle all the silver pieces, and Seles went in front calling on all to make sure of their children, and look before they crossed, and at avenues he stopped the ponies until chariots and wagons were safely out of the way.

A baker came cloudy with flour to the door as they went by, and blew on a ram's-horn long as his arm to tell all that breads were come from the oven. The wineshop on the corner had only the vintner and a boy at the counter, and outside a man twining straw to make cradles for the wine jars. The bazaar was closed for the afternoon rest, but the stalls were all tidily piled, and green fern garnished the floor ready for the evening's custom. The goldsmiths' and stonecutters' and glass-blowers' shops were all closed with canvas blinds, but the scribes were busy on the street corners with people dictating at every desk. In the Street of the Lean Days, families of beggars clustered in the doorways, whining, and pointing to their sores.

"Curious," Garvan said. "Nobody told me Rome had any beggars."

"Rome has made a million beggars," said Lydia. "Why should she have none? All the other provinces have to send food to the city itself or the people would starve."

"How is this?" Garvan frowned. "Rome is starving?"

Lydia motioned to a new building of many archways guarded by sentries.

"This is called the Street of the Lean Days because the collections of food from all the southern provinces are brought here for shipment," she said. "Romans have become too proud to work on the land. They all want to wear the toga and pace the streets and attend the games. They ape the patrician. But small pride has its price. Without Caesar's help, they'd all starve."

"And what is that building?" Garvan asked.

"That is headquarters of Annona," Lydia said. "Help for the hungry people of Rome."

"This is a weakness," Garvan said in surprise. "Who thinks of such things, looking at marching legions and the fleets of ships?"

They passed by the theater, among acrobats and dancers amusing the crowd waiting to go in, and turned into the Place of Hercules. A marble statue of the god, higher than any building, stood in the middle of a fountain. Flower sellers ringed the basin, and dozens of fortune-tellers sat among groups of people, and some burned colored lights, and others threw bones, or stones, or tossed animals' intestines, and called out their readings of the future. Against the wall of Hercules' temple a score of women wept aloud, and drank the tears of their husbands, or sons, sent to them from legions serving at the outposts.

Garvan watched the reflection of white marble in the green water of the fountain basin, and the faces of children sailing their ships in the water.

"In return for your kindness to me, how may I be of service to you?" he asked. "How, think you, could I help Genessa or her mother? You had the thought. But then you told me no. How is this?"

"Your talk with Genessa was overheard and told to me," Lydia said, looking out at the street. "I thought you might add a plea to Sulla Pinarius. Assuredly, he knows of Genessa's interest for you. But he insists she shall go to Caesar's temple at Capri to serve her term. Therefore, say nothing. You could bring his anger upon yourself."

"I'd bring down more than that for her," Garvan said. "How was our talk overheard?"

"The terrace walls have their own ears," Lydia smiled. "Air-slots. Your voices were clear."

Garvan heard a note in her voice, whether of warning, or a hint of fatter things in store, or not, he was unable to guess. But he felt impelled not to ask questions, first because he refused to discuss the master of the household where he was to be a guest, and secondly, he was angry that she could tell him, without apology, that his talk had been overheard.

"I am a Gaul," he said. "What Romans do is no affair of mine. We have no air-slots in our houses. Ears are not ready to gather speech. Let me thank you for your kindness, and for my present good health. Apart from that, I am content."

He saw her frown, and then she laughed, and her hand touched his foot in a gesture of comfort.

"When in Rome, become a Roman," she said. "Those at the air-slots in my house might have been the servants of Diana. They came, following Genessa, but they found others before them. She never moves these days without a strong guard. We were ready. And here is my advice to you. Have care in everything you say. Genessa is more than a daughter of Sulla Pinarius, and a favorite of Caesar's. She is to be a vestal-in-honor of Diana. The priestesses know her value to them. They know you to be a danger."

"I?" Garvan said in loud amazement. "How am I a danger?"

Lydia laughed the little laugh.

"Is there no thought of something more in your mind?" she asked. "If she married, their closest link with Caesar is gone, and so are their dreams of greater power and gifts of land and wealth. Therefore be careful of your words and actions."

"These things are so for me, an unimportant one," he said. "How is it that you, of real importance, are allowed to say anything so it please you?"

"Thirty years and more I have worked with the imperial government," she said. "And my father before me. The Navy uses my ships. I clothe many of the legions. Caesar's officers require loans. Is this enough?"

"Enough," said Garvan. "But you have great trust in me that you say so much."

"You know little that others have not been told," she said. "But you also drank your mother's tears in my house. Should I not trust you?"

Garvan looked along the Street of the Darts of Eros, watching a crowd mostly of seamen kneeling before a shrine to Lakshmi. An effigy of the goddess, painted in bright colors and draped in strings of glass beads, looked at all men with a bold eye, showing herself stark and shameless. The sailors joined hands and sang, and squatting priestesses, clothed as their goddess, laughed up at them.

"All men worship," Garvan observed. "Whatever lands they visit, some new god they find. How long until the last god is found?"

"What then?" Lydia smiled. "How great the harvest!"

"These things interest me little," Garvan said. "I find no joy in burning doves or blooding lambs. Mithras takes fine cattle, but the meat goes to poorer men, that they might eat of the best with the wealthiest. How is it that you, the Anointed, worship in a secret room? Is some evil done?"

Lydia sat back, laughing.

"Ah, Garvan!" she sighed. "Such a youth with questions! No. We are taught not to make a show of ourselves, but to go into a room, and shut the door, and pray to our Father in Heaven."

"Heaven," said Garvan. "Here is a new land?"

"The land of our Father," said Lydia. "The land of everlasting life."

"These are new matters, and strange to me," Garvan said. "I had thought only the gods immortal. But are the Anointed to be the only immortal ones?"

"All may be," Lydia said. "Barbarian or Scythian, bound or free, Greek or Hebrew."

"But these are foreigners," Garvan said.

"And which child is foreign to the Father?" Lydia smiled. "But no word to Sulla Pinarius in this. He is loyal only to Rome and the belief of Diana. All others, in his mind, are fools and criminals. And there is his weakness. For how strong is a bridge that stands no weight except its own?"

Seles came to the side, bowing low.

"The Praetorians bar the road and examine all who pass, my lady," he announced. "We are five, one freedman, two in bond, and two slaves, in service to the Senator, Sulla Pinarius, and to Rome, and faithful to both!"

Lydia nodded dismissal, and looked at Garvan.

"They search for the unwanted," she said.

A file of Praetorians came shoulder to shoulder across the street, stopping passers-by, and going into the houses and bringing out those inside. All were questioned by a young officer, sure of himself, and in no hurry. He came over to the equipage, haughty, and curt of address, aware of his golden armor and the red plume in his helmet. But he changed in the moment he saw Lydia, and saluted, laughing, at ease.

"My apologies to Your Ladyship for the nuisance," he said. "Please go on!"

"Why is this necessary?" Lydia asked with unusual sternness. "Why are people to be stayed on the street?"

"We seek to fill the prisons," the officer said, and turned a confident eye upon Garvan. "What is your name?"

"I am Garvan, Prince of Gaul, and Captain of the Gallic Legion in the Imperial Bodyguard," said Garvan, throwing out an air.

The young officer's face became staring stone, and he straightened, and saluted.

"This, Lord Prince, I beg you will forgive," he said in a loud voice. "I am Claudius Felix, Ensign of the Legion of Augustus, on public duty!"

"You seek to fill the prisons?" Lydia interrupted. "Why is this?"

Claudius Felix smiled.

"We need labor," he said. "There is much work to be done on the roads. Jews, Essenes, and Christians shall supply it."

Lydia flung off the silken cover, and stood out in the street.

"Therefore you should take me," she said. "I am what others call a Christian."

Claudius Felix looked at her, and his mouth was a little apart.

"Excellent lady," he began. "This is a serious matter. Such things are not lightly said!"

"They are not, and neither was it lightly meant," said Lydia, less cold and in some way almost in welcome. "See, I wear the scarlet!"

She pulled aside the saffron toga, showing a scarlet chiton underneath.

"Now add me to the Hebrews and Essenes," she said. "I will help them build your roads. And why not? It is written that we should be obedient to them that are our masters, but with good will, doing service as to the Lord, and not to men. Where are they, that I may join them and share their blessing?"

Claudius Felix turned to Garvan.

"Lord Prince," he said. "There is sickness in this woman. I place her in your care. Proceed then, to the house of the Tribune. I shall report to him."

Lydia went with him willingly enough though she refused to enter the Pinarii house, and on her promise to return to her own, Garvan let her go.

The Pinarii house was quiet, and nothing was said among the family, or among their friends when they met for dinner. But after the wine had passed, voices became loud, and the Tribune raged.

"Hear these Christians speak of blessing!" he shouted to the ceiling. "How else than under Rome's benign laws could they flourish, these useless weeds? Where does Caesar profit from such? How am I to face him and say, 'Lord Caesar, this is your friend, Lydia, once more confessing herself a Christian, and in public, before your dutiful troops'? When will he lose patience and consign her to the lictors?"

The Lady Thalia covered her face.

"Silence in this," she whispered. "Silence, I pray. Our guests become uneasy!"

"Properly so, since their lives come in question," Sulla Pinarius said. "I once thought in Nero's time, we dealt too harshly with them. I thought the Emperor overused the sword and torch. Now I'm certain he was right, great Roman that he was. If I had my way, I'd loose all the troops in the country and give prizes to those bringing in the greatest number of Christian noses and ears and right hands. They'd be a nuisance to us no more. Julian, how say the aediles? Is nothing to be done?"

Julian Potitius pulled the flesh from a shoulder of lamb, and washed his fingers in the ready-held bowl.

"Until Caesar gives us word, nothing," he said. "There are reports to spare at the Curia, all of them valid. Caesar must first take back his order."

Garvan watched angry faces under lamps giving off scented light that also shone among the gold and crystal on the dining table in the Pinarii triclinium.

Twenty guests lay among the cushions of couches around three sides of the room, and ate from dishes brought one after another by a team of slaves. Publius Marius, Consul of Pompeii, and his friend Rufus Nonnius, fat ones both, of great wealth, with commercial houses in Pompeii, blundered along the couches and went out to the vomit hole, and knelt, letting a slave thrust a feather in their gullets to bring on sickness and empty their stomachs ready for another filling. Admiral Pliny, sitting at the right hand of Sulla Pinarius, and his adopted son Pliny Caecilius, sitting beside the Lady Thalia, spoke quietly together. Opimius Balbus, a proconsul from the East, and Gaius Colcis, proconsul from Britain, with their wives, sat next, making well of the meal, and then Genessa, with Garvan at her right hand.

Beside him there rested a thin-faced elderly woman in blue silk robes, heavy with gold, wearing about her head a wreath of lilies made of jewels. The Mother Hemera, head of the College of Diana, and Genessa's tutor in chief, had little to say.

Garvan wondered at the difference between this woman, almost, Genessa had told him, as potent in the empire as Caesar, and the Lady Lydia. Remembering the cool gray eyes that smiled as if lamps were lit, he looked at the eyes of the Mother Hemera, which seemed to match those of any of her priestesses, black as stones, seeing and sightless, smiling only in a wrinkle of the eyelids, and always watching here, there, as the weasel in a poultry pen. He found it strange that Lydia chose the dangers of serving a God of no Name, and so making enemies of powerful Romans, rather than joining her abilities with the College of Diana. But even a thought of Lydia brought a sense of freshness among the rich steam of sauces, whereas the priestess wore her share and more of attars and musk, and made him think of an old clothes-chest, full of stuffs for winter and packed against the moth.

Garvan tried to talk to her, but she nodded as if she feared her wreath might slip, sitting still, eating nothing, and speaking only when Sulla Pinarius, or the Admiral Pliny called remarks from their places, or when Genessa leaned to make the priestess an offering of a tidbit. Beyond her was Julian Potitius, and his mother and father, and then Tercena, assistant to Hemera, wearing a wreath of jeweled lilies, but smaller, and blue robes with less gold.

After her, Balchus Dasius, Colonel of the Praetorian Guards, and his wife.

"They crawl in Britain even now," Gaius Colcis said in the silence. "There's little sense in being blind when we see. The Christian is not of the Eagles. What say you, Colonel?"

"What was done in Palestine could be done throughout Rome," Balchus Dasius said. "Nothing is wanting except the command."

"There's the problem," said Opimius Balbus, pale and wasted, with healing pocks in his face, and almost pushing his bones through his golden consular robes. "Start the killing, and all others panic.

Troops won't make any difference between a Christian or anyone else. When they start killing they kill good and bad alike. I've had the same trouble. Half the place destroyed, thousands unburied, and the rest fled to any haven they can find. Then sickness."

"Then what's to be done about them?" Admiral Pliny asked in a sharp, scholarly manner. "I've seen no plan, except slaughter. It's done no good in my time, and I see no reason why it should in the future. Are we so helpless? Why have we never found the reason for the Christian recruiter's success? Nobody's ever been able to tell me the attraction of the Christian over any other religion. It has no priests, no temples, no money, no literature, nothing. Yet it has strength. Why?"

Seles, in his banquet uniform and black wig, came in and struck the floor with his staff of office. Flute players and drummers in the gallery above the top table played music from Arabia, and a line of slaves came in bearing white peahens, swans, and herons, all in their plumage and dressed on silver dishes among lake grasses and bulrushes made of green sugar. The women clapped to see the procession, and the wine bearers went about to change the goblets, and pour from new flasks.

"What thinks a Gaul of these things?" The small voice of Mother Hemera was as much a surprise to Garvan as the candor of her smile. "What standing have the Christians among your people?"

"None, good Mother, that I know," said Garvan, taking a warning nudge from Genessa. "And in three years of constant travel, I never heard the term."

"Fortunate boy," she said. "I hope that nothing more of them shall touch your life. What will you do, now that you stay here?"

"I shall study with the Senator, and at the library," said Garvan. "I shall perfect where it is possible my Latin script. But mostly I shall go swimming and fishing. I am sad to think of going home——"

"Ah, dearest city!" Mother Hemera clasped her fingers, ringed each one with two or more, and shook her hands, thick at the wrists with bracelets. "She sets her braids upon you. Rome is a place of wonders, all agree. But here, in Herculaneum, is more."

"I believe it to be the most beautiful of all cities in the world," Garvan said. "A city templed for a poem, and her name you know!"

"From one I had presumed to be an unbeliever, this is a noble compliment to our Mother Diana," Hemera smiled. "Let us drink to her in your words."

They drank, but Garvan lowered his goblet after a sip, following Genessa. In the busy talk that came after, he bent toward her.

"You are the poem," he whispered. "And this is not the wine that speaks."

"Close that Gallic head," Genessa whispered. "Here is no place for such talk. How can you lower your mind to empty phrases when disorder threatens our city?"

He drew back, looking at bound golden hair intertwined with pearls, at the wide stare of eyes sea-blue in that light, at the maenad's mouth set in stronger lines than he had yet seen, and at her hands without rings or bracelets, folded before an untouched platter.

"What now?" he demanded. "Are we to speak so at our place of eating? I'd thought this a family affair, of friends and laughter?"

"With the blood of rioting not yet wiped from the streets?" Genessa said. "Know that Romans love Rome. We hate what goes against us!"

"But these were not Christians fighting and smashing," Garvan half-laughed. "These were Romans. Why hate Christians for what Romans do?"

"They were the cause," Mother Hemera said in a smile that sharpened her voice. "They were the loyal ones, making known their anger. Lawless it was, and rightfully the Senator sent the troops. But that Samarian deserves to die."

"But what is her crime?" Garvan asked. "If she says she is Samarian and Christian, is she more at fault than I for saying I am a Gaul and a believer in Mithras?"

"You are a young man, unlearned, and in our eyes, barbarian," Mother Hemera said in a sudden quiet. "In matters of Roman loyalty you have nothing to say!"

"Here you are wrong," Garvan said, pretending not to feel a tug at his other side. "I am son of my father, and I shall one day rule over others. Should I, in that time, come to you for advice when in this day you are yourself in need of it? If the Lady Lydia is free by Caesar's

direct order, why does a loyal Roman question his decision? Where
is loyalty? What is it? Or has every one his own?"

"The guest in my house has strange reasoning, dear Mother," Sulla
Pinarius said, holding out an arm toward her, with a smile crusting
grim displeasure. "Say no more on this, Garvan. I fear this night will
lose the Senate chair for me!"

Colonel Dasius threw aside a peahen's breast, half eaten, and stood,
rattling in his chains of honor, pushing past his wife toward the vomi-
tarium. He stepped in front of Garvan, pointing his finger and closing
one eye.

"There is a difference between a nation and a sect, young man,"
he said. "Learn that lesson first. You Gauls are a nation, and I for one
am glad we are at peace. But these Christians? They are sheep. They
die as sheep. It drives a poor soldier mad. I've had companies of men
throwing down their arms, and refusing to kill any more. Think of
this!"

"The Army cannot deal with them?" Admiral Pliny laughed through
a pursed mouth, turning to Sulla Pinarius. "We've had no trouble in
the Navy, you'll notice? The slightest sign, and they go overboard!"

"How long shall the empire last if all passes in this manner?" Colonel Dasius made query as an orator, holding out a hand to the top
table. "See how defenseless we are. We are defeated, first, by the trai-
tors here, in this city!"

"I shall be glad to add your argument to mine, dear Colonel,"
Hemera said in the high, sharp voice. "We agree these Christians must
be destroyed. But we have a better plan. They should not be killed, or
maimed or chained. They should be allowed to work. They need no
supervision. They never try to escape. They work far better than any
slave. Why should they not be found, and challenged, and then, on
admitting the disease, be put to work to strengthen the empire they
work to destroy? We need roads, public works, aqueducts, harbors, sew-
age systems, houses, and tilth of field and forest over all the empire.
Let them supply it at no cost, and thus pay for their belief."

Opimius Balbus lifted his goblet with both hands, and the golden
robes slid down his thin arms, showing muscle in the width of string.

"Hear this piece of statecraft!" he said in a shaking voice that brought his wife's arms to hover behind his shoulders as if she feared he might fall. "Let us drink to our Mother Diana, and to her Collegians. Not for the first time they present sound advice. Triumph, Diana! Great Mother, triumph!"

"Let them serve a vessel here." Colonel Dasius reached, jovially drunken, over the table, swallowing bile. "I served in Gaul with Sulla, Lord Prince. A splendid land. My lady wife I found in Aquitania. You must meet her. She faints to speak her Gallic tongue again."

"The health is up, good Balchus," Sulla Pinarius said. "Come, lift a goblet. Let these nameless creatures use themselves as oxen. And let them wear the Roman yoke for Diana's sake. Triumph! Great Mother, triumph!"

A slave put a fresh goblet into the Colonel's hand, and another poured wine. But the wine splashed into the goblet and out, and over the cushions, and on the floor.

Shouts came from outside, and more in the house, and Colonel and slave fell, and women among the guests were shrieking. Vases and lampstands fell, and the walls of the house moved, and the tables tipped, and the couches shuddered. Flames spread from fallen lamps, and burning oil caught clothing. Men threw themselves on smoking fabric, and tore. And the earth moved underfoot, and Garvan felt as if he stood upon the back of some great animal, with no rein, or any hold.

A bossed gong, a ton of metal, swung from side to side upon the wall, and fell on its edge and toppled almost upon the Mother Hemera. Garvan saw it, and put out his sound foot, holding it off until Genessa pulled her away.

"Hold, now!" Colonel Dasius shouted. "Are we to run for a shift of earth?"

Garvan tried to lift Hemera, and cursed his leg and arm for being like sheet anchors. But then, as a vaulter in turning sees the world turn, and standing again finds the world where it was, so the room stilled, and the floor was firm.

"Nothing," said the Colonel. "I said it was nothing. An earth tremor, no more. I'll bring the others back."

Genessa knelt, taking Hemera's head in her arms, and trying to take off the jeweled wreath. Tercena, the assistant, came over, holding a cloth to a bruised head. Hemera opened her eyes and sighed.

"I have Prince Garvan to thank," she said. "That gong could have crushed me. Come, Tercena. We must see what is done in the temple. Genessa, send one for my coach."

Genessa ran, but Garvan had felt that pressure on his shoulder, of a hand that spoke its thankfulness. Sulla Pinarius helped his wife to her feet, and went to the wife of Rufus Nonnius, a heap of trembling silk with a slipper hanging off one foot.

Seles came in, with a line of slaves, and every eye was bloodshot with fear, and many a back showed the marks of the whip.

"So, a fortunate end," said Sulla Pinarius to the Mother Hemera. "I expected the house to collapse as it did some years ago. But you see? You were here with potent prayers, dear Mother. Let us hope others were as well served!"

Lady Thalia saw to it that her women guests were carried out, and came over to Garvan.

"Garvan, forgive us," she began, holding her husband's arm. "We must go into the city to see what help is needed. Would you think us heartless if we left you in an empty house?"

"Leave me," said Garvan. "I'd give this leg to be of use to you. Let me have an arm to take this useless carcass to my room. And take my prayers for your work this night."

Corbi waited outside, to lend a strong shoulder. Garvan bade them all farewell, and Sulla Pinarius followed him to the stairway.

"The house is safe," he said, and shook Garvan's hand. "Do you know what a friend you made? How well your courage served you?"

"As a cripple?" Garvan laughed. "I did nothing!"

"You earned the friendship of the College," Sulla Pinarius said, grave and smiling. "In this, there is great good. Sleep in peace."

Garvan went up the first flight, cursing a helplessness that sent him to bed instead of roaming the streets, ready to help. At the second flight he halted at a door of hammered gold.

"Let us see if all is well with our Mithras," he told Corbi.

The old man took down the key from its place, and opened the door.

A light burned over the slab of red marble, lighting white roses spread about the crossed feet of the god standing as if he leaned against the wall, fingers to cheek, head turned ever to the right, looking always along the way that men must travel.

No sign of damage appeared, not even a crack in the golden ceiling, or in the walls of glossed leaf-green.

"See how he rests!" Corbi whispered. "So a god should be. Unmoved."

There came to Garvan in that moment a curious feeling that in the upper room in Lydia's house there had been not stillness but a movement, as if the air itself were breathing and all thought lived in royal commotion.

Here what life was in the air came from dying roses.

"Let us go up," Garvan said. "The day has wearied me."

But beyond the door Genessa waited, wrapped about in a fur cloak. She came to him, and kissed him upon the left cheek and upon the right. And, barely touched, the cheeks burned as wounds, for where her lips came, they left a little of herself.

"For my mother, and for me," she said, tender and hurried at once. "The city is not damaged. But people are frightened, and we shall drive, and where help can be given it will be got. Think nothing of the great flame in the mountain. They say the god is angered, and tomorrow we shall sacrifice. Think of me, and sleep well."

"These go not together," Garvan said, but she was halfway down the stair. "Genessa, why do you not wait to take a kiss from me?"

He had to laugh, hearing the whole heart of her laughter.

"Have it ready for the giving or I'll never wait," she called. "And make no point of it. I am allowed to kiss. But you may not. Be as a Gaul, durable and cold. This is my wish. Corbi, see the lord Prince well. This, too, is my wish. And Diana, great Mother, smile upon us both!"

X

Garvan felt a deep pleasure in living at the Pinarii mansion, and after a few days he felt he had never been anywhere else. The household's silence commanded his respect. All was in order throughout the day. Every room was gay with flowers in gold, or silver, or crystal, or black and red terra-cotta vases, and each room had its own bouquet. No slave appeared until a bell was rung, or unless fingers snapped in sudden need. Then one, and often two, came barefoot, with Seles always near to supervise. Nothing was wanting that could not be got, if not in the house, then by messengers sent outside. Garvan's favorite places were the terrace looking up to Vesuvius, and the library windowed out to the garden. The days passed usefully, and with serenity, and hour by hour he felt his strength return.

But there was one great disappointment. After that first evening he saw Genessa only once in the week following, and then to wave and call farewell.

She kept his room fresh with flowers from the first morning. In their scent and color he tried to find solace. Her mother explained that she had to be out early to practice for the temple rituals and dances, and she had to study late with her tutors to make her mark with the examiners.

"Her father is determined she shall be prize scholar in Greek, in mathematics, geometry and in geography," Lady Thalia told him. "Fortunately she has a good mind. There, she follows her father. I cannot tell one glyph from another. My house is my book."

"In this, you are my mother," Garvan said. "But I dream a little of her company."

"Gentle sauce for your next meeting," Lady Thalia smiled. "Afra the weaver comes tomorrow. You shall exercise an hour or so, and as the days go, longer. In a little time, you'll be able to move without carriers or sticks. By then, Genessa will be free."

"But how long until she goes to Capri?" Garvan asked. "And must she go?"

Lady Thalia looked up from her lace frame. For a moment Garvan thought he saw a little of Lydia's directness. But then she went on with the lace-hook, and her eyes were hidden.

"Sometime during the nones of August there will be the feast of Diana," she said. "After that, ten days of rest, and then she begins a year at Capri. Six months at the temple here. Six final months in Rome. No other girl in all the empire has such opportunity. Her father is driven mad in pride of her."

Garvan heard the flat tone, but instinct warned, and he kept his mouth shut.

"I know nothing of Dianic custom," he said. "What goodness has Diana that she so envelops Rome?"

"Romans worship her strength," Lady Thalia said, still at the lace-frame. "Caesar is bound to her. There is reverence for Cybele and Rhea and Minerva and Juno, and the Egyptian gods of the legions. But those are for the herd. Diana takes our leaders because she rules without sentiment. Genessa has been trained in her ways. In the Capri temple, she will meet the power of the Court. She will know the prayers, and the secrets, and the ambitions of every man of any rank. She will know all those who rule in every part of the empire. Think, then. What shall be her value as a wife, knowing all these things?"

"Fit for an emperor," Garvan said. "Is this her destiny?"

"It may be so," Lady Thalia said. "I'd wish her more of quietude. Had her brother lived, perhaps her father might not have set his heart on her advancement. She is the last of his name. Therefore she must be glorious for his sake. He thinks of a place as consul."

"It is close in my heart to marry," Garvan said. "We are of age. I have a fitting station. My house shall match this for beauty. My future lands are a kingdom. It's been a thought of mine, once I am afoot, to speak to Sulla Pinarius."

Lady Thalia gathered her lace-frame, and the satchel and her parasol, and stood.

"This must be your own decision, and I am not a guardian but hostess," she said. "You are here as guest of Caesar. But I beg you think well. You are young. There is time to spare."

"There is much I have to do," Garvan said. "I must go home when health allows. There are duties to be done as son of my father. Now is the proper time to think of marriage."

Lady Thalia pinned a gold fibula in another place on her shoulder, and draped the toga folds over her forearm. She seemed to want to smile.

"This would be dearest answer to my prayer," she said in a sudden turn toward him. "Yes, ask him. I'd add my words for you if I thought I could help. But I cannot."

"In this I am surprised," Garvan said. "I had understood this to be the city where women rule. Is this not so?"

"In all things except where they touch Caesar, this is so." Lady Thalia hesitated. "Even Caesar may be influenced. But not by wives or daughters. Let us not speak of this again. And say nothing to Genessa before you speak to her father. Farewell!"

Garvan saw the goodness in Sulla Pinarius's scheme, and in every way except one he sympathized. There was sound sense in wanting a daughter placed in position of such power, and it was a daughter's duty to help her father. A man lived to make his mark in time. If Sulla Pinarius wanted consul's rank, it was proper in him, and a sign that he welcomed responsibility and the honor of serving his country. And at all times Genessa and her Roman husband, whoever he might be, would make strong allies.

For himself Garvan saw that, with Genessa for wife and with Caesar's favor, he might look to a career far more illustrious than any Gaul since Aruborix, his great-great-grandfather. To bring all the people of the Keltae under one throne, with power equal to Rome's, and the daily fare level with the best Romans'; that was the dream lighting his mind.

But plainly he saw that her usefulness to her father was little enough if she married a Gaul, whereas by marrying any well-born Roman with a brain they might between them achieve power enough to make the Pinarii something more than a family of city guardians. He felt weakness in thinking that he might have to leave the house, and the city, and the land itself, and go back to Gaul with no hope of seeing her again except as another man's wife.

He made the decision there, looking over the terrace garden to the cone of the burning mountain. Almost he could imagine the flame coming out of himself. From the first moment he had looked upon her he realized that no other thought had been in his mind except that they must marry.

Think well of things well to be done, and those things will be well done, Mithras said. Think sure in yourself and other things will be sure. He set his mind that Genessa must be his wife, and put the matter aside, and asked Corbi to wheel him along the corridor to see the Greek painter and his men at their work in the main room on the upper floor.

The walls had been stripped down to the stones, and plasterers were filling the panels with a cement of lime and eggs. Phocis the painter sat in the middle, strictest of masters, watching every move. But his workmen were also strict from training, and they rarely needed any word. Master and men worked in short tunics with a sweat bandage about their foreheads. Phocis of Corinth was plump, with many chins, and the merriest black eyes, and a ready tongue for a joke, and a great thirst for the wine of his country, which to Garvan tasted like a varnish for leather.

He stood and bowed, taking off his sweat bandage, and when Garvan was seated, he unrolled the colored drawing plans to show the new features.

"This is the chief work, Lord Prince." He smoothed a cartoon of Apollo and the Muses, washed in color on cloth. "It will take the end wall. On either side of the window, we shall have panels of cupids at play among all the instruments of music. Opposite, on the west wall, a painting of the harbor by night, when Apollo sings and Diana Artemis makes prophecy. On the south wall, more cupids at play in panels beside a portrait of the Lady Genessa and her friends. By her father's wish."

"A noble wish," said Garvan. "This might even be called the Room of Genessa. But it seems to me that many cupids might dispute her for the honor."

"A woman's world," Phocis said in a sniff. "Think what I could have done here. That end wall should have been pulled down, and joined to the corridor and the main staircase. In that noble vista, I could have painted a procession of Dionysius from start to finish. There's challenge for a painter. No. They have to build a storeroom in the middle of the corridor, if you please. Romans have no idea of planning. None!"

Garvan thought of the many times he had looked through an oar vent, watching Roman generals and admirals in conclave on a nearby galley, placing flags on a map nailed to the deck, and planning by the hour. He thought of an empire won by those methods, of thinking, and moving, and thinking again, and moving, slow, inexorable.

"Tell me," he said, unwilling to enter a domestic matter. "How is it that Greeks are so advanced in matters of device and ornament? In that country how do masters grow?"

Phocis laughed, and his black eyes went into pouchy flesh as coins drop into a purse.

"We have time to devote to study of the mind, and not alone to foray and battle over strange terrain," he said. "We have no empire to suck our young men into useless service. We have time to school and to enter the workshops of masters if that's our wish. I started as a child of five."

"You never served as soldier or sailor?" Garvan asked, surprised.

"My forefathers did it all," Phocis said. "We fought for a thousand years, and we made ten thousand heroes. At the end, we had nothing except genius. We put it to work. At this moment, all Greece is a Roman province by force of arms. But all of Rome's provinces belong to Greece by force of mind. In this city, what is excellent that is Roman? The buildings? By Greek architects. The streets? Greek engineers. The ornament, in metal, stone, or paint, Greek without question. And the language most honored? Greek. The sciences? Greek. The customs among the wealthy? Greek. Which god founded the city? Hercules, a Greek. How then will you deny me?"

Garvan fell silent. It seemed, now that his eyes were open, that what Phocis said was correct. He could find no flaw. Even Genessa's studies were all in Greek, and the Dianic games and dances she practiced, and even the costumes she wore came not from Rome but Greece.

"Here, again, is weakness," he said, almost to himself. "Perhaps there is some greater weakness."

"Perhaps that one discussed by Cicero," Phocis said. "Remember? He writes, 'We are alive only to the worth of the material and not to the genius of the artist.' There is profound weakness!"

"But moral," said Garvan. "I mean one that could destroy them."

Phocis covered his eyes.

"In these things I have nothing to say," he said in real fear. "I speak of my own work abroad. That is my opinion. But in matters affecting the State, I speak no word. I am metic."

"Metic?" Garvan inquired. "What is this?"

"One who lives in the land as an alien, and has hospitality and the chance to offer his work," Phocis said, looking uneasily at his helpers. "One who pays taxes, but has no vote or other citizen right. And I pray you, good Prince, beware. The city crawls with spies. No man knows which he is, or where."

"Wait, now," Garvan chided. "A question. How strikes you this religion of Diana? What are its virtues for ordinary men above any other? Isis, or Rhea, or Urania, or how many more?"

Phocis rumpled his forehead and took most of the lines out of his face. But the rumples stopped where his hair had been, and the flesh on his pate and above his eyebrows was smooth, but in between his eyes and chin a mass of furrows changed places moment to moment with the roving effort of his mind.

"Here's a tight one," he murmured. "How should I answer this? You must know that Diana was daughter of Zeus, and sister of Apollo? She is protectress of youth, and a maid ever, and love is foreign to her. She is the moon, cold, lighting all and affecting all, but untouched herself. Her worshipers pray that her coldness may come into them, that their faces may be turned from softer ways. This is the creature of the Roman strength."

"Then"—Garvan hesitated—"if this is so, what is the use of the vestal, or of her junior, the vire? What purpose do these maids serve? How should one, all warmth, become moon-cold?"

Again the furrows crowded and Phocis watched his workmen and his hands and body were still. Garvan thought of a scout watching the enemy. But when Phocis turned his head, he was shocked to see the black eyes were hard with hate.

"You do me wrong, Prince Garvan," he said, almost in a growl. "Before these men, all witnesses? If so much is wanting in your knowledge, let others supply it. I am a painter, and a Greek. Enough!"

Garvan tried to find his breath, much less a word. Phocis picked up his board of color daubs, and tapped a workman on the shoulder, and together they bowed, and turned about and went out.

Corbi stood, looking down at his hands, and either he trembled or he was nodding his head. The workmen went on with their business, as if no word had been said. The bare room that had been so full of work and life before seemed comfortless as a lime pit.

"Why did he say that to me?" he asked Corbi in the corridor on the way back.

"The Lady Genessa is to be a vestal," Corbi said gently. "This is her father's house. How could he say things that might tell against her?"

"Against her?" Garvan pulled himself about to look at the old, patient face. "Tell me, now. What might be said against her?"

"Against vestalism," Corbi whispered. "I am old, and no follower of Diana. I am a slave to the household, Lord Prince. If it were told of Phocis that he spoke even with the sound of his voice against vestalism, he would die. And I, the same, but worse. Therefore we say nothing."

"But if you speak well, how can you be punished?" Garvan demanded.

Corbi stopped the wheeled couch before the door of the room.

"Phocis is a freeman, and a master, and I am a slave," he whispered. "But in this we are one. Every server in the house and any slave hates vestalism and all in the bosom of Diana. I lost three daughters to the temple."

"Tell me," Garvan shouted impatiently. "What is this you say? Tell me instantly!"

"I said nothing, Lord Prince, except that now is space for nooning, and perhaps wine and a biscuit would be preferred to the broth of camomile?" Corbi bowed, watching the approach of Seles. "I am a slave. I have no mouth!"

Garvan found he had to keep his patience. Several times he raised the bell to talk to Seles, but each time he thought better. It went against the dignity of the house, if not his own, to ask any deep matter of servants. It worried him that a slave could hate Diana and all her dealings and risk death to say so. And yet the head of the Pinarii, patrician and lawmaker and a man most careful of his name, not only worshiped the goddess and favored her priestesses, but offered two years of his daughter's life in her service.

Relief came in seeing Afra tap his way onto the roof and walk to a place out of the breeze and point to the spot he chose for the loom. When the servants had gone he sat.

"Lord Garvan, good Prince," he called. "Come, let us spoil thread together. It's long since we talked."

"There are air-slots here, perhaps," Garvan said. "Is this the place to speak? Or have we another warren holed by Diana's lizards?"

"Have a care now." Afra turned his blind face, without laughter.

"Before this, you were of the galley, nameless, and wanting all except your blood and birth. Now you are replete. Let not a sense of rank be wanting."

"A torn fig for my rank," Garvan whispered. "Let me know this of vestals, and assure me you speak in knowledge. What do they in the temple? Why do the basest men speak against them?"

Afra closed the weaving bar, and pushed the loom away.

"I agree the day sits hot, Prince Garvan," he said loudly. "But I fear there is no weaver in you, except of rude carpets for drunken buyers. You have a prince's mind, feckless. And a prince's tread, reckless."

"You have a mouth," said Garvan. "Let it say something."

"We shall talk on the lawn of the gymnasium," Afra said, almost in a whisper. "I shall bring wool and explain to you what makes a thread. Should you walk, or shall Corbi attend you?"

Garvan raised his stick.

"Let Corbi rest," he said. "He knows enough."

"Too much," Afra agreed. "Let us go by the outer stair."

Garvan followed with slow step, but desire to hear an end to his doubts made him strong, and he hobbled the better, glad to be free of wheels and a couch. But he was gladder still to be with Afra, for the crowds made way for the tapping stick, and they might have walked in an empty city.

Afra turned out of the crowded square of Apollo and into the Street of the Caduceus. Pharmacists and midwives and bonesetters and spellmakers had their shops and stalls along the way, all noisy with people, mostly servants, and rough underfoot with beggars.

"Why is it they allow these?" Garvan asked, pulling his toga from the clutch of a hand. "In such a city?"

"Riches have twice their worth when beggars hold the mirror," Afra said. "Who enjoys health without the salt of others' sores? Do you suppose people are sorry for me because of my blindness? They sorrow, thinking of themselves if they were blind. Turn here, at this gate. Find us a quiet corner, but away from shadow or any hiding place."

Garvan chose a square of grass along the colonnade, but in the open, near the fountain of the Five Bronze Serpents. An attendant from the gymnasium brought two chairs, and they sat in the sun. Men ran and jumped and boxed under the shouts of trainers in the games park, and a line of men waited at the door to the public bath.

"Phocis told Seles of your talk," Afra began carefully. "Seles told Yosef. Yosef told me. I also know from Chote, through Corbi. It is a dangerous matter, and one to be explained with care and then dismissed. This is Rome, and Romans are jealous of all things Roman. Do you see anyone near us, reading, or thoughtful, or talking to his fellow with an eye elsewhere?"

Garvan had a careful look to the sides, and behind, and in front. The shady length of the colonnade held a few strollers, but far away. Workmen painted on a cradle high up the wall of the gymnasium and talked to women at a window.

"You chose well," he said. "We are alone."

"First, fit these details in your mind," Afra said, barely above a whisper, at the same time holding up a hank of wool and plucking at it. "This is washed wool from sheep of the Abruzzi. It makes a fine thread suitable for tunics and heavy togas. It dyes well and won't shrink. That's if any should ask you why we speak. Now, the substance. These Dianists are powerful in all the empire. Their priestesses accept only coins or jewels or property. You see why it's a religion for patricians, the wealthy? Plebeians, with nothing except a dove and a prayer, may choose another's altar. Look about the garden. Do you see anyone?"

Garvan looked well, and saw none.

"The religion is ruled by women under Caesar," Afra went on, twirling the wool into a long thread. "I never heard of a priest except among the legions. The daughters of most important men become vires from the age of six years, and train to be vestals-in-honor. But they have much to learn, in ritual, and dances and music."

"I see nothing in this to make men fear," Garvan said. "Why did Phocis turn hate upon me?"

"You may speak of Diana only in a certain way," Afra warned. "Any other way is death. Do poorer men speak with hate? Perhaps their daughters were sold as vires to rich worshipers."

"Genessa was not," Garvan whispered.

"Indeed not. Perhaps many a vestal-in-honor has gone into a temple and hasn't been seen again——"

"Not Genessa!"

"Never. Vires, we know, have been sacrificed by knife and fire——"

"But her father will protect Genessa," Garvan said.

"Go to the temple," Afra said. "Seles will take you and prepare your entrance. If further doubts trouble you, come to me. But say nothing to others for your own sake and theirs!"

A hand bright in a sword glove reached over his shoulder and snatched the wool. Shadows fell across them. Garvan looked up, at an officer and four men in the blue and silver uniform of the temple guard.

"You spoke of Diana, Queen of all praise." The officer pulled Afra to his feet. "Explain this matter!"

"It is simple." Afra laughed his silent laugh. "I had warned my friend he'd never keep his secret. He learns the loom from me, not as weaver, but as one bringing use to his bones, broken in the arena under the aegis of Caesar——"

"These things we know," the officer said. "He is the Prince Garvan——"

"As I said, how could he keep a secret?" Afra laughed. "Thus he reasoned. He works some hours every week with me. Better than weaving for weaving's sake, he wanted to make a mitra for the Lady Genessa to wrap about her head when she practices the dances for Diana. Behold, in your fingers, the very stuff!"

"What stuff is this?" the officer asked Garvan.

"Of the sheep of Abruzzi," Garvan said. "How was our talk overheard?"

"You were lip-read." The officer handed back the wool. "Let me say this word. It is best not to talk. You, weaver, remember this."

Garvan watched the officer march his catfooted band along the colonnade.

Afra put a coin on the chair for the attendant.

"As I suggested," he whispered under cover of gathering his cloak and fastening the neck chain. "You are watched at all times. Someone is not friendly, Lord Prince. Who? For what reason? I made the choice of this open, public place. But had we gone into the darkest cellar, we would have been disturbed just the same. Who is not friendly? For what reason?"

"Perhaps because I am a Gaul," Garvan said. "But still why, if I live at the house of Sulla Pinarius?"

"Indeed," Afra nodded. "And who else lives in that house, with even a little more to do with Diana's business?"

Garvan thought of Genessa, and made no reply.

Afra tapped his way to the colonnade.

"Care," he murmured. "Care in all things. Since our Lady Lydia opened her mouth there has been need for care. The College of Diana would call a feast in the moment of her arrest. Who hates the Fisherman more than Artemis Diana?"

"Who is this Fisherman?" Garvan asked.

"Lydia serves Him," Afra laughed, and turned off on the avenue to Pompeii. "I will help you across the traffic, Lord Prince, and leave you. Remember, if she were found to be suborning Caesar with her talk, there would come death to many. This is my fear. I have lived too long in the night. It has grown warm about me. It is my kingdom."

Garvan thought of Titus Caesar, and of what effect Lydia's talk of a God of no Name might have. But he shrugged it away.

"Rule on, good Afra," he said. "Here is my street, and here my hand."

"Do you go to the temple in the morning, Lord Prince?" Afra asked.

"That, rest on it," said Garvan. "Farewell!"

XI

Long before first light of dawn, when Genessa and her maids had
left the house in laughter and a barking of lonely spaniels, Garvan
went out with Seles and mounted a chariot waiting for them in the
square. Lamps were alight and, early as it was, the streets were busy
with men and women carrying flowers or coops of birds and some
with trussed animals, all in dark hurry toward a place of worship.
Grottoes and shrines were filled with kneeling people, and the smoke
of sacrifice blew sweet in every street.

Diana's temple threw mauve in the sky. They turned into the avenue behind the Forum and left the chariot, going on foot toward the
gardens and joining the singing crowd along the paths leading to the
temple steps. Trees were lit in many colors from fires in shrines set
under the foliage, and everyone tossed coins and sang a prayer at every
shrine, and every tree stood in its own bright mat of flung gold.

Braziers flaming here red, and there blue, stood between each column and washed the entrance in red and blue, until they met in purple toward the roof. A mighty group, in gold, of Caesar carried in a chariot with four prancing horses, divided the stairway, and women went to one side and men to the other. Main doors of silver bossed with gold were closed, and wreathed with myrtle. Worshipers entered one by one through small doors at the side, throwing an entrance offering into gold bowls, each watched by a squatting priestess; and as the coins clashed, she gave a blessing and handed the donor a wreath of laurel.

Garvan put on his wreath, and at Seles' sign he wrapped the blue veil, mark of the unbeliever, about his face and took off his shoes, and followed into the vestibule, to the tables of the money-changers. He waited his place in line, watching all ages of men in rich temple robes, some come drunken from an entertainment, others barely awake, and a few with worry haunting their eyes. But all were combed and shaven, and all sang prayers, many by themselves, and sometimes leading a great chorus. Garvan was surprised at the largeness of their gifts. An old man brought servants carrying bags that held a thousand talents. The stacks of gold coins were paid off on metal, so that all heard a true sound, and black-veiled women in black robes rattled the count in their fingers, calling the numbers for the scribes to make a total.

But all the old man got in return was a small square of bronze with Diana's head impressed. For one talent, which he had thought far too much to spend, Garvan was given one of the same pieces. His pride was trodden to hear his one coin called after the old man's thousand, though nobody took notice either of the old man or of himself. The man behind gave two hundred talents, and a young man in the next line had with him eight slaves, each bowed under four leathern bags all filled, doubtless, with gold.

Garvan marveled. Mithras said that giving was itself a gift, the more of one the greater the other until a man might give himself the world. It was time, he thought, to lose the frugal ideas of a Gallic upbringing, and to adopt the Roman style of making gifts, which seemed to leave no thought for the future.

Seles touched his arm, and led through the curtains into the warm, frankincensed air of the temple.

And he saw that marvels and shocks of wonder were only begun.

At the end of the great hall an altar of gold shone red in fire from the sacrificial hearth. Some hundreds of women in blue and white stood in banked rows on either side, hands together, heads bowed, chanting. Altar servers moved in ritual on the steps and in the broad space dividing the choir. Worshipers stood in groups on varying patterns of colored marbles set in the white paving, of stags, and sheep and oxen, and archers, and fruit and vegetables, all repeated, over a tall bronze grille dividing the temple down the middle, on the women's side. Beyond the columns holding the roof wide cloisters were alight with shrines, each with a priestess on a small throne behind open curtains.

"Diana is goddess of all things in the field or in the forest, and mother of all things giving kindlily to men," Seles whispered. "Therefore, where you have interest in lands and produce, you choose the sheep and oxen, or if your interest is in a business requiring search and pursuit, you stand on the archers. In that way, each shrine, and each oracle, deals with the same matter and there is no confusion."

Galleries one above the other all around three sides were filled, and golden rails were spiked by singing faces looking down, but the sound rolled in the roof's gold raftering, adding to the echoes of the choir.

Garvan propped himself in the shadow of a column on the white marble in a space between crowds. The chant became a clear song, and the worshipers joined in. Drums, cymbals, and sistra beat and clashed in many rhythms, and a priestess's voice called, and all answered, and she called again and was answered.

"Help us, Diana!" she sang.

"Help us!" the worshipers sang.

"Great Mother, prevent misfortune!" the priestess sang.

"Help us!"

"Dry our tears!"

"Help us!"

"Mars, Jove, Quirinus, Vesta, send your strength!"

"Help us!"

"Zeus, Great Father, smile upon your daughter, Diana!"

"Help us!"

"Let her triumph!"

"Triumph!"

"Let Diana Triumph!"

"Triumph!"

The choir sang loud, in chords, and the worshipers went to their knees, singing with them. The hearth below the altar burned a bluish flame, and the drums beat until the color was brightly purple. Trumpets sounded above the voices. Pipe music skirled, and the worshipers all stood, and went to the side, under the columns, baring the great space of the hall.

From both sides of the altar processions of girls came out, through the choir, and down, into the open space, carrying garlands of flowers, with wreaths of lilies in their hair, and necklaces of lilies about their throats, and belts of lilies about their waists, but with no other garment. They danced, one long line to the women's side, and one to the side for men. The line separated on the patterns in the marble paving, and each faction made a ring, dancing to priestesses playing pipes and sistra in the middle.

"These younger are the vires," Seles whispered. "The older vires train to do the work of vestals-in-honor. Watch for the women in the white with purple, and a gold diadem. Those are the vestals. Above them are the priestesses. They wear the blue and white."

Worshipers shouted the time and clapped their hands in rhythm, and the dancers wheeled one way, and another, and went into the middle, and turned one to another, and wove in and out, always faster, until the wheels of flowered bodies and flying hair became almost solid circles. Voices grew louder, and the clapping was joined by stamping, and every man shouted with all the force of his lungs and clapped his hands faster than eye could see, and stamped in time with his hands, until men fell with weakness, and some of the dancers fell. People screamed over the music, and the choir set up a great shout, moments long, and then silence.

In a blast of trumpets the altar's gold doors swung out, and the choir, dancers, and worshipers fell to the ground in prayer, and a great stillness came over all. Seles tried to drag Garvan to his knees, but the leg was not to be bent, and he bowed, low, held by the column.

White light from a thousand small lamps showed a figure recessed in the darkness, almost the height of the building and broad as the altar space. A crescent moon shone above the head as a crown, and the eyes blazed red, and light fashioned the roundness of a woman's form, with a torch in its right hand and a wreath in the other. Gongs and bells beat, slowly and softly, and faster and louder until the ears could have bled, and then smoke puffed from the altar, and when the cloud was thick, and the lights were dim, the altar doors swung inward, and closed.

Men wept, and tore at their hair and their robes. Loud as the men shouted, Garvan heard the women's louder screams. The circles of vires stood, forming in lines facing the altar. Most were young, scarcely from their mother's laps, and few were more than the earliest age for marriage. But the white limbs, and glossy hair all flower-crowned, and the blue-painted eyes and red-painted mouths gave them all, even the youngest, a strange likeness to older women suddenly become children.

Women in white robes striped with purple, and wearing plain gold crowns, came from the altar, carrying silver bowls in outstretched hands. Worshipers ran, and knelt, putting their hands together as a cup.

"Here are the vestals," Seles whispered. "See, the vires serve each a little, that all may eat of the life force of the goddess. This is the *mola salsa*. Put out your hands."

A vestal passed, tall, and in a gaze hard as the statue's behind the altar, and calm, with no color in her face except the whiteness of denial. A vire dipped into the bowl and took a little of the black, warm ash and put it into Garvan's palm. Other men put it to their mouths, and ate, mumbling prayers. But the pellets had the feel of charcoal, and Garvan opened his fingers and let the offering go as dust to the floor.

He caught the eye of Seles. Other worshipers had gone back to the marble patterns in the main hall, mixing with the vires. The gold curtains in all the shrines had been drawn, and guards stood with swords that none might enter. But Seles looked away, toward the altar, and

Garvan, standing a head taller, saw beyond the nearer lines of vires, to others waiting on the pattern of stags.

Genessa's golden hair, lovelier than any, gleamed among them, and she was laughing at Publius Marius, the Consul of Pompeii, and he stroked the hair lying along her shoulder. She drew away from him, but he followed, taking her by the hand.

Garvan moved, but Seles had him by the painful arm, which felt it might break in his grip.

"I beg you, Lord Prince, be still!" he whispered. "Let nothing disturb you. Any outcry, and not you, but the house of the Pinarii will suffer!"

All the worshipers were mixing on the patterns of their choice, greeting the vires as old friends. Many of them went on their knees, whispering. Genessa repeated what was told to her, and ran to the shrine, passing the guard and going behind the gold curtain to the throned priestess.

"They speak their prayers to the older vires, and the younger ones listen to learn," Seles whispered. "Now the priestess makes appeal to the oracle, and the vire brings back the reply. Let us go forward. But no sign, I beg you."

"Do you fear death?"

"No, Lord Prince," Seles said. "To die is the sooner to live another life. But our duty is not to die."

"But why do these men set hands upon them?" Garvan whispered. "Are not vestals supposedly of all women the most chaste?"

"They betray their feelings to the goddess," Seles said. "They caress to show themselves as children in need of help."

Genessa came back, and went to her chair. Publius Marius fell on his knees before her, and she took his head in her hands to whisper the oracle's reply in his ear. Evidently all was to the man's liking. He raised his hands to the roof, and shouted, but the sound was thin in a general shouting. And when he sought to kiss Genessa in gratitude, Garvan turned his back, unwilling to see more.

"We shall go," he told Seles. "Upon these things I shall inquire further. Tell me, in this charnal house, what is the value of their prayers?"

Seles swung his eyes all the way from this side to that, but the noise seemed to reassure him.

"Depending on rank and circumstance, Lord Prince, every value," he said. "These prayers are for certain works, certain contracts. All men pray for success. Both the prayer and the sum he has paid are recorded by a scribe. The oracle tells if he may expect success. These things are known because Diana controls all."

"It is, then, more a place of trade than a place of worship?"

"Romans are practical people," Seles said. "They demand their religion be practical, that is, to produce benefit. What use to give, if nothing comes back?"

"And other religions?" Garvan asked. "What of poorer men?"

"They too can profit," Seles said. "But in lesser ways. All things have a price."

"Then a vire trained to be a vestal could indeed become learned in the affairs of commerce." Garvan turned to watch Genessa. "And also in affairs of state?"

"For that they study," Seles said. "Some become priestesses. The chief of them, those of the College of Diana, are sage women. They know men's minds. Think how, knowing all things, they may advise Caesar and his council."

Garvan limped toward the shadow of the column behind Genessa's chair, and he had to push among the crowd to go close. A hand touched him, not with courtesy.

"Keep your place, cripple," a familiar voice said. "Your betters are before you."

"Straighten your speech," he said through the veil to a tall man, with cropped black hair and a scar down his left cheek. "I have no betters, and I'm not a cripple——"

The big man reached to tear off the veil. Garvan brought the heavy stick off the floor and hit him under the chin with the metal handle, closing his teeth in a snap that resounded. His eyes looked to his nose, and he dropped in a sprawl.

A shout went up, and the nearest men drew off, leaving Garvan in a space with his victim. In a gap between those nearest he saw Seles, with his hands over his eyes as if he feared to see what might follow. The gesture brought anger and contempt.

But before he could move, a white figure leapt beside him, and he caught the scent of lilies, and he was pushed toward the drawn curtains of the nearest shrine, and through a doorway beside the altar, and hurried as fast as his walk would allow down a wide corridor.

"I prayed that you might join Diana," Genessa whispered. "But you go constantly afoul of what is proper. Why did you strike Tabis Netto?"

"He was discourteous," Garvan said, and laughed. "But now we are level in score. Was he not captain of the city police? He struck me across the mouth. Repayment of just debts is worthier than many prayers. Am I now able to ask you questions?"

"I have work here until the forenoon," she said. "Then I attend the games. Tonight, I shall finish the music examinations. Go home, dear mule. I'll tell Seles, if he isn't outside waiting for you!"

"How did you know about Seles?" he demanded. "It was secret between us——"

"—and everybody," she laughed. "I permitted him to bring you. Who has secrets?"

"You," he faced her. "I want to ask many things of you."

"Tomorrow." She pulled the curtains about her. "I'm frozen, and there's work. Go in peace!"

The door slid shut in front of him, and through the bars he heard her thank the doorkeeper, and then go off singing.

Seles stood in the empty Forum at the chariot side, glum.

"I thought you lost, Lord Prince," he said. "No man may offer violence in Diana's presence."

"One of her brood began it," Garvan said. "Did he expect me to stand there?"

Seles shrugged, nodding to the driver to start.

"No other man would have dared," he sighed. "Has the morning been a teacher?"

"Let me think on this," Garvan said. "I went prepared for disgust. I saw nothing of sacrifice except in money, which caused no pain. Why do some men with daughters hate the Dianists?"

"If they live, three more fathers hate at this hour," Seles said. "For when the altar doors opened, three maidens died by the knife. And when the doors closed, the bodies were burned, and the ash was mixed with their blood. That was the mola salsa. Which, in common with the rest, you held in your hand."

"But did not eat," Garvan whispered. "Lord Mithras, you were with me!"

XII

After a bath, and a kneading and twisting of the arm and leg by the Numidian, Garvan sat out in the late sunshine on the terrace, and made certain of his decision about Genessa.

Whatever her religion and its claims upon her, he made up his mind to marry her. But he also made up his mind that the conduct of the male Dianists was far from what he thought proper toward a future princess of Gaul. It followed that either she must stop going to the temple, or if she wished to go, the men must be warned to keep their distance and put their requests in a manner fitting to her station.

Moreover, she must wear more clothing.

He saw little wrong in the plebeian habit of wearing a scrap or nothing during the day's heat. But people of family found no need to make a show of themselves in public, and even less in a place of worship, whether customary or not. He found himself shaking with anger at any thought of another's hand near Genessa, or any lightest kiss for her but his own. He acknowledged that she had taken little notice of any of them. A piece of wood might not have shown less feeling, but the process went against his idea of what was right and wrong. There was something comical in any notion that he could become a Dianist, and make bribes for favors, and whisper secrets to the half-grown for oracles to answer.

Even for Genessa's sake he would not. It also came to him that whether from the Lady Thalia, or from Lydia or Seles or Afra or anybody else, nobody had told him what more Genessa would have to learn in two years of training. But he began to wonder if all, slaves as well, were not praying for a champion strong enough to defy the power of Diana, and Caesar, and all the Roman Court, and take Genessa away from them.

There came a desire to walk in the city, and perhaps to go to the theater if the bill promised well. He swung a cloak over his shoulders, and took his stick, and went down the terrace stairs into the Street of the White Peonies.

He walked for some time, enjoying the cool air among the city strollers, and turned into the Street of the Crying Quail, and knew himself to be near the cookshop of Chote the Carthaginian. He felt drawn there, if only to savor a meal he could pay for in memory of the ragged guest of a blind weaver.

The shop was crowded under the hanging vines by a shouting mob of cripples and beggars. And he stood there, and stared, for at the table in the corner, Tadmon, hero of the wineskin, had his teeth in a haunch of suckling. His shout of welcome and the backslapping and laughter brought Chote from the kitchen, and potmen cleared a place for a knife and a trencher of bread, and in shortest time Garvan shared the meal.

"See how fortunate I've been," Tadmon laughed through a mouthful. "And what do I do? I'm a stoker of the furnace at the public bath. Where I heard all about you."

"About me?" Garvan frowned. "What now?"

"Talk of the city, that's you," Tadmon grinned. "But nobody knows

from me that a couple of ragtails met over a splash of free wine. Your
fortune makes me happy. But you have enemies."

"Nothing of these is known to me," said Garvan.

"I listen to what's said in the baths," said Tadmon. "There's the
place for chatter."

"Steam comes from a bath," Garvan said. "It passes."

Tadmon chewed a piece of crackling rind, and drank from the flask.

"Enemies are not killed off by turning the back," he said at last.
"You are thought to be a companion to Christians."

"I stay at the house of their enemy," said Garvan. "Where is my
crime?"

"You lifted your hand in the temple," Tadmon said. "You were
saved by one carrying the favor of Caesar."

"Let her name be unsaid." Garvan took water and washed his fingers. "How may I be of service to you? Might I try to find your wife
and children? Is there hope?"

Tadmon dropped his knife, and closed his mouth, and his eyes
dulled, and the years came upon him.

"Aye, hope!" he groaned. "Hope of sticking a knife in a hundred
gullets——"

"Let us see, first, what may be done," Garvan said. "Their names
and where captured, by whom and whence taken. A woman, Lydia, a
Christian, will help us in this."

"See how they make the world their own." Tadmon pushed away
the food. "Even Vesuvius shakes all, and rests. But with these Christians, nothing is still."

"You know about them?" Garvan asked eagerly. "Tell me, since
we are friends, what do they offer? Where is the gain in being a
Christian?"

"It is told by them that they shall have everlasting life of another
kind beside this." Tadmon grimaced. "They say that when they die
they shall be raised up, not in this earth, but in another, where all live
in peace. But also, and more to the taste, they do very well in this
life. All I've met have paying work, and fat living. They want for
nothing."

"These things I do not understand," Garvan said. "How are they supplied when all Romans hate them?"

"Not all Romans," Tadmon smiled. "Christians cherish their own kind. But they live too few years to grow fat. The aediles sweep them up as blasphemers and unbelievers, and they die. But they die gladly."

Garvan remembered the words of Colonel Dasius, and his complaint about the willingness of Christians to die.

"What is it that makes them so?" he asked. "What new spine straightens their backs?"

Tadmon shook his head, holding up his palms.

"This mystery comes clear only by joining their temple," he said, and leaned forward. "The Dianists are saying that Caesar himself is infected. They put their heads in a basket to see what may be done to save him."

"These things you hear in the bath?" Garvan inquired. "Free talk, certainly. Are these my enemies?"

Tadmon started eating again.

"You design to take from them their dearest bait," he said. "A vire, soon to be a vestal——"

"Make her no name in this place," Garvan told him. "Where is their bait?"

"Titus Caesar spreads his feet toward his fortieth year, without wife or any issue," Tadmon said. "This girl you speak about wants yet a little toward full growth as a woman. She has name, blood, rank and beauty. The College of Diana makes her prime favorite. And why? Might she not bring the First Roman back to Diana? And keep him?"

"But would those virtues keep him?" Garvan asked. "He knows them now. Yet you say they think him infected?"

Tadmon pushed away the suckling carcass, and scraped grease and bones and bread to one side, and dipped his hands in the bowl, and splashed his mouth, and wiped himself.

"I am father of daughters, and one who has never missed a temple to pray for them," he said. "If they are dead, I will exact a toll. I enjoy my hate as I savor my food, though sometimes both sicken me. Yes, brother-ragtail, this nameless vire is a Greek gift to Caesar."

"Greeks make gifts expecting favors, but this is gossip of the bazaar and the bath," Garvan said. "How could a man of rank offer his daughter?"

"How is it that when men tread the gutters they see, and speak, and deal honestly with themselves?" Tadmon asked the roof. "How can it be, that with a little more food, and clothing, and money, that then they change, and turn away, the better not to believe what life in the gutter has taught them? This man of rank will give his daughter for the sake of Rome. This is worthy in him? He thinks so. He will give his daughter for his love of Diana. This is meet in him? He thinks so. He will sacrifice her to the Roman lares and penates that Caesar may be held from any other faith. This is love of his country's ideals? He thinks so. But are they so? All Romans are ambitious. Who, next to Caesar, is most powerful in the empire? The Empress. And who, next to her? His favorite!"

Garvan had a feeling that once again the Numidian had flung him into the icy bath. But instead the sweat broke wet on his forehead, and the blood drummed, and the knee and the shoulder became sore, and he felt tired.

"If this should happen, I'd fall upon my spear," he said.

"Here tragedy would spin both head and tail," said Tadmon. "Lord Prince, I call you so this once, but never more until we meet, armed and helmeted, as equals. But know me, however lowly in this time, to be your friend. And remember, when I send a message, act upon it as you once drank wine on your knee. In trust."

"Why should I trust you?" Garvan asked. "In what matter?"

Tadmon laughed, but no smile was in his eyes.

"In the matter of ragtails, brought to account," he said. "My message will tell you when you may expect to die. In what place, or at which feast. And beware the Roman fish. It comes sweet-cooked. But the flesh is dead. Chote is paid, and so is the potman. Your trust you may keep. Farewell!"

Tadmon went out, through the cookstoves and beyond, and neither did he turn. In a few moments the man had come upon a rare dignity, and his years sat with all their weight. His warning was a double shock, for if a stoker in a public bath could know so much, then those speaking must know much more.

Garvan went through the noisy room, giving away the coins he might have spent, and into the street, fresh with a breeze from the sea, and he took it in for tonic, walking toward the busy, flare-lit avenue to Pompeii.

Among all the people he trusted there seemed nobody better to ask for advice than Lydia. On the corner of the Forum he called chairmen, and told them to go down the Street of Lean Days to the harbor. He sat in the leather-lined box, and the men set their poles in the sockets, and lifted, and started their jog.

Streets were bare, and cleaners were gathering the day's refuse, and teams of women scrubbed the paving. Windows were lit on second and third stories, and police stood about sparking braziers on corners. Flowers gleamed beside doorways and under windows, and flame was bright in many a niche along the walls, marbled as shrines to Vesta, and stuck about with waxen tablets cut with prayers.

He paid the men off beyond the Square of the Singing Muses, and walked through the street past the baker's shop. Lydia's house showed no light, and there was no watchman. Tapping on the bronze-studded door was waste of time. He went around to the terrace gateway, and felt behind the loose stone where Yosef always left the key for Afra. He could have laughed aloud to pick it up, and he opened the door and locked it behind, and went up the stairway to the terrace, almost with a feeling of coming home. His old room was empty, and the corridors outside were dark. He went to the main stairway, and felt his way down. The atrium was silent, and the stars sent light among the columns of the garden, showing stools and benches against the walls, and twists of wool and silk hung by the dozen on racks. Light came from the doorway leading up to the women's side of the house. He walked down, hoping to come upon a sleeping servant, but he was at the foot of the stairs and still he saw nobody.

But he heard a chant, low, deep, in many voices, that caused the stair rail to vibrate under his hand. He went up, one step at a time, soundless in soft leather on stone. Where the stairway turned into the passage, a wooden screen closed the way.

A woman's voice called from a little distance, and other voices answered her in unison from the other side of the screen.

Garvan went close, looking through the space between the hinges.

The door to the private room was open, and its light showed the passage filled with kneeling men and women, most wearing scarlet and others in black. Afra knelt before the open door, and beside him Seles, and a serving-woman he had seen in the Pinarii household. Beyond, an old man, but he knew the face and then he remembered Uriel, the fisherman of Agrigento. Yosef knelt, facing the stairway, and he saw both his old nurses.

Shadow fell, and Lydia came to the doorway, carrying in one hand the pannier filled with pieces of bread, and in the other a cup.

She held out the pannier to a woman kneeling beside the door, and the woman bared her arm from black folds to take a piece of bread. And her hand came into the light when she dipped the bread in the cup, and when she raised the sop, he saw the Lady Thalia. He heard Lydia tell her to take, and eat, and all the voices joined together in answer.

But he came away from the screen, and went down, through the atrium and up to the terrace and he locked the door and hid the key. And in all he did he refused to think of what he had seen, and turned his eyes from any memory. By long practice in the oar banks he was able to clear his mind of most thoughts bringing discomfort. Even so the night passed restlessly and he slept little.

At first light, before he was out of bed, Corbi came in to announce Seles.

"Lord Prince, morning greeting." He stood, pointing toward the hills to the north. "The signal fires are lit. They tell that the oracle spoke in augury an hour ago, and Diana will hold her feast tomorrow night at Lake Nemi. The Lady Lydia takes ship today at the tenth hour, and offers a guest place to the Lord Prince. Tomorrow is the greatest day of the year, and all Rome will be at Nemi!"

"My compliments and thanks to the Lady Lydia," Garvan said. "I shall accompany her. Take this message to the Lady Genessa, that I offer devotion new as the morning and old as my life."

"The lady and her maids are gone, Lord Prince," Seles bowed. "They will be there before you."

Garvan went down to the harbor in good time. The vessel was new, and larger than any flagship he had ever seen, and painted in white, with a blue sail. A pattern of three fishes, in silver, shone in the peak.

"Welcome to the Ark of Tarsus," Lydia greeted him. "This is the workshop of my fleet. But you must excuse me during most of the day. I have a great deal to do, and little time. Why did you enter my house last night?"

They were standing on deck above the busy quayside. Garvan kept his eyes on the head of Hercules rising high above the roofs. The great face stared as if it felt his surprise.

"I came to ask your advice," he said. "About Genessa. But I saw nobody."

She looked at him with her head bent, and although the gray eyes half smiled, he felt cold.

"Others saw you," she said. "I told you to be careful of your movements. What did you learn on the upper floor?"

"I have no memory for others' business," Garvan said impatiently. "I am filled with my own. Is this reason for making me guest? Here, call a chariot and let Diana feast without me!"

"Not so." Lydia put out her hand. "Be patient, Garvan. You should know that Genessa asked me to offer you passage. There was no way for her to take you, and her father goes direct with Caesar from Capri. You could have gone by coach, but here am I going to Rome, a little way on. Therefore, I asked you as my guest. What trouble had you with Genessa?"

"The trouble of one jealous of Diana and those who worship her," said Garvan. "I fear for the time she must spend in Caesar's temple."

"As do we, her mother and her friends," Lydia said, almost with relief. "Here is not the place or time to talk. Later, where there are fewer eyes. Your cabin is prepared. Go, rest, and be at ease."

Most of the day he sat and drowsed, or walked the decks, watching the coast line and the mountains. The ship sailed with fair winds, creaking her content. He was introduced to men and women and he remembered their names only for the moment he held their hands. They seemed plain people of small speech, and most of them spoke Greek though with an accent, but all wore the scarlet. In the evening he sat with them in the main cabin on couches set about a long table

with two wings. The place in the middle of the long table was dressed
with flowers. An old man called Joseph lay to the left, and a woman,
Aquila, to the right of the place, and Lydia lay among those at one
wing, with Garvan next. But nobody lay in the place in the middle.

At a sign from Joseph they all stood, and put their hands together
and bowed their heads, repeating a prayer in a foreign tongue. They
broke loaves with a cross baked into them, and dipped small pieces
in wine, and ate them, and Joseph made another prayer.

"This is my work-ship that visits over all the seas," Lydia told him,
in the general talk when they had eaten well of fish, and fowl. "We
go to Rome to meet the brethren there. Come, let me show you how
we work. When you take your place in Gaul, you might invite me to
open a school. This is how it would be done."

She led the way into the lower end of the deckhouse, through a
curtain, to a space filled with small looms each in process of weaving.
Around the walls material of every sort hung from rolls, and swatches
of cloth were threaded on leather thongs.

"These are models of the looms we build anywhere we can," she
said. "These are the different types of weaving. Below in the hold,
we have the dyes and raw stock. This ship we send wherever a captain
can make a landing. If the country's ruler is friendly, we invite him to
send his women on board to make a choice of materials. Then we set
up the looms ashore, and teach them to weave. So we build."

"And where you build, there also comes word of the Anointed?"
Garvan asked, daring her eyes. "Thread by thread. Isn't that it?"

She nodded, smiling.

"We teach," she said. "And now, Garvan. What of Genessa?"

"I have no hope," he said. "What shall I say? If I plead with her,
I ask her to throw aside love of her family and respect for her duty.
This, from one who worships her?"

"Titus Caesar will be at Nemi and so will Sulla Pinarius," Lydia
said. "At this time, and never after, you will have opportunity of putting your case for marriage with Genessa. Consider. As prince of
Armorican Gaul, you are allied by blood to the most powerful and
numerous peoples in all the empire. The Alemanni, Marcomanni,
Suevi, Tungri, Helvetii, Celtiberi, Britannici, Gothini, Osi, Vindelici

—these are only some of them. What greater stroke could be laid for peace than for a royal son of all these peoples to be married with one of Caesar's choice and with his blessing?"

"Why do you tell me these things?" Garvan asked. "Why have you always shown me kindness?"

"You will presently bear responsibility for your people," she said. "They will look to you. They are in wretched state from war. Mithradites do not persecute those of other belief. Neither would Genessa. As to kindness, what is this but common duty? And also, think well, you spoke first in my hearing of conscience."

"The teaching of Mithras," Garvan reminded her.

"Many of our converts come from the Mithradites," Lydia smiled. "They have faith, and hope, and an ideal."

"Are these not enough that they must come to you for more?" Garvan demanded.

Lydia shook her head.

"There must be charity," she said. "A knowledge of the dearness of people, one for another. Faith, hope, and charity. These lead to love."

"You have no husband," Garvan said. "How is this, that one speaking so much of love is by herself?"

"Never!" she smiled, deep and content. "Love I knew when I was young. He was of all men the best I have known, a Hebrew, and a learned rabbi, the tentmaker, Saul, a man of Tarsus in Cilicia."

"He was of the Anointed?" Garvan asked.

"Of the first," she said. "He took glory at the hands of the Emperor Nero."

Garvan frowned at her.

"He died of this life, and took glory, and was risen again," Lydia explained. "Thus, his hand, with all the others, is strong upon us. The grave had no victory."

"But if the Romans killed him, and others with him, down to this day, is this not a Roman victory?" Garvan asked. "If a battle is fought, and the field is bloody with the loss of one side, and the other side has no loss and flies its flags of triumph, how is this a victory for the losers?"

"How is he a loser who gains everlasting life?" Lydia said. "And more of us are left. For every one that dies, two step in his place. Where is the Roman victory?"

Garvan shook his head.

"These things have the smack of the labors of Hercules, which also I do not believe," he said. "How is it that you, a woman of great wealth and power, can believe that the dead rise up again in a Kingdom of Heaven?"

Lydia took his hand, and he felt the roughness of the loom on her fingers.

"Mithras teaches that the dead earn in this life a place in the next," she smiled. " 'Those who soil the status of Man by living as pigs will rise to pigdom in another life.' Is this not so?"

"So I was taught," he said.

"We were taught differently," said Lydia. "We were taught to believe that love of Man, and for Man, will make him into his true self, a son of the God of no Name, the eternal Father, maker of all things in heaven and earth. Him we serve. And since He made all things, should we choose the best or the worst?"

"The best," said Garvan.

"So, we choose love," said Lydia. "But there is no love without service, and no service without work. Thus we love, and serve, and work with all our hearts and with all our minds, that all men may come into the Kingdom. That is our faith. Sleep well, in peace."

She left him, and he walked on, through the deckhouse, passing the long table. A flask of wine and a pannier of bread were set before the flower-wreathed place in the middle, and a single light burned clear flame above. And again he felt the silence quiver, as if the air held life.

A squeaky lullaby of rope and tackle sent him to sleep, and anchor chains awoke him. He bathed and went on deck, in clear sunlight, seeing a high mountain green with vines, and a harbor filled with ships. Lydia's coach, of plain wood, varnished, and drawn by eight grays, waited at quayside, but such was the pressure of ships in arrival that the Ark of Tarsus had to lie out, and Garvan was rowed ashore, waving to Lydia and her staff, all in white, leaning over the rails.

Neptune's City, a little more than a few lanes of fishermen's cots about a fortress, was crowded with traffic. Three hours, Lydia had said the journey would take. But at the third hour they were still crawling and, during the fourth, they were put off the road by cavalry, and Caesar and his staff passed in gold coaches. Late in the afternoon a guide in the Pinarii house colors met them, and led the way to the imperial park.

The Lady Thalia met him with less than her usual warmth of welcome.

"This night I think I have feared all my life," she told him. "I prayed it might not come. But Diana triumphs. From this time on, I am no mother, and mother of none. My son was taken by war. My daughter by Diana. After Capri, one will marry her. Her sons will go to the Army or Navy, and the daughter, again, to Diana. So goes Rome. I can hope no more."

"Then I have chosen my time well," Garvan said, standing. "Strengthen your spirit, and wait for me."

He went to the tent set for him in the garden. Corbi was ready with clean clothing and a fine toga of white and dark green and red in the colors of the Keltae.

"Hasten," he told Corbi. "I am the same man in rags or with the toga, but I will dress well for Caesar. Where are the tents of the Grand Council?"

"The equerries' tent is that with the Praetorian's Eagle outside," Corbi pointed. "The vestibule is beyond. The Lord Prince would speak to Caesar?"

"That," Garvan said, busy with a towel.

"This is not the dress," Corbi said with big eyes. "Caesar sits among his officers in war panoply. Tonight is the swearing of oaths and the dedication of the Eagles——"

"Tonight is the yes or no," said Garvan. "If I return a corpse, then bind me well and send me back to Gaul. Make way!"

He went out, and limped down to the left, toward the lights of the imperial camp. But many dignitaries waited in state robes, with their staff officers about them, and an equerry told him that no place could be made for him, and neither could he promise any hope, for most appointments had been made a twelvemonth in advance.

Garvan felt the cold trickle of defeat. Then anger came, and a desire to do something more than stand as an animal waiting for one to open a cage. A group came bowing from Caesar's presence. An equerry signed to the next in audience. Before he could announce the names, Garvan flung the curtain aside and walked in.

And stood still, in smoky light from torches.

Caesar sat, helmeted, and in gold armor, in a half-circle of his officers-in-council. Garvan felt a sense of lean power crushing the smallness of his errand. A marriage and anyone's happiness seemed of little moment before an assembly of the Roman will.

"Lord Caesar, Garvan, son of the King Orberix of Gaul, salutes you!" he began. "There is this crisis in my life. One man may give me hope with a word."

Caesar raised a finger, no more, to send the equerries away.

"Be at ease," he said quietly. "Speak."

"It is my prayer to go one day into my father's place, though let that day be distant," Garvan said. "Armorica is only part of the peoples of the Keltae. But with patience, all might be brought under one banner. For this I would work. I require to marry, and the wife of my choice is Genessa, daughter of Sulla Pinarius. She, Roman, and myself, Gaul, in marriage would unite not countries alone, but different bloods and make into kin what before was alien."

Nobody moved in the half-circle. Eyes stared in shadow of helmet visors, and torchlight flared on the figured gold of breastplates, in buttons, on sword hilts.

"It pleases me that you come yourself to ask," Caesar said. "That the union might strengthen us in Gaul is of interest. It shall be discussed at a proper time. You are almost well?"

"Soon I shall use a sword and walk without a stick," said Garvan.

"We must see that you are invested with your toga," Caesar smiled. "You will then have no excuse for appearing before me improperly dressed."

"Despair was my driver," Garvan said.

"I shall not punish you," Caesar said. "But you cannot choose your time to come to me. You were thoughtless. You may go!"

XIII

Garvan was surprised at the smallness of the new Dianic year ceremony. Hundreds of private boxes and tents were built in levels one above the other from the imperial pavilion at lakeside. Each held a few adults of one family, mustering in all barely a couple of thousand people.

The lake filled the floor of a blown volcano, and the sides went up steep all around making an enormous bowl alive with gardens and forest. At one end of the lake Caesar's golden barges were drawn up in line, and at the other the silver barges of Diana faced them. In the middle there floated a circular platform hung with blue and white banners on silver standards, and in the center a tall lily-wreathed pylon held a wooden statue of Diana.

The College buildings on the opposite steeps were lit by blue fire, and torches along all the pathways shone in the golden roofs and domes. From the temple came the chorus of a hymn, and music of the harp and pipe. Trumpets sometimes sounded from the imperial camp, and commands to troops often rolled across the water tiny as if dwarfs were being drilled.

"There are few people because Caesar willed it so," Lady Thalia told him. "The Dianic oracle gives just time for those in Rome and Herculaneum to reach here. In that way, there is no great crush of plebeians. The ceremony is the quieter, and private."

Garvan thought of the upper room, and a ritual of bread and wine shared with slaves and servants.

"Do you attend each year?" he asked.

"I was born to Diana," she said, looking away. "I have always attended. This is my last year. No more!"

"Do you hate Diana so much?"

"I do not hate. That is the most severe test, not to hate, or fear. That is the task."

"Who sets this task?"

"Let us say, Conscience. And Conscience tells me there is love. There is forgiveness. I don't wish to speak more."

"I respect your wish," Garvan said. "But does Genessa know of your feeling?"

Lady Thalia's eyes were dark and sad, looking over the smooth water.

"She knows how I've hated the thought of her at Capri," she said. "Other things she could only know from you."

"What things are these?" Garvan heard his voice, light from guilt. Lady Thalia laughed at him.

"I was told of your visit," she said. "Lydia said I was not to fear. Is this so?"

Garvan nodded, without words.

"I know I should confess in public," Lady Thalia said. "I should be brave. I want to be a Lydia. But I haven't the real faith. Only hope. That's why I wear the black. I pray for strength to wear the scarlet."

"This wearing of scarlet," Garvan said. "Is it a sign?"

"Of faith, outwardly." Lady Thalia took his arm. "Those wearing the black are the learners. I must think of my family, and the ruination. And yet, for all this, and the terror, I dream of wearing the scarlet."

She went from him, and into the main pavilion, and he heard her voice, gay, in talk with Sulla Pinarius, in his senatorial robes and wearing the golden wreath. The wine cups were being passed, and then Sulla Pinarius caught sight of Garvan.

"Toward the morning, some great thing will be said about this young man," he laughed. "Let it be known that he enjoys the Lord Caesar's highest favor, and that we go now to appear before the Mother Hemera. Triumph, dearest Thalia. Triumph!"

He kissed his wife's hand, and she stood tiptoe to kiss his cheek. She walked with her hand in Garvan's to the entrance, and he felt the pressure on his fingers, and he could have laughed aloud, remembering another touch that was daughter to this, that also spoke of trust.

"We have little time," Sulla Pinarius said, climbing into the palanquin. "Indeed, the night has been so filled that I am hardly myself. The Lord Caesar enjoyed your manner of getting things done. The Grand Council in full session, with the Proconsul of Iberia waiting, and in bolts a wild-voiced son of Gaul in robes fit for the street, to talk of a marriage? Such a thing has never happened. Too fearsome to think about!"

They stopped at a gateway on the other side of the line of Dianic barges. Temple guards with torches flanked them to curtains of blue silk covering the College entrance. Hidden lights showed a great hall of white columns with a blue floor, and incense filled the air, and silence. They took off their shoes, and a guide led them to a small room. The Mother Hemera sat in a chair raised on squares of black stone. She wore blue robes and a golden diadem laced with jeweled lilies, and her eyes were painted with blue shadows and black lines, and her cheeks were pink, and her mouth was red, and silver powder glittered in her hair.

She made cordial greeting, and servants brought chairs, and wine, and biscuits shaped in Diana's torch and her basket of flowers.

"It would please us greatly if this union were made," she told Garvan after Sulla Pinarius had spoken of the joy of the Pinarii family. "But I wished to talk of one matter above any other. The ceremony we attend tonight brings Diana newborn into the Roman world. When Genessa marries, she will take the great mother wholly with her, and since a house cannot be divided, her husband also must be part. Are you ready to plead for Diana's favor?"

"This favor is my father's," Garvan said. "We are of the Mithradites. What could we find with Diana?"

"Let us look closer," Mother Hemera said, and stayed Sulla Pinarius with an open hand. "What favor has already been found? Have there been prayers to Mithras? Only by your own people. Yet they received news of your safety from Roman sources. Dianist, in other words. And your present condition? Due to prayers of the Mithradites? Or to the god himself? But what of Diana?"

She snapped her fingers. A priestess came with a papyrus wrapped in brocade, and at Mother Hemera's sign she unrolled it, showing a long list, page after page.

"There you see the number of prayers said for you in the high temple of Diana," she smiled. "You also see by whose plea they were said. And who paid for them. I do not deny Mithras his part. But let me see such proof as this before all credit leaves the great mother. What will you say?"

"Little," Garvan said. "These things I had not known. Genessa prayed for me!"

"Since you met," said Mother Hemera. "And Sulla Pinarius paid."

"With a glad heart," the Senator smiled. "Think what victory if Diana were established in Gaul!"

"Here we travel overfast," Mother Hemera said. "Prince Garvan, you saved me from injury not long ago. I will show you my gratitude by making your path easy. Your plea shall be made tonight, at the ceremony, and your likeness shall be carried in procession. Do you seek Diana's favor, and the wifely kiss of her daughter Genessa?"

Although no ropes were about him, Garvan felt them rough and drawn tighter with the moments. Genessa's prayers shown in long lists made day after day had been a hotly pleasant shock. There could surely be no harm in joining himself to a goddess that worked so well for her children, neither could there be harm in believing as Genessa.

There was always time for her to believe more, with him, in Mithras. To say No, here and now, was to go off empty and hopeless——

"Yes, Mother Hemera," he said. "I seek Diana's favor——"

Sulla Pinarius gave him no time to finish. The Senator threw himself before the small shrine, lighting a taper from the sacrificial fire, and murmuring his thanks.

"See how dutiful a son," Mother Hemera smiled, holding out her hand for him to kiss the blue stone of a ring. "And how happy we shall all be to sing of you this night!"

A guide led them down a flower-strewn path to a torchlit place near the lake, guarded by temple sentries. The pavilions and tents on the side to the left were white in a rising moon. From the gates of the College came a mass of torchbearers carrying flaring lights of different colors. After them, the temple musicians and behind, a choir in white with silver powder in their hair. Torches began to light the imperial pavilion, and little figures in golden armor filled the viewing space.

"See now." Sulla Pinarius took his arm. "When the moon lights the altar, there, in the middle of the lake, and Diana's eyes take fire, then the priestesses will go out in their barges, and on the other side, in Caesar's barges, the proconsuls and priestesses of the outer lands of Rome will come for the high blessing. There, see, the Mother Hemera sails."

A procession led down from the lower door of the temple to the lakeside, and robed figures went into the silver barges. From the other side of the lake there was movement of torches among the barges of Caesar. But the main procession along the avenue never stopped, and girls in thousands, clothed in blue, sang up at blue flames carried high among them. White-clad girls followed, with effigies of the goddess in dress proper to each of the territories, and portraits of the Caesars, and of the high priestesses, and after them long lines of singing girls among red, and blue, and white flares.

A chorus of maidens robed and veiled in silver lifted singing mouths to flares of palest white, glinting on silver crowns and in the silver plumage of wings outstretched from their shoulders. Among them temple guards carried a figure of Caesar under a silver canopy. Behind, an effigy of Sulla Pinarius dressed in the golden robes of a proconsul sat on a golden proconsular throne. Garvan shouted joy at honor that brought the Senator within a rank of Caesar's, and made him and his family Caesar's cousins.

But Sulla Pinarius lay face down in the earth, holding in both hands the ruby amulet he wore about his neck and praying his thanks to the lares for noble fortune. Garvan might then have gone to him and offered his salute, but he stood, instead, with open mouth, watching his own effigy, painted by a hand he knew instantly as Genessa's, borne high among banked red and white roses, with the blue and silver Dianic hood thrown about the shoulders.

Roses pelted from the singing chorus's ranks. Genessa passed before them in silver robes and wearing the outspread wings from silver cross-straps and veiled so heavily that Garvan saw her only because she turned her shining eyes to him and threw a garland. Sulla Pinarius knelt, and threw up his arms, and laughed at the stars.

"Ah, Garvan!" he shouted, small in the chorus of passing voices. "What glory is in this night! Who lives, except a Roman?"

Garvan felt the denial come swift to his tongue, but he held peace, for there was little sense in argument at such a time. They stood together, watching older priestesses in silver cars pass by, and then the youngest vires, all flower-crowned, and, in rear, the temple guards.

"Now to the Shrine of Nemi," Sulla Pinarius said. "Ho, palanquin! Ho!"

The chairmen ran down under the eyes of the sentries, and Sulla Pinarius climbed in, sighing with relief. Garvan watched the Dianic barges sailing out. The first, larger than all, reached the circular float before any, but the people in her were too far away to be anything but figures. Caesar's barges, raising purple sails, went alongside, and uniforms glittered. Great flares threw plumes of color from the College quayside, setting splashes of red, blue, green, and yellow mixing among myriads of swans, each swan pulling a float in the shape of a lotus leaf, and, on each, a vire standing with the reins in one hand, and in the other a Dianic torch held to stream its flame above her head.

The moon's white showed clear of the crest, and in a gonging of

bells the rays lit the eyes of the statue on the pylon, and they burned
red. The flares died, and the thousands of torches were mirrored in
the water among the swans. A shout grew as a swift breath, and roared,
and trumpets cut the phrases of the imperial salute.

People left the center float once more to go aboard the barges. One
small figure took a torch, holding it against the pylon. A flame crept
in golden rags up the garland of flowers, and longer flame took growth
on the pylon's supports. The little figure crossed the gangway into the
largest barge, which cast off, turning to meet the swans.

The burning float massed in flame and sparks flew into the upper
air, covering the statue of the goddess. As suddenly, the flames went
out, and the structure turned over and went down, and the waters
smoothed and settled.

"So dies the year," Sulla Pinarius whispered. "So goes the wish
denied, the prayer unsaid."

The doors to the College water gate opened in red flares, and a huge
statue of Diana was drawn by boats toward the imperial pavilion. The
moon paled the statue's silver, gleaming among all the silver-robed
and winged vestals grouped below its plinth. The golden roofs and
domes of the College gleamed in light, and a choir sang with harpists.
A mighty harmony of trumpets sounded from the imperial camp.
Torches were alight in ranks of Praetorians guarding the massed
Eagles, and Caesar stood alone, on the edge of the lake, holding out
his right arm to the goddess floating ever nearer among her fleet of
swans.

"Now is Diana born!" Sulla Pinarius shouted. "On your knees,
Garvan. Shout triumph! Triumph, Great Mother. Triumph!"

A burst of scarlet and blue flame lit the base of the statue. Priestesses
stood at the altar. Knives shone in their hands, and splashes flew dark
on the white slab above the sacrificial fire.

"Yes, they sacrifice," Sulla Pinarius said without surprise at Garvan's
question. "What then? Do not Romans die to bring others the Roman
law? And can others not spare a little of their blood to bind the
bargain? To strengthen a prayer for peace? Must we of Rome do all
the dying? That is not our belief."

"What is the Roman belief?" Garvan asked, watching bound

women lifted onto the altar, and a burnish of steel in the priestesses' hands. "Is it proper that women should die in such a manner? What if Genessa were one?"

Sulla Pinarius stopped the chairmen at a barrier, and got down, helping Garvan. They went through a row of sentries, onto a broad stone walk toward the ranks of Praetorians.

"My son was one who died," the Senator said. "Genessa might also go to sacrifice if Rome had need. What greater honor than to die for Rome? That is our belief. Hasten. We are in good time!"

The float touched the quay, and ropes were fastened. The silver-robed vestals-in-honor went on shore, standing in a group about Caesar. A ritual started, of prayers and chants. Titus Caesar walked with Mother Hemera before the line of effigies. In front of each they paused a moment, and the Mother Hemera splashed water with a silver ladle, and they went on to the next.

But at Garvan's effigy Caesar stopped and spoke to his equerry. Sulla Pinarius walked out, and stood, bowing.

"Ah, good friend!" Caesar called. "You see how we reward our Sulla? You go to Gaul as our proconsul. And where is Garvan?"

Sulla Pinarius took Garvan's right hand. Among the vestals-in-honor Garvan saw only one.

"A son in place of one I lost, Lord Caesar," Sulla Pinarius said.

"Garvan, you are come to us at the birth of Diana," Caesar smiled. "You shall marry in Diana. You shall guard our mother in Gaul. This is our Roman wish, to make the nations one under the Eagle and in the temple. Is this your sworn desire?"

"It is," said Garvan, watching eyes behind a veil.

"We give you Roman greeting," Caesar said, taking grip of his fore-arm. "We are one in blood and in will. Good Mother, set Diana's sign upon him!"

The blue and white hood was unhooked from the effigy, and the Mother Hemera took it from an assistant, and slipped it over Garvan's head. A hymn was shouted, and the vestals-in-honor danced about him. But they broke on signal.

Caesar came toward him, holding in both hands a folded garment.

"With us, you share the purple," he said. "Here is your toga, sign of your right as citizen. So, Gaul becomes of Rome, and Rome is of Gaul. Triumph, Diana!"

Voices and trumpets shouted together, and Garvan felt many an arm about him in hearty wish of good fortune. But another sound was louder, of women's screams, and officers calling commands, and the clash of swords on shields.

Plainly a battle cry was shrieked, and then a shout in answer. Senators, judges, and priestesses turned one to another, and then about, and then they were running. A guard of Praetorians closed on Caesar and marched away. Vestals-in-honor ran in cover of the marchers, but in all the scurry Garvan kept an eye on one, and went to her.

"I am unarmed," he said. "Yet, of all those ready for battle, I am most prepared in arms and armor."

"A conundrum," she whispered behind the veil. "Where is your sword, shield, armor, charger?"

"Beside me, with her hand in mine," he smiled. "What other guardian would you have?"

"None," she said, and threw aside her veil. "It will be good to die with you!"

"Rather speak of life as a Gaul," Garvan said. "Come, who are these upon us?"

"Runaways," she said, as if she spoke of insects. "Slaves, and broken gladiators, and hirelings taken to the mountains."

"And is Caesar not warned of such?" he asked.

"Warned, and contemptuous," she said. "As I. As any Roman."

Garvan looked at her eyes, brightest blue, or gray, or green, but without a blink of fear. Her hand in his was firm and she was still, and her mouth was a maenad's, smiling, without tremor. They stood, alone, on the wide stone quay littered with toppled effigies and trampled blossoms. Only Garvan's effigy stood upright, with the candles burning bright about it.

"Your hand caught me well in painting this," he said. "Did Phocis the Greek help you?"

"Every line and tint my own!" she whispered in anger. "What, because a Gaul is clumsy, is this reason to suspect a Roman? Pity, I gave the eyes less a squint!"

A boat hook with a barbed harpoon of bright steel lay on the quay-side. Garvan picked it up, testing its balance and finding it to his lik-ing.

A group of attackers, black with sun, whiskered and ragged, broke through the ranks of the temple guards, running down toward the imperial pavilion in hope of loot. For a moment Garvan was tempted to cheer them on in memory of himself not long before. But when the leaders saw Genessa they broke their run, and advanced, leaping high.

"Swim," Garvan told her.

"Never," she said. "Unless we go together!"

"I cannot run from these," he said.

"Expect nothing less of me," she smiled. "Rome, too, has its mules!"

"A kiss for each long ear," Garvan whispered. "I give you, dearest mule, to Mithras. Stand out of reach!"

"Diana, Great Mother, preserve him!" Genessa called. "Triumph, Garvan. Triumph!"

A swordsman came on, laughing. Garvan had a leg and an arm to work with, and a leg and an arm to hold him back. Exercise had done much for the arm, and especially the stretching drills became useful now, for in quick thought, he ripped off the toga and cast it as Zetak threw the net except that he wound the heavy silk about the man's sword arm, and pulled him, in a stumble to the lake's edge, and in, to a cheer from Genessa.

A second man broke his pace and came on, with another to the left, and one to the right. Garvan tried an old spearman's trick. He whirled the weapon about his wrist, and hopped forward a couple of paces, and pulled the spear out of its whirl, and jabbed the spike-shod end at one, and took him through the head, and with the point speared the other in the gorge. He took a long lunge, at the third, and a fourth got the return jab. A man, tall, bearded, and slavering at the mouth, ran at Genessa. She straightened herself, facing him, but she gave no ground. Garvan hurled, and the weapon passed through the man and splashed in the water only a moment or two before the body. He picked up a sword, but, stoutly made as it was, it had the feel of a toy, and he threw it at a man edging about, and broke his knee. He picked up another, and hopped on the good leg to Genessa.

"Now is the time for prayers," he said. "We are come to a tooth-pick, and I cannot lift a shield."

"I am your shield," she laughed. "Diana, great huntress, triumph!"

He put his arms about her, and she came close, but then she screamed, and he swung around to face attack. But the ruffians were on the run, and Praetorians dropped out of pavilions and boxes, and came from aisles leading from the hillside.

Equerries and an escort of Praetorians came toward them.

"Lord Prince," one hailed. "Greetings, in honor!"

He turned, pointing to a dark patch on the steeps near the imperial camp.

"The Lord Caesar watched the battle from that place," he said. "I am instructed to accompany you to his presence. Carriers are here if they are needed."

Garvan offered his hand to Genessa.

"We shall walk together," he said.

"Mules, in pair," said Genessa. "But I insist that we ride. Your limp hurts me. I will say more in the proper place!"

There was little enough for her, or anyone else, to say in the tent of the Grand Council. Ceasar was pale, and his eyes stared bright as metal.

"I made good choice in you," he told Garvan, but with barely any voice, as if he had shouted himself out. "It was my intention to make public notice of your marriage. The disgrace of this night prevented it. I shall choose another time. Your defense was greatest credit. We shall meet at Capri. Farewell!"

"Those are the softest words he's spoken in the past hour," Sulla Pinarius whispered on the way out to the palanquin. "These mountains run with escaped slaves and runaways of one kind or another. Who could think they'd brave a time like this? And come within a finger of success? But now the order is given. All runaways and those unable to account for themselves, citizens or not, are to die where they stand. These mountains will be raked and sieved. This, never again!"

"But are the Romans killed without trial?" Garvan asked.

"By Caesar's pleasure," Sulla Pinarius said. "And any ruffian now in prison and awaiting trial shall also die. See, the orders go by signal fire!"

He pointed to bright points of light burning high on the mountain.

"A moment," Garvan said, looking at Genessa, and thinking of Khefi, Stavros, and Zetak. "How is this? Any man in prison? Should I not also be in prison. As a runaway?"

Sulla Pinarius dismissed tracts of the empire in a wave of his hands.

"The Court leaves at first light," he said. "Genessa and her mother return with the College sometime later. I can find a place for you, or the Potitii will take you back with them."

"No," Garvan said with a notion growing stronger with the moments. "I will first present my compliments to the Lady Thalia. Then I will go to the Master of Horse and find myself a coach. I hold captaincy of the Gallic Legion. I am entitled to six horses and their changes."

"It had not been in my mind," said Sulla Pinarius. "Thus, you may travel when and how you will."

"Have you such hurry to be at Herculaneum?" Genessa asked.

"To welcome you," said Garvan. "And to prepare a ship, that we may sail and swim——"

"I have one week free before I go to Capri," said Genessa. "We have ships to spare——"

"To Capri?" Garvan said, rounding the words. "But you will marry me. You will come to Gaul——"

"After she has served her term at Capri, dear son," her father said.

Garvan looked at them in the darkness of the swaying palanquin.

"I had thought her given into my keeping," he said.

"Thought does not alter fact," said Sulla Pinarius.

"Where shall I find the Master of Horse?" Garvan inquired in voice enough. "If there is only a week, there is too much to be done to idle here!"

"My son!" Sulla Pinarius leaned, laughing, to pat his knee. "How excellent a Roman, dear, dear son!"

XIV

There had been little delay with the Master of Horse, and after saying good-by to the Lady Thalia and the new Proconsul, the coach went off with an escort of legionaries along the road south to Herculaneum. For worst of company, Garvan took with him a certain curious glance of Genessa's, not a smile and not a frown, that seemed to be in equal parts of quietest regret, and an almost weary yielding. There was no chance to speak. He could only look at her, and stumble over words, and go.

His leg and arm were overstrained, and the coach rolled on the stone setts, but after Corbi had strapped him to the cushions he slept. Dawn was well up when he awoke among the crags of the coast road, hearing the trumpeter sound a warning to the post ahead. They dropped to a walk to make way through herds and flocks, and mule and donkey teams going to their markets. While the horses were changed and the legionaries ate their meal, he got down before a tavern seeing that another tavern faced it, and farther toward the sea, a third, and all of them crowded.

Corbi chose a table, and from the landlord borrowed linen and a knife, and a good chair, and a glass for wine. Garvan went into the pump house to wash himself awake under a torrent from the mountain. While he dried himself he heard a knocking that at first he thought was a hammer, and then a woodpecker. Afra, with combed hair and a fine toga of bleached wool, tapped along the path. Garvan stood until the shepherd's crook might have touched him, but Afra paused, and stepped to one side, and Garvan followed, and Afra stepped more, and Garvan stepped again.

"Who is this who cuts a jig?" Afra demanded. "Shall I have you thrown in the cess?"

"Fine greeting from a friend," Garvan laughed. "How is this, did you sleep in brier?"

Afra laughed with him, the silent laugh, up at the sky.

"Let this be told to unbelievers!" he whispered. "Lord Prince, I am on my way to Rome to the Lady Lydia, and we shall sail back after tomorrow. Yet I had prayed to speak with you before that time. And here we stand!"

He opened his hands, looking up at the sky, and bowed his head against the shepherd's crook.

"Come, little time, many matters!" he said suddenly, and turned toward the tavern. "Lord Prince, a quiet place and a sharp ear for words barely spoken."

Garvan took him to the table Corbi had set, and Afra warned everybody off by turning his face toward them, all around, grinning, and rolling his eyes.

"Here, then, the marrow of this," he whispered, sitting and filling his mouth with bread. "I'll speak as I chew and so make stuff for any lip reader. The Lady Lydia knows danger. If Caesar takes away his favor, she dies within the hour. Many are her converts. The Lady Thalia, one——"

"This is known?" Garvan whispered.

"If you know, why should others not, whose only business it is to find out?" Afra grinned. "But here is concern of yours. The Lady Genessa was promised in marriage to Julian Potitius. How will that family accept a contracted wife going to a foreigner?"

"A sour plum for all the Potitii," said Garvan.

"Well said," Afra grinned. "But the son, Julian, is Aedile. A man of civic power. So far, because of that contract, he has done nothing to take the Lady Thalia out of her Christian way. But what if Sulla Pinarius were told? Where, then, would be your marriage?"

"It would make no difference," said Garvan.

"Wrong," said Afra. "He and his wife would have to leave the public scene. Would you see his daughter again?"

"I should prevent her going to Capri," said Garvan. "This has the taste of aloes to me."

"Aloes shrivel the mouth with bitterness," Afra said. "Let them also shrivel talk. There is safety at Capri. Safety in dealing soft with the Aedile. Safety for the Lady Thalia. For the Lady Genessa. For Lydia. For me, and others dependent."

"What is to be expected at Capri?" Garvan swept the table clear and leaned. "Let me know rest from these doubts."

Afra wiped his face and his fingers.

"In this time you have learned the Roman mind," he said. "Caesar is Rome. His command is law. The Lady Genessa will follow the orders of the temple, and the commands of Caesar."

"What orders and what commands?" Garvan shouted.

Afra gathered his toga, and picked up the shepherd's crook, and stood.

"Loud voices make fools wise," he said with his hand over his mouth. "Rome can do no wrong. Therefore, all that Caesar does is lawful."

"Speak plain words," Garvan whispered savagely.

"Plain words in such a matter before a rabble?" Afra laughed, still hand to mouth. "Let us say she will have reward for companionship to Caesar and those princes and emissaries in his favor."

"A courtesan," Garvan whispered.

Afra shrugged.

"Not in Caesar's eyes," he said. "Not in the eyes of any Roman."

"My eyes," said Garvan.

"Romans find them as useful as mine," Afra smiled. "Remember Lydia. And her friends!"

"I shall not forget," Garvan said. "But why did you pray that we should meet?"

"Did not the signal fires say last night that you were turned to Diana?" Afra laughed. "Where should I find a stronger friend? If a Lydia or a Thalia were taken, where is Afra? In this black world, where does he turn?"

Garvan looked at the quivering, closed eyelids and at the nervous hands.

"I am your friend," he said in pity. "Lift your heart!"

Garvan went, leaning on Corbi's shoulder, to the coach and gave orders to the petty officers to make best pace to Herculaneum. He gave the tavern keeper a gold piece and waited for change, noticing a worn sign of three fishes, plaited, burned on the moneybag.

"What sign is this?" he asked, thinking of those in the upper room at the house of Lydia.

"Of the Anointed," said the tavern keeper, counting change without raising his eyes. "This tavern is one of three blessed by the presence of Paul, an apostle, of Tarsus. His sign is on the right-hand side of my door."

"Are you then, of the Anointed?" Garvan asked.

"I am," said the tavern keeper, keeping count. "I wear the scarlet. Is this something to you?"

The question came gently, and Garvan was lost for a word to say.

"I spoke with another of your belief these moments ago," he said. "You seem many in number."

"We work and earn," the tavern keeper said, and raised clear, smiling eyes. "You spoke to one? The blind weaver, a brother to Judas Iscariot?"

"I know him only as Afra," said Garvan. "Who is Iscariot?"

"One who loves and dies every moment," said the tavern keeper, paying the last coin. "Afra is one among us, but not of us. He has his place and his glory. He wove the shroud of the Son, our Master. For that reason, he is venerated."

"The Son, your Master?" Garvan repeated. "Is he the Fisherman?"

"Him," the tavern keeper said, and bowed. "His blessing follow you in all your ways!"

The hours went by in hard thought, but wherever he turned there built a web. On the approach to Herculaneum he ordered the coach to the Curia. The city appeared empty. But Corbi gave the reason while he brushed the travel dust outside the Law Court's inner door.

"The search squads have been abroad since before dawn, Lord Prince," he whispered. "They say the execution parties have worked till now."

"So, and so!" Garvan spat. "Let us talk with this Potitius!"

The court was in session, and the public places were crowded with the relatives of those on trial. City police and prison guards dragged howling men and screaming women from the cages and out, to the barred carts taking them to death. Julian Potitius sat on a gold throne in a court open to the sky. Lawyers and scribes sat before a long table in front of the Aedile, and the prisoners stood to one side, and the witnesses came to the other. Garvan raised his hand in salute, and the Aedile recognized him, staring for a moment at the toga's imperial purple, and made haste to rise, bowing.

"It is good to have one, fresh with honor, dignifying our city court," he smiled. "Is there some matter touching on justice which brings you, Lord Prince?"

Garvan had instant notion that the purpose of his errand was known. He sat in the chair brought for him, and without detail he told of his interest in Khefi, Stavros, and Zetak.

"The case shall be brought forward," Julian Potitius said, and gave a scribe an order.

Garvan looked around at a shout from the main doorway. Ultor, in white and black lawyer's robes, came through a crowd all pressing forward to kiss his hand or touch his garment, and none seemed to care that the guards kicked them.

"He seems well loved," Garvan said.

Julian Potitius laughed, showing an empty space in his bottom teeth, and eyes that looked as if he had bathed them in hot water.

"Indeed," he said. "He carries some magic, supposedly. We'll see its efficacy here. Bring out the prisoners!"

Stavros came first, and Khefi and Zetak, in prison garb of loincloth and sweat cap, each bound about the arms and ankles. All three looked at him without a sign that they had met. Charges were read, of breaking in, and of threatening a citizen. The lawyer for the city made a speech about the serious nature of the crimes, and demanded penalty of death. Ultor stood forward on a sign from the Aedile, and first proved that the accused were not in city bounds when they were arrested.

"And how did these break in where there is no wall?" he asked. "Is it breaking in to walk a mountain? To sleep in a cave? I ask dismissal here!"

"Dismissed," said the Aedile in a small voice. "What of the threatened citizen? Let Tirius Porrius stand forward."

The man Garvan remembered, wearing a fine toga and carrying a gold-handled whip, walked from the crowd and went to the witness stand.

"How do you believe?" the court officer asked him.

"On Mars," said Tirius Porrius.

"As son of Mars, should you expect the flails of his wrath if you lied?" inquired the court officer.

"That," said Tirius Porrius.

"Say what you know of these men," the court officer said.

Tirius Porrius gave a plain account of his meeting, and of trying to spring a trap, and changing his mind because of the gift of his life.

"Your life was in danger?" the city's lawyer asked.

"I would not have given a snip of twine for it," said Tirius Porrius. "Except that the honorable citizen pleaded for me, I would have been dead."

"Which was this?" asked the lawyer.

"That one in the purple beside the Aedile," said Tirius Porrius.

People in the court raised a sigh of surprise, but lawyers and scribes sat straight, and the Aedile swept flies with a horsetail switch, unmoved.

"Let the Lord Prince Garvan stand before the people!" the court officer shouted.

"Hold!" Ultor raised his hand. "The prisoners by common consent refuse the Lord Prince's services as witness. They would plead their case by merit of circumstances——"

"Which I refuse," the Aedile said in his small voice. "Death, all three!"

Guards took them by their bound arms and swung them toward the door.

Garvan stood.

"A moment, Aedile, with deference to the court," he said. "If they refuse my service, they cannot refuse my request, which I make to the court, that I be placed among them as a prisoner."

"On what grounds?" Julian Potitius asked with no sign of surprise.

"We had sworn an oath together," Garvan said, looking at Khefi. "We had said that if one were taken, the others would not live until he were free, or they dead."

"Conspiracy," the city lawyer said.

"I wish to plead." Ultor raised his voice.

"Let me put these facts upon the scroll." The Aedile turned to the scribe. "First, three make escape from the galleys. They land. They trespass. They attack a citizen. They attempt kidnap. They prepare a false defense. All these crimes carry penalty of death. But who appears for them? One, Ultor, a Jew, resident in Transrhenana, but born in Palestine, and practicing law in defense of Christians, Jews, Essenes, and other criminals. What is his purpose? To cheat the law by crafty use of words. The penalty for this is death. Who is his patron? One, a woman of Samaria, Lydia, a known and shameless adherent of the Christian sect. You, Ultor, how do you believe?"

"On the God of my father," said Ultor, "and on His Son, our Master, the Christ."

The Aedile held out his arms, grinning at the loud cries in court.

"We are into a den of Christians," he laughed. "Arrest him. There is penalty of death!"

"After trial," said Ultor with no sign of distress, taking his place between the guards.

"Oh, after trial, certainly!" the Aedile said, pretending impatience that any could think differently. "Take him away!"

"I am a citizen," Garvan stood, addressing a bronze statue of the wolf suckling Romulus and Remus, the founders of Rome. "I have rights before the law. There are penalties, but there is still the law. We, all four, were taken from our homes and imprisoned by soldiers of Rome——"

"Soldiers of Rome are under command of the Lord Caesar," said the Aedile. "Caesar does no wrong!"

"But were men born to suffer capture without making an effort to escape?" Garvan demanded. "Is this the Roman way, to sit in chains——"

"You were not of Rome," said the Aedile.

"Neither is the law," Garvan said. "The law has no Caesar and no slave. It is the law, what may be done, and what may not, and it serves all, with no favor."

"This is a busy court," the Aedile said. "What would the Lord Prince do? Make charges against himself? Will any of the three prove his guilt? Come, one of you. What was his crime?"

Khefi looked at the other two, and grinned.

"The noble Prince speaks no word to us," he said. "Him we never winked an eye at before. What have we to do with those wearing the purple? We wear the shackles. And we shall die, remembering others who wore them with honor!"

"Is there no right of appeal?" Garvan asked.

"First to the Senator, Sulla Pinarius, joint guardian of this city, absent on imperial duty," the Aedile said. "Afterward, to Caesar. Should either be angered with this?"

Afra's warning came clear in Garvan's mind. He heard the whisper, urging him to think of Genessa. Instantly he brought his anger in control, and turned the pitch of his voice.

"I think not," he said. "I would prefer to speak with you in the matter. I go soon to Gaul to pay duty to the King, my father, and return then to my place with the Imperial Bodyguard. But I would think little of a man if he forgot his friends or those who helped him.

I look to you, Aedile, since at this moment my friend the Lord Caesar is far away!"

A change came into the face of Julian Potitius. The laugh and part sneer went, and in its place came wariness, but pleasanter.

"The court is ready at all times to perform its duty to Caesar," he said. "We shall meet at some proper time. Until then, the three shall be remanded."

Garvan saw the three look at each other with hope's wide eyes. He knew that Stavros would be thinking of Diana, and Zetak with him, and that in the moment they reached the cell, Khefi would have to argue with them between her saving powers and the claims of Zoroaster. Thought of them able to quarrel, even for that short period, was reward in itself.

"Nothing more, good Aedile," he said. "I am content."

Corbi came in at dawn to announce that the Aedile, Julian Potitius, waited to talk to him. He flung aside the sleeping-rugs, and ordered his visitor shown to the terrace. The Aedile was unshaven and uncombed, and his eyes looked ready for a fever.

"This is the only free time I have," he explained. "For three or four more days I shall be busy at court. After that, I go to Rome. Have you thought of any way that I might help?"

Garvan felt a moment of shame. Here was one not much older than himself, heavy with duty, spending time he might well have used for rest to come visiting, bent on help.

"Truly, this is the Roman generosity," he said. "In your place I'd sleep every hour I could. Let me confess I'd thought you young for such important business."

"I have advisers," Julian said. "Mine's the responsibility, heavy

when Caesar is near, or among us. But my father is jointly guardian
of this city with Sulla Pinarius. Thus I must please this one, and that
one, and endure all sorts of disharmonies for their sakes. How may I
help you?"

"In the matter of my friends," Garvan said. "They are good men
brought to crime by circumstance——"

"So often it is said before me," Julian smiled, taking a bowl of
chicken broth from Corbi. "This is lawyer's talk. They talk differently
on the other side. Crimes were there, and they must die."

"Rome needs good men," Garvan said. "None are better than these
three. What is gained by killing them?"

"This, that they are dead." Julian wiped his mouth and eased his
cheeks of shreds. "We have no need of such. We are greatly troubled
by those who threaten the civil peace. I shall hope to hear nothing
more in the matter of pleas. In any other matter, I hope I shall prove
less intransigent."

"That, for example, of Ultor," Garvan said.

"A Jew and a Christian." Julian barely shook his head. "Making
trouble by playing word games with the law. He and his patron, Lydia,
are at root of the disturbances here. In Rome they treat her highly.
She has great influence. But let Caesar revoke his word and she'll find
little to avail her in any court, foreign excrescence she is!"

"Yet greatly of use to Rome," Garvan said. "And a noblewoman,
one given to charity——"

"The word sickens me." Julian stood, wrapping his toga. "The
Roman is not a beggar. The Christian and his charity would make
him so——"

"Here we disagree," Garvan said. "Lydia of all women is dedicated
to work, and all those with her—"

"To the destruction of Rome!" Julian shouted suddenly, staring
over his shoulder. "She and her miserable proselytes. Let me give you
warning, Prince Garvan. I came here, not to waken you, or to drink
your excellent broth. But to say to you that championship of any
Christian will bring you into odorous company and high disfavor."

"I shall do all I may to help my friends," Garvan said. "How does
warning apply here?"

"Know that the Lady Thalia is gone to these Christians," Julian said. "Prime work of Lydia. Here is reason why I make no protest against your marriage to Genessa. I do not build my life upon such evil ground."

"You are well informed," Garvan said.

"I am chief of aediles," Julian smiled, and held out his hand. "Visit your friends as you please. They have at most four days to live. The Lord Caesar freed you by act of clemency. They have no escape."

The word stuck as a flaming spear in a straw roof.

"That is a matter for justice," Garvan said steadily. "Let me thank you for spending your time."

Garvan went to the terrace door, and watched Julian take the reins of the black and gold chariot and drive off. His mind was settled in what he must do, and he told Corbi to hurry his dressing and call a chariot. He drove direct to the prison, and with no question the guard commander let him pass.

The yards and cages brought memory of the oar banks. Khefi, Stavros, and Zetak were among countless others, men and women, in a compound, chained to stone blocks. They lay in the sun, with no cover except their sweat caps and loincloths. Their faces were blank of welcome, and neither did they raise their heads when he stood over them, a little out of hearing of the guard.

"Go from us," Khefi said into the sand. "We want no help of you. Should four die when three suffice?"

"Number four is a free man," Garvan whispered. "Tomorrow night we'll all be so, or sharing a grave. Remember the ship we left in Uriel's care? The fisherman? I'll send one to make it ready. And when you are free, clear a way that these others may also go."

"Most of them Christians," said Khefi. "Jews, the rest."

"They mislike the term," Stavros said. "It is thrown in hatred of their country, Judea. Call them Hebrews. Let them have honor. Braver have not been in my sight."

"And the Christians!" Zetak whispered. "For other gods I have bought enough goats to eat the bloom off mountains, and chickens to stuff a thousand feather beds. What did I get? Even Diana is gone against us, and I had given her a cow, white, without a mark. But what God is this, which needs no cow or goat or any chicken, and yet gives courage to send His people singing into death?"

"We have seen for ourselves," Khefi said, drawing patterns in the sand, a face with long hair, a body with short arms, and a six-pointed star on each side. "They sing till the blood is out of them."

"Then make the way easy for these others," said Garvan. "Where is Ultor?"

"In the cells you pass to leave the prison," Stavros said. "I saw him taken there. They scourged him."

"Send us a hot meal," Khefi said loudly. "Why talk soothing words to us of what you shall tell our mothers? We are dying men. Give us filled bellies to die fat on!"

Other prisoners cheered, and even the guard laughed.

Garvan caught the barest wink from Zetak, warning enough. He left them, cheering, and went toward the cages beside the gate. Blood-caked, moaning creatures with torn fingers and pulped faces sprawled on the stones behind the bars. In the last a man's gray hair showed through blood. He sat against the wall as if he slept. His beard was half gone, and raw flesh showed where the roots had been pulled.

"Ultor," Garvan said clearly. "My respect. My grief, to see you here. My prayer, for strength."

"For all those, my thanks," Ultor said, trying to open swollen eyes. "My time is not long. I am beyond them, and able to pray for them."

"This is far from my understanding," Garvan said.

"So said our Master," said Ultor, closing his eyes, and leaning against the wall, and speaking as if he took comfort. " 'But I say unto you, "Love your enemies, bless them that curse you, do good to them that hate you and pray for them which despitefully use you and persecute you, that ye may be the children of the Father which is in heaven." ' That is our faith."

"A father who lets others beat his children and kill them, he should also be beaten and killed," said Garvan. "Who is this Father?"

"One who makes the sun to rise on us, evil and good," said Ultor. "As the rain comes upon us, just and unjust."

"I would help you," said Garvan. "Food, clean clothing shall come in."

"No," Ultor said. "When I am risen, I will wash and array myself."

"Risen," Garvan said.

"With the Master," said Ultor. "The time is at hand."

"You lent me gold, a coin," said Garvan. "I would lend you hope."

Ultor tried to raise his hand to reach through the bars.

"Peace be with you," he said, and his head rolled, and he fell.

"Let me see the Aedile," Garvan told the guard. "This is not a criminal, and he has had no trial."

"He is not a citizen, Lord Prince," the guard said. "The orders are to find the names of the Christians in his nest. If he opened his mouth, he'd be comfortable enough. Stubborn ones have to be taught."

Garvan left him, and hurried over to the Curia, into the same babble as on the day before. Julian Potitius sat in the same chair, and Garvan had a notion that all had stayed as it had been, and would ever stay as it was, with people dragged in, and lawyers speaking, and a Potitius ordering death.

"Aedile," he saluted without preamble. "A man of learning and dignity is brought down in blood and disgraceful hurt. Where is Rome honored in this?"

"You speak of which man?" Julian asked.

"Of Ultor, a Hebrew, and a lawyer, respected in all of Rome," Garvan said.

"Jews and Christians have no respect." The Aedile sat straighter, and his voice was sharp in a quiet court. "He refuses testimony. He suffers for his contempt. Have you more to say?"

"Let him be released in my bond," Garvan said.

"He is held." The Aedile waved his hand. "Be wise. Go to your business, and leave Jews and Christians to theirs. Proceed!"

Anger that had been held took Garvan and shook him as if by a hand, and he trembled, going through the crowd, barely able to see, and hardly able to listen to covert whispers of encouragement from one after another of those making way for him.

Outside the Curia, in the sunlit Forum, he stood for a moment, looking at the water springing silver from the fountain, and wishing he could take one pot of it into the prison. In the shadows of the bronze nymphs combing long hair in the spray, he saw Khefi's pattern drawn in the sand, of long hair, and short arms, and a star on each side.

Chote, the Carthaginian, came into his mind.

Khefi might have been telling him, beyond the guard's knowing, to talk with Chote, the cook, friend of the friendless, of the milch-cow smile that hid a ruined face.

He called a chariot and told the driver to go to the Street of the Crying Quail.

Chote's cookshop was empty because of the early hour, but the cooks were busy, and dozens of women peeled vegetables in the space beyond the kitchen. A potman went running, and Chote came, with the dark-eyed smile that made all troubles less, and Garvan started to whisper his plan. But he was stopped by a baby hand flat on the table. Chote signed to him to follow and they went to a place in the kitchen, and Chote stood where he could see all that went on in the shop, though none could see him, and over any speech lay the noise of working cooks.

The smile did not lessen in Chote's eyes. Garvan used his mouth to form the shapes of words, and in detail he told how he would break into the prison, and how many armed men he would need, and what he would pay them. He told of the ship hidden in the cave of Uriel, and how to find her. Chote put a finger over his mouth, and nodded out at the shop.

Corbi stood there wringing his hands, and pleading with a potman. Chote went to the serving panel and smiled, and Corbi ran in, falling to his knees.

"Lord Prince, the city guards are outside with Captain Tabis Netto," he whispered. "Make no move to go. Let Chote hide you——"

"Should I not be here?" Garvan demanded. "I am free, a citizen——"

"This is a cookshop for beggars, thieves, and bondmen from prison," Corbi said in fear. "What does a guest of the Senator do here? they ask. Why should a prince so demean himself? Let Chote give you safety. These guards would burn his house and think no more!"

"On that account, but on no other I will go," said Garvan.

He followed Chote through the kitchen and up a back stairway.

Shouting came clear through the walls, but Chote made no pause. He unlocked a thick door, and locked it after them, and went through an outer corridor into the next house, and the next, and down a stairway to a cellar door, and through, to the smell of old wine casks. Garvan saw only Chote's white bulk in front, wondering how it would be if the man were a traitor.

Chote knocked on iron, and a grille slid open. A noise, not a scream and not a whine, sounded between the cat-purr of his breath and the door opened, into lamplight and bare white walls.

Garvan went in at Chote's nod, and understood from the play of baby hands and a milch-cow smile that he was to trust the doorkeeper to see him safe. Chote went away, and the weight of the closing door shook the building. The doorkeeper was stooped, tall, in a scarlet toga, with a fillet of leaves about his forehead. The cellar had a great length, and a high roof painted with fishes. Mats and pillows were spread about the floor, and couches filled the spaces between the stone pillars.

A fine aroma of incense reminded him of the shrine in Lydia's house, and the scarlet dress of a dozen or so men and women reclining about a long table brought further memory of the scarlet worn aboard the Ark of Tarsus.

All stood when he came in.

"One needing help," the doorkeeper said.

Everyone smiled, and sat again. Garvan thought of startled birds settling wing pinions to nest. The doorkeeper took him toward the table, and into the light of a stand lamp. In a space between the stone supports a man sat by himself writing at a small table.

Even in scarlet there could be no mistaking Maximus Potitius, father of the Aedile, Julian.

Garvan made no move toward him, but followed around the table set for a meal, with a white cloth, laced, and flowers in gold pots, and golden wine flasks and bread dishes and a seven-branched candlestick, unlit. Couches stood about, but the couch in the middle was larger, and the back was garlanded with white flowers.

Maximus Potitius saw the doorkeeper and smiled. His eyes shifted and lit, pale, and froze. But then he stood, flinging out his arms.

"Lord Prince, such pleasure in this welcome!" he laughed. "How are you found here?"

"I escape the city guards," Garvan said. "For some reason they follow me. Chote was my guide."

"The Captain, Tabis Netto, perhaps," Maximus Potitius said. "I'm told he has no liking for you."

"Then we are pot and cover, for I have none for him," Garvan said. "I came hoping to find men enough to break into the prison and free those of my friends in chains. Ultor is there, in bad case and bloodied to die. He was kind to me."

Maximus Potitius shook his head.

"All must be done according to the law," he said. "We must obey the law that exists, not the one that we wish for."

"You would let Ultor die without an effort to help?" Garvan demanded. "What manner of men are you?"

"Of the Anointed," said Maximus Potitius gently. "Those who live by the sword shall die by the sword. That is our teaching."

"We must go," the doorkeeper broke in. "I was told to pass him to the street without delay."

"We shall meet again at the proper season, good Prince." Maximus Potitius held out his hand. "Peace among us all!"

"Words," Garvan said. "Prayers cost nothing. A sword stroke for Ultor might cost your life!"

Maximus Potitius laid his hand upon the scarlet.

"This life is given," he said. "In sword strokes are the lives of other men. Would Ultor take his freedom in their wounds and death? We have the strength to suffer if we must."

In spite of rage Garvan knew respect. He had a thought that he stood in the presence, not of a mere soldier, but of a warrior of some new kind.

"I was impatient," he said. "You must use yourselves as you believe. I will do what I must."

He followed the doorkeeper into the darkness beyond the table and turned into an angle set apart. A single light threw a sheen in curtains of scarlet silk covering a square on the end wall, and beneath it an offertory with a knee-rest. Incense burned on top, and to one side a pannier held a loaf of bread, and on the other, a flask of wine glowed in a cradle.

And on the walls on both sides were paintings in silver of three fishes interlaced.

The doorkeeper went through a curtained arch, and along a passage with a light at the end. They walked a winding distance of four or five houses through cellars, and halted at a stairway. From a niche in the turn of the stair another man, also in scarlet, held up a light.

"Up, and to the left, you shall find the house of Petrus Borbo," he said. "Look for his sign, a carp, holding a twig of laurel. Go to the corner and you will find the Street of the Acanthus. To the right, you'll see the Temple of Vesta. Go toward it, and there's the Street of the White Peonies. The Pinarii house is not far down——"

"Whom may I thank for this courtesy?" Garvan asked, going one at a time up the stairway.

The man at the top laughed with the doorkeeper.

"Let us thank the God of no Name," he said, and held up the light. "Peace comes from our Father."

The door shut, and Garvan walked away, almost willing to believe he had dreamt the time since leaving the prison. But Khefi, Stavros, and Zetak were still in there, and something had to be done to release them.

Petrus Borbo's sign hung over a shop on the corner. Garvan remembered the name from his first meeting with Ultor, and hesitated, and then went in. A wide place opened onto a yard where a score of men pestled colored powder in stone pots, and each man was stained head to foot in his own color, and those working in white came among them as phantoms.

Petrus Borbo hurried to him, wiping his hands and smiling in a manner that Garvan was beginning to know was mark of the Anointed, a straight look in the eye, and no slavish trace of fear. He was white-haired, and lined, and his hands were a little of every color.

"Ultor once told me of you," Garvan said.

"Then you are a thousand times more to be welcomed," Petrus Borbo said, with no sadness and no surprise. "What shall I do for you?"

"Give me six men with swords," Garvan said. "I'll break into the prison and have him out. With others."

Petrus Borbo shook his head, looking across the road at a nursemaid trying to soothe a squalling baby.

"He will be taken out in proper time," he said.

"He bleeds," Garvan said.

"Without complaint," Petrus Borbo nodded. "So with us all, I suppose."

"You cannot, or you will not help him?" Garvan asked.

"Must not," said Petrus Borbo. "It is the Will that he should be taken or not. What have we to do?"

"Are all these of the Anointed?" Garvan motioned toward the workmen.

"All," Petrus Borbo said.

"And not one of them would help another?" Garvan asked. "By help, I mean striking a blow?"

"Not one," Petrus Borbo said. "For consider. If he should strike, and wound, or kill, where is he different from the damned of Satan?"

"Who is this Satan?" Garvan asked.

"One fallen to evil and become a prince of darkness," Petrus Borbo said, making, as Lydia, a sign between his head and breast.

"I know him not," said Garvan, out of temper. "But I hope he shows more courage, and better feeling toward his own than you do!"

He went for the street, wiping the rage from his eyes. Farther along, the temple of Vesta poured smoke from underground gratings. He walked, trying to think where he might recruit help, but the Anointed were useless, and all Romans were out of the question, and there was no sense in going back to Chote's.

Good humor came to see Corbi waiting for him on the Pinarii house steps. The old man was silent, and from undressing, to the bath, to the massage table, to lying on the couch, Garvan heard no word.

"How was it you knew I had gone to Chote's?" he asked.

"Others followed, and I followed them, Lord Prince," Corbi said. "There is danger in this city for you. From city guards and from those under the sign of the fishes."

"That also you know." Garvan felt no surprise. "What do you know of fishes?"

"You are guest of the Senator, Lord Prince," Corbi said. "If you acted against the law, and what you did became known, would the Senator regain his seat? Or would his party disown him? If it were proven that he had sheltered a traitor, he might even be cast into prison with his wife——"

"He knows nothing——" Garvan said.

"Ignorance is no defense in law," said Corbi. "You share his roof. He is responsible for you."

"We met on a happy day, Corbi," Garvan said. "I shall do nothing."

Corbi bowed, and took a pile of clothing, and went out.

Garvan breathed long.

Never had it come to him that a host might be held to account for the actions of his guest. He could make no move to help those in prison while he stayed under the Pinarii roof. He first had to move. But there was nowhere to go. Taverns there were, out along the roads, but none in the city. Workmen's hostelries he had heard of, but his presence would rouse suspicion even if they let him in. But lying there, easy among the cushions, he imagined Khefi, Stavros, and Zetak chained in the heat and dust, and he thought of Ultor perhaps at that moment under the whip. He raged, but there was nothing to be done.

Someone pit-pattered down the corridor and rang the bell outside the door, but then he knew, for the jingle was Genessa's, and he leapt up to meet her.

She carried flowers and a package, and she wore a dress of the material that Afra had woven, scarlet in one angle, blue in another, with a thread of gold, and when she came into the light, she seemed clothed in violet, and her eyes appeared the same color, or blue, or gray, or if something of each and in between he could never tell.

She smiled, looking at him as though from a distance, full of a mystery, and gave him the package.

"Now we may talk," she said, and put the flowers down, and went to sit on the window sill, looking out across the vineyards to the slopes of Vesuvius.

He tried to take her hand, but she made the slightest gesture of withdrawal.

"I am a squeezed orange," she said. "There is nothing left in my brain. I have no energy. I'd give anything to sleep."

"Sleep, then," Garvan said. "I'll watch over you."

"Weakness," she sighed. "I must be strong. Fifty at dinner tonight, and then a ceremonial service for Titus Caesar. I could sleep standing up. If only I could break my leg and have excuse to sleep!"

"If I were your father I'd break others' legs for allowing this," he said. "What use to spend your time in a daze? This is no natural thing for a girl."

"Gauls have other ways," she said in dismissal. "Will you open that package, or shall I throw it from the window?"

Garvan made haste to undo bindings and unfold a tunic of white silk, bound at the edge with the colors of the Keltae, key-patterned with the purple, and embroidered on the breast pocket with his initial and a coronet.

"Where did you find time to warm my heart?" he asked softly.

"I sewed while I memorized," she said. "Hour after hour through the weeks. It kept me awake. In that tunic is the entire psaltery of Diana, stitch by stitch. In your initial is every step and place in the altar ritual. In the coronet is all I could remember of our law. If Dianists took rank by quality of dress, you'd be first among us all. Instead——"

"Instead?"

"You are, of all, the most backward and idle and worthless!"

"What is this?"

"Have you once been to the temple since your return?"

He shook his head.

"There!" She sat back, nodding. "You were admitted under imperial auspices. What thanks do you give? None. Your first visit should have been to the temple. Instead you went to the Curia. How could you be so thoughtless? What do you suppose will be thought of my father for permitting it?"

"These things are foreign to me," he said, pretending disdain but conscious of wrongdoing. "Tell me what I should do."

"Take a thousand talents to the temple. Implore forgiveness. Swear that you will do all that you should in Gaul, all that may be asked of you. Then ask for the release of your friends from prison, and ship them away. On one count, at least, you shall be at peace!"

He stared at her and thought raced, and her smile became beautiful.

"In this I am wordless," he said. "Is Diana more powerful than the Curia? Are her priestesses given more authority than the Aedile?"

She laughed aloud.

"Julian? Sitting there day after day, with death in his mouth, and punishment at his finger-ends? He has become a monster from the boy I knew. But his father refuses his place, and Julian must serve instead."

"His father should sit in judgment?"

"Turn and turn about with my father. They are the city guardians. But Papa is Senator, and Maximus Potitius should do duty in his place. He has no love of it. He prefers his library."

"If Maximus Potitius sat in judgment, people would know gentler dealing."

"That is why Papa seconded Julian. For his harshness. I do not agree."

"I thought Dianists must be cold, and given to harshness."

Garvan saw the faintest pink come to her cheeks.

"Suitably harsh in their dealing," she said hesitantly. "Forgetting self for a higher purpose in Rome. Sacrifice of self."

"Which self was forgotten in adorning me?" Garvan held up the tunic. "Was there no other to inspire you?"

"No other except Papa is worth the trouble or the sore fingers," she smiled. "The silk is from Lydia's private stock. Even I have nothing to compare with it."

"I am a Gaul and there is none to compare with me, and that has been said before," Garvan grinned. "There are two questions I must ask you. Now, without further delay. They will not be polished in the Roman manner, but barbarous and fitting to my condition."

"Speak on, barbarian."

"I am told that you were given by contract to Julian Potitius for marriage."

"I was first to speak against it when I came of age. Julian feasts until the early morning, he and his mother and their friends. That shall not be my way. So I told Papa long ago."

"He agreed?"

"Gladly. He has no respect for Maximus Potitius. He says he doesn't trust his look."

Garvan thought of the man sitting down in the cellar under the sign of the silver fishes.

"Thus," he went on, "there is no great obstacle to your marriage with some other——"

"Provided I have seen him and dreamt of myself with him. This, I think is proper to marriage. I do not like the fashion of the older time. I am not a heifer to be given on a piece of parchment."

"That you are not. And I come to the second question."

"Speak!"

"Very well. Since most men die early in their years by war, the Gauls marry young. It is my time to marry. Even if it were not, since first I saw you my brain has turned and I see nothing before me. Except you. I pretend to think of other things. But I think of you. I try to ponder questions of philosophy befitting a student. But I think of you. I work at mathematics, knowing them good for the tendons of the mind. But I think always, everywhere, at any time, how or wherever, of you. I look into your eyes, which seem to have within them high noon forever bright with beauty's own sun, and I take your hand thus—permit me—and I ask you now, in finest Latin that is a foreign tongue to me, why it is that I am gone a madman, and filled in place of blood with gentle thought of you?"

"A passing sickness."

"When these limbs are sound, I'll show you health. No, make no move away!"

"But I have guests——"

"I asked a question."

"Perhaps your faintness persists. The faintness, remember, when you slept into seven weeks."

"Is this faintness in my eye? Or do you hear some weakness in my voice? This arm about your waist, is it woven soft? Or is the sinew true? And this kiss, this Gallic kiss——"

He took her strongly, and felt her yield in part, although while he kissed the soft of her lips, she struggled, and pushed, and made sounds. He released her, little by little, until his only touch upon her was in the kiss, and still she struggled.

"Lustrous girl, ever loveliest," he whispered. "Marry me and come to Gaul. Let us together build a kingdom for ourselves as well as for those put in our keeping——"

"First there is Capri——"

"I will plead against it with your father——"

"Hopeless!"

"I will face Caesar!"

"Worse. At all times he relies on the advice of the Mother Hemera——"

"I'll go to the Mother Hemera this very night!"

She looked up at him and showed the maenad smile.

"Now you use your wits. The Great Mother has far more in the way of favors to ask of you. Diana needs five full years to take root, and twenty to bring the first children from vire to vestal. Two years at Capri will not serve me in Gaul——"

"You will? You'll marry? Genessa!"

"Wait! There are many things to be done——"

"Everything is done!"

"The lares and penates must be appealed to, and the College of Augurs——"

"First I'll go to the temple with one demand, and one request. But at what time? And where shall I get money at this hour?"

"Seles will have it ready. Be at the temple at sunset."

"Shall you be there?"

"Certainly not. But one, Euthylia, will attend you——"

"You had planned it so!"

"What use to stand, woodenheaded——"

"Genessa!"

"No!"

But he took her, and despite her struggles, kissed her.

"We should not," she whispered. "This is not the Roman way——"

"True," he said. "This is of Gaul, and with this Gallic kiss I sear the Gallic brand. I promise it will ever stay, and torment in or out of speech. Remember this!"

She ran from him, and turned in the doorway, and her smile seemed to light the shadows.

"How it burns, this brand!" she whispered. "What flame is in me to keep it so. Plead, Garvan. I fear the thought of Capri. And take those flowers. Show them, and Euthylia will go to you!"

What he put on, or how it was got on, or if he had anything on or not was small matter from that moment. In a singing, sunlit blindness where he saw everything clearly and not at all, he arrived by chariot in the Forum, and Seles came behind with slaves carrying the bags of coin.

At the temple he heard his name called for one thousand talents, and when the vires came, he stood forward with the flowers, and one made way to him before the ranks were still. She repeated what he said, and took the flowers, and he watched her go into the shrine. But while he waited he found himself praying to Mithras. The vire came laughing from behind the curtains, and took his hands, and told him to go to the prison and find what orders were given. His shout of joy turned heads, but he was careless, and Seles had to run to catch him at the chariot. But city police barred his way a street and more before the prison.

"The Christians are out," an officer said. "They crawl from every hole. You'll have to walk over them."

"I'd thought them all in chains or dead," Garvan said in surprise. "You permit this?"

"The prison is full," the officer said. "One more, and the walls would burst. So they creep from every crack and kneel, praying. And what? If we go among them with the sword, still they kneel. So let them kneel and pray for all of me. I am of the civil police, not of the butchery and graveyard. Let be!"

Garvan pushed through the standing crowd in the avenue, and heard the singing, and the cries of people entranced. But he stopped short at a kneeling mass of men and women, some in scarlet and others in black, all facing the prison gateway, and at signs from a man standing in front, raising branches of palm and shouting together.

Garvan stepped a pace at a time, and the depth and fervor of their voices entered into him and he was willing to call them brave. He halted a little way from the gate, looking at the man giving signs and calling prayers.

Petrus Borbus smiled and beckoned him on.

"Here are more than six of spirit, Lord Prince," he called. "And for swords we carry the palm of peace——"

"I have no understanding of this," Garvan said. "Where does howling from without succor those within?"

"In the single purpose of our prayer," Petrus Borbo said. "That the Will might be done."

The doors in the main prison building screeched open and an officer came out with a file of prison guards. Behind them Khefi, Stavros, and Zetak, burned and dusty, stared in the manner of men left too long in the sun and touched in their minds.

"Water," Khefi said through a cracked tongue. "Make no further work with us, towhead. Leave us. Go. But water."

People of the Anointed picked the three up and carried them toward the lane into the main avenue. Garvan made half-hearted attempts to prevent them, but they were moved faster than by their own feet. The singing went to a high note, and held. The scarlet and black concourse stood together, and raised their arms, and all the branches waved.

He felt the earth give underfoot, and slide away, and he fell. A crash of tiles from the roofs came among screams, but ever all the singing steadied in a chant. He got to his knees, but the ground lifted under him. Stones fell, and parts of the prison wall, and dust blew, yellow and thick, and rolled.

Still the Anointed people sang, and Petrus Borbo stood in white, with his arms toward the sky, and called out, and they answered him, but fear was not in their voices.

A great cracking and grinding, and a slither of stone burst in whiter dust. The Anointed people walked, singing, toward the prison walls, scarlet and black figures going into shadows and beyond. Again the ground shook, and again Garvan had to grope for support even to kneel. Yet the Anointed people walked, and sang steadily. Sunshine came, lighting the dust in a speckled swirl of golden motes, picking bright green in the raised branches and glittering in the eyes of men and women laughing while they sang.

The dust shifted, and settled, and a shout went up, and Garvan stood, looking at gaps in the prison walls, at piles of stones, and at the black and scarlet crowd walking up, and over, into the prison yard.

Prisoners dragging their chains crawled and walked, or were lifted out, and looked to the left and right, and chose a way and ran. A plain chant began inside the walls, and a clapping of hands, and a jingle of sistra. Petrus Borbo, in a scarlet tunic, led over the heap of stones, and his white garment wrapped a man carried on the shoulders of those behind.

The crowd chanted, and the branches were held high, and the procession went on, passing the staring, helpless sentries.

And Garvan saw that the man they carried was Ultor, the lawyer, and the bruised eyes were closed and the face was set in peace. He wanted to follow, but he felt put aside, for men and women, old and young, all went together, arm by arm, shouting the words of the chant, and there seemed no place for him.

XVI

The Pinarii house was calm. Seles told him that the tremors had barely been felt in that part of the city, not even enough to shake pollen from the vases' blooms. But the dinner had been canceled, and the Lady Thalia and Genessa had driven to the temple to see that any needed help was given, and might not return until late, and the Senator had gone to a meeting of the City Council.

Garvan felt at loss. The evening lay empty in front of him. There was plenty to think about, but he refused his mind, although he wondered how Caesar might be affected by such a show of Anointed strength. Rome and Diana depended upon steel and soldiery. It was something new that a simple one with a prayer and other simpletons with branches of palms could break down walls and release prisoners. Dianic arts, Corbi assured him, had no compare.

"Doubt works in the city, Lord Prince," he said while Garvan dressed. "It is on all tongues, how the God of the Anointed tore down the prison walls."

"It was a movement underfoot," Garvan said.

"But while they sang," Corbi went on. "They say it was a miracle——"

"No more in this," Garvan said. "If I am accountable to my host in conduct, should I speak of Anointed ones, or miracles in his house? What plays at the theater tonight? My brain requires a turn."

"Something droll, so Phocis tells," Corbi said. "A Greek work, where frogs speak as men."

"Then I shall go," said Garvan. "Perhaps the frogs are wiser."

"Indeed," said Corbi. "For they shut their mouths to speak."

Garvan went out, along the Street of the Lean Days. People were in the roadways, looking as if by the moment they tested the steadiness of the ground. Shops were all shut except the wine sellers'. The theater was crowded, and he had trouble to get a seat, and that on the side, even by extra coins in the ticket seller's hand. The actors wore gold masks, some with the mouths turned up in a grin defying the Fates, and others with the mouths turned down in defeat. For the rest, he understood one word in three of the Greek, though others about him roared at every line and thus called note to themselves as wise ones, if not as scholars. But under the night sky, looking up at Vesuvius's flaming shaft, and the flat cloud of smoke made fiery in its underpart by the glare beneath, he listened to the voices, and taunted himself with lack of study that made him ignorant of almost all they were saying.

He felt a pluck at his sleeve, and turned to send away some impertinent hawker. Instead he saw a head of red curls, and a face drawn in heavy lines, and eyes tragic with appeal.

Tadmon clung to a ledge, looking over the sill of an arched window.

"I had to climb as a fly over the building to find you," he whispered. "Your slave told me you were here. No other can help me!"

A shh! started among the patrons, and Garvan signed he would go into the street. He went down the flights with his mind set to have more to do with frogs when he knew more of the Greek.

Tadmon stood in shadow behind a statue of Julius Caesar.

"I need money and your help," he began. "My wife and daughters are brought from Eire, and they stand in the night mart to be sold. I have not enough money saved to buy them. And I am not a citizen and cannot. Help me. I give you myself!"

"Come," Garvan said, moved by the eyes of a begging dog. "A chariot!"

They rode only a short distance from the Forum. Torches flared from sconces set in the walls, and platforms of a man's height were built around a square. Grown males roped together filled one, and in another youths and boys. Opposite, a platform was filled with grown women, and on the next, maidens and little girls were crowded, too thick to sit down. The square was full of people listening to callers reading out descriptions of the lots to be sold. Tadmon hurried, and Garvan was pressed to keep up, for the man almost wept with impatience. He went to the side of the platform, among many squatting on rugs, and looked about, and whistled. A woman got up and came to him, and Garvan recognized a face that might never have been young.

"They were left in the yard," Pharia, the public nurse, nodded across the road. "The dealer says they might go for little. They have no flesh from voyaging."

"Let us see him privately," Garvan said.

Pharia looked, but she said nothing, and he was unsure if she knew him. She led around to a tent of mats and went in, to many tables, and men eating and drinking. One man in a corner she went to, and whispered, and he spoke through mouthfuls, and his tongue trapped rice grains on his chin.

"There is no choice," he said through food. "They are taken in a lot by the Temple of Diana. I have many better to tempt your pocket——"

Garvan moved before Tadmon. One kick sent the table over and knocked the dealer out of his seat, and the steaming pot splashed over him. His shriek brought others off their couches, and blades and swords flashed. But Garvan looked about, and Tadmon stood beside him, and steel whispered away, and all went back to what they were doing.

"It is finished," Tadmon said in a strong voice, out in the square.

"I shall go into the temple to find them. We live together, or die."

"Let us go to the temple," Garvan said, thinking of Genessa. "Perhaps there is one we might touch with a word."

Pharia stood near to Tadmon in the chariot, and she would not be put off.

"How then?" she asked with tears. "Can a woman not help here?"

"You have helped enough, good Pharia," Tadmon said. "Since we met, you have been truest friend to me——"

"You were gentlest of any I have known," she whispered. "Let me help to find the women nearest your heart——"

"Let it be so," he said, and took her hand. "A public nurse, a stoker, and a prince. Here, Diana, is mixture enough!"

But the gardens were dark, and the temple was shut. A beggar told them that a side door was open, and they hurried into the street, finding ranks of chariots and wagons and the drivers lying about on the lawns. Pharia went among them, and came hurrying back.

"Here the goddess lifts her hand!" she laughed. "They are taken in this side, underground. But the nurse is known to me. Give me money. She has a tooth for coins!"

Tadmon caught her by the robe.

"You risk much," he said.

"I have seen you," she told him over her shoulder. "What should I fear?"

She turned to Garvan, and he threw all the money he had into the fold of her toga.

"So, sprig," she smiled. "Are these the coins you promised me? See, in what straits they're paid!"

She went, blowing a kiss, and ran among the trees to the lighted arch of a gateway.

"Wait," Garvan said. "I'll go in."

Tadmon nodded, watching the lighted arch.

Garvan went to the side door, which was open, and looked in at the cloister thronged with priestesses and vestals, and matrons and their daughters. A priestess took him to a group over in a corner, busy about a table filled with bandages, rolls of linen, and small pots. Genessa filled bottles with liquid, and her mother mixed an unguent in a bowl. He kissed his fingers and laid them on their hands in greet-ing.

"Many are hurt in other parts of the city," Genessa told him. "We make stores for the physicians. We are soon done. Did you fear for me?"

Garvan swallowed the ready lie.

"No," he said. "I shall never fear for you."

She smiled, the happiest and laziest smile.

"It is well," she said. "And are your friends released?"

"By a miracle," he said in all truth.

"And a word from Papa, and gift from you," she said practicably. "Put all things in their proper place!"

"A serious matter for your hearing," he whispered. "A family of women is sold to the temple. How may I restore them to my friend, the husband and father? Do you know a man's eyes that see his wife and daughters lost?"

"Was this wise, to busy yourself in this matter?" she asked.

"Now I wish I were of the Anointed," said Garvan. "To break these walls in a prayer. Must children be slaughtered for the sake of bar-gainers?"

"No more!" Genessa caught him by the arm. "A word and we are thrown to the guards!"

Garvan took her hands and held them.

"Enough," he said. "You are my first thought."

Genessa told the Lady Thalia, and they went together to find the Mother Hemera. But she and her staff were at the Curia in attend-ance on Titus Caesar. Lady Thalia said they might call there on the way home, and they went out, through the laughter, bowing to friends' waves and bows. Tadmon was not under the trees, and Garvan spared no time to look for him. The Pinarii coach took them to the Curia and they walked into the large court, filled with civic dignitaries, law-yers, and soldiers, silent, listening to a voice that brought Genessa to clutch Garvan's arm, and stop.

The Lady Thalia went on, to a farther column, and stood in shadow looking at her husband.

Caesar sat beneath a canopy, with the Mother Hemera at his right

hand and a dozen standing about him, all in the purple. Lawyers
and scribes sat at the long table. Sulla Pinarius stood in the prose-
cutor's place, facing an elderly man in the prisoner's box. His back
was turned, but Garvan knew him by the scarlet toga and the white
hair. Julian Potitius sat behind the judicial bench, watching, elbow
on knee. But nothing in his face showed that his father, Maximus
Potitius, was on trial.

"These were the duties of my joint guardian," Sulla Pinarius was
saying in an almost friendly voice. "Yet, knowing that the prison walls
were breached, he caused one, Ultor, to be taken into his house. On
this, his more dutiful son reported the matter, and his wife, the Lady
Cleona, left with her children and servants. I went to him, as guardian
conjoint with me in the conduct of the city's affairs, to ask for an ex-
planation. He met me in a scarlet toga. The man I have known for
fifty-odd years, Lord Caesar, is one of these that infest us. A Christian.
I ordered his arrest. And now I demand his death, with one grace.
That his lady wife, and his innocent children, dutiful citizens, go free
with all his goods, lands, and chattels intact."

"What say you?" Caesar asked the prisoner.

"The facts are correct," said Maximus Potitius. "I am of the
Anointed."

"When did this fall upon you?" Caesar asked again.

"The yoke came upon me over ten years ago in a meeting with
Peter, an apostle, at Rome," Maximus Potitius said.

"Let his sentence be yours," Caesar said. "You lived in honor. You
die in disgrace, and infamy is your portion. Is this sufficient reward
for your Anointed faith?"

"Our Master said, 'Rejoice in that day for in the like manner did
their fathers unto the prophets,'" Maximus Potitius said softly. "Earth
will be a joyous place when all these things are passed——"

"Let the court be unburdened of this incubus," said Caesar. "It
should be understood by the lower courts that no mercy is to be
shown to this sect. They shall work as slaves until they die. Those
too old, and those weakly, and those not readily confessing shall die
where they stand."

"But it was said by the Christ, the Anointed One," Maximus

Potitius called in a loud voice. " 'They shall fall by the edge of the sword and shall be led away captive into all nations. And there shall be signs in the sun, and in the moon, and in the stars, and upon the earth distress of nations, and the sea and the waves roaring, and men's hearts failing them for fear . . .' "

Over the smoky light of the torches a pink glow flushed in faces and reddened white marble. A murmur started, and then a shout. Behind Caesar men pointed over his head at the sky.

Garvan turned, seeing the fright in Genessa's eyes, but the words of comfort stuck in his lips.

Vesuvius had thrown a tall red pillar into the sky, and the clouds coiled in crimson and, as the moments passed, the pillar grew brighter, almost to gold, and sparks flew up and down and the clouds stretched wider, and higher, and the light grew redder.

"A sign!" A voice shrieked. "See how I am strengthened. I believe!"

Garvan saw the Lady Thalia tearing at her mantle, but Genessa moved first, and even so, she was too late. The mantle fell, and the Lady Thalia showed herself in scarlet, pale as a flame in the strong light, and walked toward Caesar.

"I am of the Anointed, Lord Caesar," she said clearly. "Give me place beside my brother——"

She held out a hand toward Maximus Potitius, but guards dragged him back.

Genessa ran to throw herself at her father, but he threw her off, and Garvan caught her and held her, screaming and kicking to be freed. Sulla Pinarius drew his sword in a blue arc of steel and went close to his wife, and turned his back, and stabbed, and she fell. Genessa breathed long and went limp, but Garvan held her. Sulla Pinarius took the sword hilt, and pulled out the blade.

"Titus Flavius, I am your friend," he called out. "I am a Roman, and my son, and all my name. Think well of us. Ave!"

He plunged the sword with both hands, upward, beneath his heart, and went to his knees, watching blood run down the blade, and turned his eyes toward his wife, and crawled far enough to touch her, and lay still.

Garvan folded Genessa in her cloak, and lifted her, anxious only to bring her into cool air. Caesar had turned his back, holding a fold of the toga over his face. His staff followed him off the dais, and he paused beside the bodies, though still with the toga held to avert the sight of tragedy.

"My friend shall lie in honor," he told the officer. "Bury him with his lady. Let no word be recorded. Let no man speak of this."

He went on, and Garvan would have followed, but the Mother Hemera and her attendants ringed him.

"Give her to us," Mother Hemera said. "There will be many tears, and days and nights of shadow. We will bring her calm, and at peace again."

Despite himself Garvan released her, thinking of her grieving in the empty house.

"I shall wait at the College for news of her," he said, watching the women carry her away. "We shall marry. We need not wait."

The Pinarii coach was not in line, and he took a chariot to the house. The streets were even more crowded, and many families were packing carts with household goods, and heavy traffic filled the avenues leading out of the city.

But a crowd had gathered outside the Pinarii house, and women were weeping on the steps.

Seles sat beside the door, with his robe over his head, and his staff broken across his knees, and an overturned bowl beside him, and his fingers were curled in death. Women slaves lay in blood, among ashes thrown in grief. Grooms and servants sprawled in the garden and along the colonnade, and red pools glimmered by torchlight.

The shrine of the lares and penates was covered, and the lamp was out, and in front the Lady Thalia's maid lay dead, hand in hand with Sulla Pinarius's valet.

"They chose not to live," Corbi whispered from the stairway. "How could they be sold, and serve another, having loved the Pinarii?"

"And you," Garvan said. "You had no love?"

"I serve you, Lord Prince," Corbi said. "The Numidian, also. And upstairs, one waits to speak. The housekeeper."

Garvan went up, and a kneeling woman got to her feet and stood beside the door of his room. In both hands she offered her keys.

"These I give to you, Lord Prince," she wept. "One other thing I have to do by order of my mistress. Be pleased, I beg, to come with me."

He took the keys, and nodded assent, and went with her along the corridor, passing the room where Phocis the Greek had worked, to a small doorway that she unlocked with one key she had kept. They went in, to a narrow passage with a lamp burning, and she opened a door, and he saw a small room of white-washed walls, and a red stone floor. A silver box lay on the offertory, and above, scarlet silk curtains were drawn aside, showing an empty space in a wooden frame.

The woman took the box and gave it to him.

"I was commanded by the Lady Thalia that if death came I was to give this into a safe hand," she said. "It is to go to the Lady Lydia."

"Is not the daughter of this house more fitting?" Garvan asked. "Should not these keys be hers?"

The woman shook her head.

"Others of the Pinarii will come, and they are senior," she said, pulling the veil over her face. "I was instructed to do what I have done. In that box is what rested above the altar. The Lady Lydia is not in the city, therefore I place trust in you, as trust was placed in me."

"You shall serve the Lady Genessa," Garvan said.

Through the veil he saw her eyes, and fright struck in her glance.

"I served those who are gone," she said. "I waited that my work should please them. Now my time is come, and I join hands with them."

She made low obeisance, and turned, hurrying, and he heard her call out in a high voice that got fainter as she ran. He followed, and he saw that Phocis the Greek had been wrong in complaining of a storeroom behind the main wall, for what had spoiled a dream of Dionysius was a shrine to the Anointed.

"First, call him who attends in death, and let all who lie here be buried with respect," he told Corbi. "Then close and bar the house. Bring the keys and my baggage to me at the house of the Lady Lydia."

He carried the box with him, and rode through quieter streets. Vesuvius was covered by cloud, but smoke lay a great distance, black against the night, and a smell of burning was on the wind.

Lamps were alight in Lydia's house, and the door was open, and in the roadway a force of police guarded Yosef and all the servants roped together. But when Yosef held out his hands in appeal, a guard knocked him down.

"The Aedile is within," a petty officer said, saluting the purple, but denying way to the prisoners. "We are at command."

Garvan looked at the fallen man, and at the others staring down at corded wrists. With slow steps he went toward the doorway. He heard the tapping stick coming from somewhere above, and stood, cut to the heart that Afra should be taken. A group of civilians and police were busy opening cases in the space beyond the atrium.

"Was there, then, no church in this house?" Julian Potitius's voice came from the first flight of stairs. "Was this not a bishopric named for the Jew, Paul? Such is my information. You were never told so?"

"Ah, noble Aedile!" Afra's voice shook in laughter. "This was always in way of work, this house. If I had sight would any woman rule me? I allowed her to prevail, and why not? My earnings equaled all others together. And who chose my stock, my dyes, my clients? She. Therefore I said nothing. What she did, was it my affair?"

"I was told that you leaned toward the Anointed," the Aedile said, coming down the stairway.

"A man as old as I must listen to many things in his time," said Afra, tapping his way down. "Whether he believes them or not is breeze from another quarter. Lydia told me she heard a Voice, and had faith, seeing nobody. But after all, I hear voices, seeing nobody. Other voices speak, and seeing none, I make up my mind for much may be told from the voice——"

"Enough," Julian said, walking into the atrium. "Be ready at court. The sooner they are condemned and stretched to dry, the better."

"What I have missed in all my life!" Afra reached the last step, and cracked the stick on the ground. "That I could see her spiked to wood!"

"Filthy scarecrow traitor!" Garvan shouted. "Is this the whiner to the Lady Lydia, and father allspice and philosopher to all else?"

"What do you here?" Julian Potitius demanded, with no greeting. "This house is confiscated!"

"I came needing shelter," Garvan said. "The Pinarii house is a tomb. How do I hear? That the Lady Lydia is held for trial?"

"And all with her," Julian Potitius said. "Fleet, houses, servants taken by Caesar. At last. What will you say?"

"In face of this, little," said Garvan. "But friend Afra is a free man?"

"Lord Prince, make no attack on me," Afra said, staring toward him. "I ever helped you. Should this woman drag me to crucifixion, and I, with no word to gainsay her? This is my work and my life. I have no faith in crosses, or fishes or in the power of bread and wine. I have faith in my fingers, and in the loom, and bread and wine is what I earn. And you? Did I not act as marriage counselor, and did you, then, mock me? Lord Prince, indeed! Romans make little of such."

Julian Potitius laughed, and officers and police standing about laughed with him. Garvan stepped forward, and slapped backhanded, and knocked Afra on his back.

"Make no advantage of age and blindness," Garvan said. "One word more of such, and I will kick you to a mash. And have care, good Aedile, or I will see to it that these smiles are scraped from your faces wth the edge of a sword!"

A trumpet call brought pause to the Aedile's angry reply, and men came in a rattle of shields and armor. Three Praetorian officers came to the doorway, and, seeing the Aedile, saluted.

"We seek a prince of Armorican Gaul," one said. "Garvan, son of Orberix——"

"I am he." Garvan stood forward. "What's your business?"

"The Lord Caesar commands your presence," the officer said. "This, with all dispatch."

"Let there be no waiting," Garvan said. "But I am not robed."

"Lord Prince, let an equerry decide," the officer said. "We come to guide you."

Garvan saw a grin in the face of Julian Potitius. For a moment he was tempted to throw everything aside only to wipe the malice out of the scalded eyes. Instead he helped Afra to his feet, and put the shepherd's crook in his hand, and followed the officers.

The prisoners had gone. A gold coach from the imperial household waited with a cavalry escort. He got in, and the cavalcade went off at a gallop toward the Praetorian Barracks. The guard passed them through the archway, and where the coach stopped an officer led up a stairway lit with lamps burning the white flame of human fat, and through a corridor walled in mirrors and jeweled plaques, into a circular room with a great window of crystal cut with the likeness of Diana.

A soldier cloaked in purple over the Praetorian uniform came in, and when he was nearer, Garvan recognized Colonel Balchus Dasius. He smiled, but there was something more than humor in his eye.

"Lord Prince, good welcome," he said, letting his voice find echoes through the vault. "We last met at the house of my friend, Sulla Pinarius, of happy memory. If you have regard for your father's place in the Lord Caesar's affections, make no argument. I say this remembering the Senator and his thoughts of you. Let me advise you."

"I am well advised," Garvan said.

"Excellent!" the Colonel nodded, and his sense of relief was plain. "Then come, we are expected. Good sense is what the night requires."

Garvan followed him to the corridor, and they turned to the left, and a servitor standing outside a closed double door knocked twice, and a leaf opened.

"Enter before the presence of the Lord Caesar," the Colonel said with no ceremony or raising his voice. "Allow me to announce you."

He went in, and stood erect, and made a slight bow.

"Lord Caesar," he said. "Your servant, Garvan, is here."

"Ah yes," the quiet voice said. "Thank you, Balchus. Let him enter."

Garvan went in, and made a bow in copy of the Colonel.

Titus Caesar wore the lighter shade of purple, and he sat low in his chair, and his mouth dragged. The room was a library, set about with racks from floor to ceiling, and all filled by scrolls and books. A scroll taken from a circular container lay open at his elbow.

"Be seated." He waved to a chair at the table. "I was disposed to be angry with you. But I account your foolishness to youththood. Mark these words, Garvan. It is not my way to speak twice in the same matter. First, let me recount, you were joined in a serious crime, that of laying hands on a citizen. You were forgiven for reasons of state. You then made yourself busy with the affairs of your fellow-conspirators in prison and awaiting trial. This was stupidity. Much more serious, you involved yourself with a nest of Christians. Whether certain of these creatures appeal to you or not is beside the issue. They do not appeal to me, and you are sworn in my service."

He spoke with calm, and his eyes, though they showed the bloody veins of fatigue, were direct, bright under the hand shading them from the lampstand.

"The Lady Genessa is not to be considered free, since she is now part of my family by my order," he went on. "Is there any room for misunderstanding?"

"I had no thought of any," Garvan said. "I would make her my wife."

"Never think of it again," Caesar said, sharper. "If you wish to marry into a Roman family, this is well, and it shall be arranged. In order that all unwanted acts may cease, you will return to Gaul. Is this understood?"

Garvan nodded, unable to speak, for the earth had seemed to slip from under him and he could only hear its rumble.

"You will leave when the ship is ready," Caesar went on. "Proper lodging will be found for you here, at the Praetorian Barracks. And remember, I take this course because I am not anxious to disrupt my friendship with your father. Is there anything you wish to say?"

"Nothing in these terms," Garvan said. "If I busied myself in the affairs of my friends it was because they were loyal to me. Should their misfortune make me disloyal?"

"Robbers and murderers," Caesar said. "They had no claim to your loyalty."

"I was stolen as a boy, but these were soldiers and Romans," Garvan said. "There is perhaps some difference——"

"An end to this," Caesar said. "What more?"

"This nest of Christians," Garvan began. "I did not involve myself, neither have I heard their doctrine——"

"It is well," Caesar said. "And enough. Do not displease me further, Garvan. Take this dispatch to your father from my hand, and give him my salute, so!"

He gripped Garvan's forearm in the Roman style, and Garvan felt the flaccid quality of his flesh. Caesar was a tired man.

He snapped his fingers, and the door opened.

"See that the Prince Garvan is made comfortable," he told Colonel Dasius. "Signal the Admiral Pliny that the prince will sail with the first flotilla. When you stand off for Gaul, think of your friend, Titus Caesar. Farewell!"

The door shut, and Colonel Dasius walked a few paces, humming under his breath.

"Far better than I'd thought," he said. "You'll sail tomorrow by the afternoon flood."

Garvan nodded, scarcely able to use his wits.

"Be of good heart," the Colonel said. "The day's events have sickened us. By sunset tomorrow, there'll be many less Christians and far more peace. This officer will show you to your quarters. Please do not leave them without word from me. Sleep at ease!"

Garvan passed through every state of mind, from hottest rage that he could be treated in such a manner to coldest fear that he might never again see Genessa. His only salve was that she was safe among those she trusted. About himself he tried not to think, for then he had to consider his father, and his people. Duty said that he must obey, and go. But a small voice said that he ought to make an attempt to tell Genessa that she would always carry his thoughts entwined as flowers about her head, and to explain that he would fight for her and steal her away, but never in the knowledge that innocents in Gaul would yield up blood for every kiss.

The window had no glass, and fog that smelled of ashes blew in. The room was any soldier's, with a table, chairs, a bed and lamps, and hunting trophies pegged to the walls. The one sleeping rug was not long enough to cut into a rope to climb down, even if his arm could have borne his weight.

At last the door opened, and an orderly brought in a tray of cooked fish, and hot breads, and wine. Behind came the Ensign Aristarchus Cornelius, and with him the Aedile, Julian Potitius, and two others, dusty from a journey and carrying cases of documents.

"Lord Prince." The Ensign saluted. "Be pleased to talk with the

Aedile. I am your escorting officer, and I am ordered to accompany you to the port of Misenum."

"I shall be brief," Julian Potitius said, and motioned to the two men. "These are prosecutors sent to make a case against this Samarian woman. Let us not interrupt your meal. Savor, and tell me if my cook has not a secret."

"I have no wish to eat," Garvan said.

"Pity," said the Aedile. "I'd thought you well disposed toward the taste of fishes. My colleagues have questions about the woman who used fishes for a sign."

"Which I shall not answer," Garvan said. "Remember, by command of the Lord Caesar I was made her guest against my will."

"Then you suspected her?" one of the visitors inquired. "Of what?"

"Of kindliness, and decency, and of most things which others appear to lack," Garvan said. "End this. I have nothing more to tell you."

"Let me remind you of your Roman oath," the Aedile said. "You swore to serve loyally."

"In that, you are no judge," said Garvan. "You were not even loyal to your own father. Leave me!"

The Aedile kicked a chair against the wall, and went to the doorway, signing to the others to leave, and turned in a grimace of bared teeth.

"Let this be known to you," he whispered. "When next we meet, you may find me Proconsul to Gaul. I look forward to many an agreeable meeting, Lord Prince!"

Garvan made effort to move, but Aristarchus paced before the door, and saluted, giving the Aedile space to go.

"Your servant waits orders with your baggage, Lord Prince," he said. "Is something wanting that he might bring?"

"A half minute alone with that Potitius spawn," Garvan said. "An hour of freedom from this prison. These, let him bring!"

"Until I report to escort you to the flagship of Admiral Pliny, I am off duty," Aristarchus said steadily. "What may happen in that time is a matter for Gallic prudence. But this room is four stories above the ground. Beyond the door are Praetorians, and you are unarmed. Add to that my sympathy!"

He gave an order, and Corbi guarded his eyes with a hand, and entered, bowing.

"Lord Prince, all is well," he began. "The smoke from the burning mountain is thick. We cannot see above a dozen paces. You should have change of clothing, heavy footwear——"

He pulled at a wrapping inside his tunic, and took off the cloth, showing a golden stopper, and the gleaming white of an alabastron.

"—and a cloak against a hard journey," he went on, speaking for the benefit of the waiting sentries. "Many send farewell greetings, Lord Prince, and one gave this for a token. Others said they would accompany you to the port and take leave with music. But Saracens and Greeks and Phrygians have no place at Misenum, or any other guarded confine."

Garvan took the alabastron, wondering how Corbi could have got it, but he dare not ask. There was appeal in the old man's eyes, as if he wanted to tell more.

"I will do well with what I have," Garvan said. "How did this message come?"

"With many tears." Corbi bowed over clasped hands. "If it were known which window was this, it might be that your friends would come to sing their joy at thought of your return."

"None may come within the walls," a petty officer said sharply. "The time is gone. Lord Prince, excuse him. I must close the door."

A barracks cat, a striped and stringy animal, rubbed itself against the jamb, and mewed, smelling the untouched fish. A light came into Corbi's eyes. He lifted the silver lid, and took the fish, and threw it. The cat leapt, and chewed, and the petty officer began a complaint about a mess on the floor. But then the cat stretched, and howled, and fell on its side in a kick.

"One bite of the Roman fish is good for man or beast," Corbi said, and picked up the tray. "I shall wait below, Lord Prince, for your message."

The petty officer kicked the cat's body outside, and slammed the door.

Garvan turned out of a stare, and shook himself. Tightly though the alabastron was stoppered, a breath of perfume brought Genessa warm beside him. He realized what effort she must have made to reach Corbi.

This, he knew, was her appeal to him, and there was no thought in his mind except that he must go to her. He remembered what Corbi had said about Saracens, Phrygians, and Greeks. His eye caught the glint of a hunting bow. He took it from the peg, and the quiver of arrows. One by one he steeped the arrows in the lamp oil, and with a dozen ready he went back to the window. In delight he found he had the strength to pull. The first arrow blazed in the lamp, and he shot it high, and it dropped, making a pale track. The second went to the same place, and a third and fourth, and then, beyond any doubt, he heard Zetak's whistle.

He sat, planning and counterplanning, trying not to notice the scratching of a rat somewhere in the wall, and even wishing he could become a rat if only to find a hole for escape.

There came a sound from the window, and he caught a movement near the ceiling. Two baby hands stretched down from the top of the arch. On the back of each was tattooed a star, and while he watched, they beat against the stone and he heard the softest scream in a cat's purr of breath. Chote the Carthaginian hung head-down from the roof.

Garvan took good hold of the wrists, and the baby hands tightened like shackle bars. Without a breath Chote bent at the waist, raising himself until Corbi and the Numidian, holding his ankles, could lift first one and then the other over the parapet. They ran across the flat roof to a couple of planks bridging to the next barracks building, and through empty rooms to a stairway, and out to a timber yard and a waiting cart manned by a couple of Chote's kitchen boys.

Chote put Garvan in the cart with Corbi, and piled bags of charcoal about them, and logs on top so that they could scarcely breathe. Then the mules were clucked, and off they went.

"None would allow me in until the Ensign Cornelius came, and I begged him," Corbi said. "Your friends urged me to find you, but I was dizzied with the rounds of the stairs. Then we saw the arrows. Chote supplies the barracks with fuel. So, we sit here!"

"How was the alabastron got?" Garvan asked.

"The Lady Genessa is held in the villa of the Mother Hemera," Corbi whispered. "Her maid, Dassi, was sent prisoner to the temple, and there found a woman of the public baths——"

"Pharia," Garvan whispered.

"The same," Corbi said. "She, and one Tadmon, came to Chote with the alabastron and this message. That the Lady Genessa, having no thought to live beyond the land of Gaul, will die at Capri."

Troops were marching by, and the cart was stopped at a command. Chote whined and purred, and a potboy mumbled, and the cart went on again. Screams and shouts came clear, and the crack of blazing timber, and the rage of a crowd.

"The Anointed die, Lord Prince," Corbi said.

"So long my Genessa lives, I care nothing," Garvan said.

"They work timber for the Lady Lydia and her fellows," Corbi said. "At noon they will hang on a cross with a bolt through each hand, and one through the bones of the feet. As the Carpenter was hanged before them."

"Who was this Carpenter?" Garvan asked.

"The Hebrew, Jesus," Corbi said, and made a sign between his head and breast. "The Anointed One."

"You, then, are also of these Christians," Garvan said.

"I am of the Anointed," said Corbi.

"Is this how you know so much of fish?" Garvan asked.

"The Aedile knows more," Corbi said. "And who cries for a dead Gaul?"

The cart stopped, and the bags and logs were pulled off. They were in the cookshop yard, and Chote led below to a cellar. Khefi, Stavros, and Zetak waited for them, and a dozen other men, and among them the red beard of Tadmon. He came running, and gripped Garvan's hand.

"Know that my family is safely aboard Uriel's ship in harbor," he laughed. "But could I go, knowing you held prisoner? I am Tadmon, Prince of Drelain, in the land of Eire. Brother ragtail, count one more sword beside you!"

"And needed," Khefi said, pointing to the others. "Come, towhead. We'll skirmish to the harbor. In thirty minutes we'll be in open water!"

Garvan felt his spirit weaken in their friendly eyes, knowing that all had risked life to help him.

"Go without me," he said. "I must find Genessa. She is held at the villa of the Mother Hemera. I shall go there, and take her. Then to the harbor."

"This, in a city choked with Praetorian cream and wet underfoot with Christian blood!" said Khefi admiringly.

"The Mother Hemera has been my friend," Garvan said. "She has ever been careful of Genessa. Should I go with a sword?"

"Go with your wits, and our prayers," Khefi said.

Garvan looked at them all, and raised his hand in salute, and left them. He went through the lanes between the houses going down to the sea. Smoke was lifting, and through the rifts he saw the blue of morning sky. The mountain was covered with black smoke and so was all of the city on its lower slope. In the houses on both sides servants were packing, and the lane was filled with wagons being piled with goods. None, servant or master, spared him a word or a glance. Twice, and loudly, he heard shrieks, and rough commands, and under all the bustle there was constant tramp of soldiery. He went into the gardens leading to the Villa Hemera, and crawled along a ditch, and climbed the wall and stepped carefully through the garden. All the windows were shuttered, and there was no sound except for dogs in a howl on the other side. He made way through the garden's darker leaves to the two spaniels roped to a bench. His heart was lifted, for they were Genessa's pets. He crawled toward them, and slipped the knot and they snuffled at him in the shadow, and ran to the terrace, and their ears flapped over the wall, but they were silent, as if they knew where to go.

Garvan bent double in a sprint across the open path, and clutched at the balustrade, pulling himself over. Two doors at each end were open, with drawn curtains. The spaniels' tracks led to that on the left. He crept, pace by pace, not to make swift shadow that might attract a glance.

The dogs howled from inside the villa, and then were quiet, as if a door had closed. Voices came loud nearby, a woman's voice in a shriek, and the drone of a man's, and another man shouting. Garvan went

across one door, and opened the curtains of the other, looking into a
shuttered room lit by a wick. At left a corridor went the length of the
villa. A door at right was curtained. The voices were clearer. The high
shriek was the Mother Hemera's. The shouter was Julian Potitius.

But the drone came from Afra.

"I rule my kingdom with a stick," he was saying. "If I am to work
for the College, then I must have my share."

"You could be forced, blind one!" Julian Potitius shouted.

Afra laughed at him, the blind laugh.

"Ruin these hands, or touch these senses," he said. "What might
then come from a loom? Better you think of a way to force Lydia."

"She dies," the Mother Hemera said.

"And with her, every secret of color," Afra laughed again. "For this
I came to you. What use to work the loom if color is gone? How
weave the purple for the Lord Caesar? Only she knows the secrets of
the dyes."

"Could she be made to tell?" Julian Potitius asked.

"She might be broken," said Afra. "She would never bend."

Garvan went inside, and down the corridor. The doors to four rooms
were all closed, and a lamp at the end shone in the tiled floor. He
listened at the first, and at the second, and at the third door he heard
a voice he knew.

Slowly he turned the handle, and went in to a small, square room.

Genessa lay on a couch talking to the spaniels curled on the floor
beside her. In the window a priestess spun by light coming through
the shutters. She looked up at the door's whisper over the carpet, but
Garvan had his mouth to her ear before she could move, and his words
stilled her.

Genessa sat up, and he went to her, and folded her, and held her,
and she held him, wordless.

"Gather what you need and let us be gone," he whispered. "We
have little time."

"But for the fog we should have sailed for Capri," she said, half in
tears. "I prayed that Dassi might find you——"

Garvan caught glimpse of a movement, but his turn was too late.

Genessa pointed to the curtains moving in the mid-wall, and she looked with fright about the room.

Faint screams, and other voices and a bell ringing and thudding feet sounded together. But then a silence, worse than noise. Garvan pushed open the shutters and took the dogs by the scruff, and put them out. He helped Genessa over the sill, and she jumped down, and he landed beside her.

Dead weight fell on his shoulders and arms, and he was forced to the ground, and he saw the steel shin armor of temple guards, and he looked up into the face of Captain Tabis Netto, and beside him, the Aedile, Julian Potitius.

XVII

"This time, the charges stand," the Aedile said. "Of entering and despoiling the peace of a household, first. Of laying hands upon Genessa Vespasianus, a member of the Lord Caesar's family, second——"

"My name is Pinaria," Genessa said, clear and strong. "There was no peace in this household to be despoiled. And he laid no hand upon me, but kissed as I kissed, in love!"

"To the Curia, both," the Aedile said.

Garvan tried to speak, but a sentry knocked him down. His hands, arms, and ankles were tied. He saw the Aedile and Tabis Netto drive off together, but he had no chance to look for Genessa. He was flung to the floor of a chariot and the guard pressed one foot between his shoulder blades that he might not rise. He smelled smoke thick nearer the Forum, but the driver went at stretch gallop. They pulled to a halt inside the courtyard, and guards ran from wagons behind to drag him into the court. In the prison cages men and women were crushed until legs and arms hung out of the bars and the faces of the dead poked black tongues. Farther back, crosses of raw wood were piled against the wall among heaps of shavings, and Lydia of Samaria stood near, chained to a group of men. Smoke blew and filled the lungs and scratched throats, and heat dried sweat, and a crowd of guards and police milled about the fountain.

Trumpeters sounded to make a way for the Aedile in his robes, leading a procession of lawyers and public men of Herculaneum, and others wearing the badge of Pompeii. Captain Tabis Netto stood in front of the judge's dais, and smiled, folding his arms.

A chamberlain struck his wand for silence, and the Aedile declared the court ready to hear a delegation from the temples of Herculaneum and of Pompeii, led by the Chief Priest of the Temple of Hercules.

He, frail and bearded, and clad in gilded lion pelts, began a history of the city, from the time that Hercules returned from Iberia to build the first house, until the present day. He went into the family history of the Pinarii and the Potitii, and told of the god's many favors to their descendants, and also to the people of his city.

"What then do we find?" he quavered. "Christians, that vile breed, allowed room among us. Did the god show his displeasure? Did he not cause movements of the earth to warn us? In late days have been processions of these scum in their scarlet, openly. Was sword drawn against them? Not until the elder Pinarius, he, joint guardian, perished in this court of his own hand. And why? Because his wife was a Christian. And whereby did she become known? Because a Potitius, he, joint guardian, was proved a Christian. And we wonder at the rage of our god?"

"What would the excellent father desire of the court?" the Aedile asked in his small voice.

"That proper sacrifice be made," the priest said. "That the godly anger might abate, we demand the body of the woman, Lydia. Let her be offered in the flames to relieve the memory of all the unfaithful."

Priests and priestesses in a body went forward shouting out agreement.

"There are other claims against her," the Aedile called. "Stand forward, Tercena, most excellent Matron of the College of Diana!"

"Hear me, Aedile." Tercena's voice came from a group of priestesses and vestals on the other side of the court. "This Lydia, a Samarian, on plaint of the College of Diana, is condemned by the court to die. But this Lydia has secrets of the loom and vat that are precious to all people. We, then, offer her the lives, but not the liberty, of her Christians, sentenced with her, for the knowledge which she has."

"Let the Samarian stand," the Aedile said. "What say you?"

"Secrets are little enough," Lydia smiled with her voice. "I will give you every secret and all the knowledge you want. But not against lives. I do not plead against sentence——"

"No speeches," the Aedile said. "Bring the woman before the court!"

Garvan felt the thongs about his wrists being cut through. Another knife was at work on his ankles. Both his guards had been replaced by others, though he had taken little enough notice. But the guard taking post near Captain Tabis Netto seemed too big for his uniform, and his red hair showed strangely under a helmet something small. At the farther door the Numidian leaned on a spear beside one with every appearance of Corbi, though he, too, wore the uniform of a temple guard.

Garvan barely turned his head. Khefi, also in uniform, stood at his side. He felt the hilt of a sword put into his hands. He turned again, and caught a half-grin from Stavros, and a glint from the eyes of Zetak.

Now he felt the pulse of his heart, and his eyes roved, and he saw that one or two guards in temple uniform stood at every entrance, and every city policeman had a guard at his elbow.

Two court attendants pulled Lydia before the dais. Her hair was cut short, and her face was stained, and she wore rags that she tried to hold together.

"Say, then," the Aedile commanded. "If these lives are spared, do you swear to give of your knowledge?"

"How is this that the Dianists are foremost where favor is shown?" Hercules' Chief Priest demanded. "What use to talk of secrets when destruction is upon us?"

"Let the excellent servant of Hercules be comforted," Tercena called out. "In place of this woman, here is one sharing the blood of the traitress, Thalia. Here is the daughter of Sulla Pinarius. Let the god know peace in her!"

Every hand was raised, and voices clamored approval. The Aedile gestured and Captain Tabis Netto came, holding Genessa by the arm.

"In this way, you absolve your name," the Aedile told her in the small voice. "Let her be taken to the Temple of Hercules. Bring forward the Gaul, her companion!"

Captain Tabis Netto straightened himself, and walked forward, looking here and there, but never at Garvan until he stood in front of him. He put his hands behind his back, and stared him in the eye, and the scar down his face turned red and a nerve beat. Garvan felt the pins and needles of blood coming back in his arms and legs, but his grip on the sword had no bite.

"First, let me be represented," Genessa called. "I am a citizen guilty of no crime. I appeal to Caesar!"

"I, too, am a citizen," Garvan said, looking the Captain in the eye. "I am more. I am Captain of the Gallic Legion, of the Imperial Bodyguard. This is not a rabble of lackeys and doorkeepers——"

Captain Tabis Netto set a hand on each of his shoulders to toss him. But even as he gripped, a sword blade flashed from Khefi's side and from Stavros' side, and steel cut through both forearms at the elbows. Captain Tabis Netto stared at Khefi, and at Stavros, and at nothing, and his eyes glazed, and his face paled, and he fell.

Sure of the strength of his limbs, Garvan unhooked a blood-spattered tunic, and let it fall, and weighed the sword, going toward Genessa. A murmur became a roar, and people ran.

The Aedile stood, signing to guards in the doorway.

"Disarm the prisoner!" he commanded. "Cut him down!"

But over the heads of shouting people a net spread and wrapped him about, and drawstrings tautened, and he was pulled away from his chair and over the edge of the dais.

Garvan leapt to the prisoners' cage, and kicked away the bar. The first wretches fell, and he helped them up, though when Genessa came with Lydia, he pulled her away, and took her about the waist.

"All to the harbor," he shouted. "Before the Praetorians are led here. Out, to the right hand. What does Zetak carry there?"

"A pretty one," Zetak called. "A mongrel in a jeweled collar——"

"My dogs!" Genessa cried. "My spaniels!"

"Corbi has them in front," Stavros comforted her. "We followed General Towhead to the Villa, but we were too late to do more than settle accounts with the guards——"

"The Mother Hemera," Genessa began. "She was hurt?"

"I have names for none," said Khefi. "A brood of hens went into flame. This, certainly——"

"Lend your mind to matters more serious," Garvan said. "What do you hear?"

A rapid and heavy trot of shod feet became plainer. Over the roof tops a trumpet sounded, and another answered nearby.

"Praetorians," Khefi said, and pulled a face. "They, of all men I had rather not meet ten to one. Or two to one. General, they will stamp you flat——"

"We have the Square of Hercules to go over," Garvan said. "If we are caught there in the open, we shall be slaughtered——"

"Remember the Sanctuary," Genessa warned. "The Temple of Vesta. They dare not enter."

"See how the gods come usefully to hand," Zetak called, panting happily under the load in the net. "Remember Khefi? You swore me for a mooncalf when I spent a coin to burn a candle for our Vesta, but see, she opens her arms to us!"

"With Praetorians to kick us into them," Khefi growled, and helped him with his load. "What's to be done with this one?"

"I'd thought him a sweet mouthful for the lampreys," Zetak said. "Remember also, he told us we'd make rare housing for maggots?"

"Who is that in the net?" Genessa whispered.

"No friend," said Garvan. "Run!"

They entered the Square of Hercules. Smoke hid the statue above the waistline. Citizens were screaming at each other and going into houses in a great slamming of doors. The crowd of running prisoners was almost all gone into the Street of the Acanthus on the harbor side.

The Temple of Vesta lay on the left of the square, a small building fronted in columns, with tiers of marble thick with years of grease from candles burned in her honor. An elderly priestess in green robes held out her arms in welcome to them, and pointed warningly over their heads.

A phalanx of Praetorians in drab war dress trotted into the square from the next street, and ranks of bronze shields flashed in vicious gleams of red.

"Is there sanctuary for us?" Garvan called to the priestess.

"For all," she smiled. "Enter!"

Garvan waved the little crowd inside the columns, to the warmth of brier flaming in the city's hearth, a circular bowl set in the floor in the middle of a dark building, charred with smoke and heavy with the odor of burned wood.

"We could take a chance and run," said Khefi. "They'll stay there and starve us out."

Garvan looked at the massed ranks drawn about the temple.

"To come within a javelin throw, and fail!" he groaned.

"Prince Garvan!" A loud voice came from the lane between the companies of troops. "I am the Ensign Aristarchus Cornelius, and my orders are to escort you to the flagship of the Admiral Pliny. Are you ready to accompany me?"

"There's your Praetorian!" Zetak said admiringly. "Give him an order, and that's all he knows!"

"We enjoy sanctuary of Vesta, and we refuge in the genius of this city," Garvan called.

"Nothing was said of this." The Ensign stood at the foot of the steps. "Will you come with me, one and one, or must I fetch you?"

"This by force of arms," said Garvan.

"Make your choice," the Ensign said.

Garvan felt a hand grasp his fingers.

"We die once," Genessa whispered. "Now, and together, were dear a time as any."

But a call brought them to look inside the columns, at Lydia. She knelt, praying, and her face was calm.

"Never did I ask a moment's help for myself, or for any of my sisters and brethren," she appealed, staring into the sky. "Save these unbelievers. They cannot suffer. They are children, and innocent——"

A whistling that picked up dust was in the air, and lifted the smoke in spirals, and made the hearth roar. Sunshine came blindingly, and the slope of land up to the tip of Vesuvius cleared, and the clouds lay behind. The great cone as far down as the olive groves was massed in a froth of flame and steam that poured lower, moment by moment, covering houses and gardens and burning the tops of orchards farther down. Fire blazed from the cone's mouth, and went up, straight as if built as a column, and splayed in a deep red cloud bursting in sparks.

Screams came from people watching on roof tops, and officers shouted among the troops.

"Make way!" The Ensign loosened his sword, and walked up the steps. "Lord Prince——"

"Save breath, and draw," Garvan smiled. "But no man brings heavier heart to fight!"

The earth moved, and men fell, and the buildings shuddered. A half of the mountain's cone broke away and molten waves rolled down, covering the froth of flame and steam, and a noise smote the ears as if the mountain had burst, and men covered their heads and went to their knees. The earth moved in broad motions, and stopped, and moved again, and a wind came down, with clouds of smoke, thick and red, and raw with sulphur. A cracking of stone began, and slabs of flooring were flung up, and tiles fell from the walls, and a column broke and toppled down the steps among the ranks of waiting troops.

Garvan took Genessa, and held her close. The earth heaved and they fell together, and struggled up, and fell again. Blocks of stone rolled down about them, and the shrieks and shouts of frightened people were louder than the wind. But then many voices joined a single scream in the red mist ahead, and men ran, and stumbled, and fell, and climbed over each other, and still the scream went on.

Genessa pointed up, at a dark shadow overhead that got darker and more hugeous. A screech of tearing stone overlay the human shriek.

"The god!" Genessa screamed. "Hercules. He falls!"

The mass of marble fell across a house, and over all the square, crushing dozens, and pinning dozens more by legs and arms. The torso of the great statue blocked the street to the harbor, and an arm and a fist of marble lay across two houses.

Again the smoke thinned. The square was littered with bodies and spread over with rubble, and fallen house fronts, and broken columns, and the troops were smashing pieces of the marble to rescue their comrades. The Temple of Vesta heaped in ruin, and smoke poured out of rubble, black, into red smoke thickening once more with the drift of the wind.

Khefi came with Lydia in his arms as a child, and Stavros carried Vesta's priestess. Garvan ran to the fallen marble, and pointed up, over marbled muscles, to the crest of the shoulder.

"Climb, and lower ropes," he told them. "Haul up the weaker."

Townspeople crowded, pleading for their children, and more were crawling out of wrecked houses. Maddened horses galloped, and officers tried to re-form ranks of troops. But still the earth moved, and sulphur choked, and all wiped tears. With belts, and lengths of torn garments, ropes were made, and Chote, Khefi, and the Numidian climbed the marble, though at the top they could barely be seen. The ropes fell taut, and the women were tied, and pulled up, with men climbing alongside to hold them steady, and going with them down on the other side, into the street leading to the harbor.

Genessa held children and helped mothers, and Garvan ran from one rope to another, making sure that his charges were all over.

A high note of terror in sudden screams brought him to face the square. In amazement he watched soldiers leaping together in the smoke as if they played a game. But then a wash of red water swept in a wave, and swiftly there came another, and the water steamed, and heat burned his face. The street up to the Forum was half under water rising higher than the doors, pulling debris along, and bodies.

XVIII

A mass of water poured into doorways, filling sewers and cellars, flooding houses and gardens, taking with it furniture and carpets and statuary, and every hapless one caught in its way. Darkness came, more sudden than night. Ash sifted down, harsh in the throat and nose, and burning the skin. Houses were on fire, and still the waves came, and the heat appalled.

Garvan lifted Genessa on to the statue's upper arm to be out of the red swirl, and held the rope steady for her to climb, but in following her he saw the Ensign Aristarchus riding a white horse, and leading another, and trying to coax them up the temple steps to be out of the water.

Garvan jumped into a knee-high scald, and ran, grasping the bridle of the second mount and vaulting up. He drove the frightened animal toward the lower slope of the statue. Those above saw his plan, and hastened down to help, grasping hooves and lifting both horses, pace by pace, and laying garments on the smoother slopes that shoes might not slip. At the top the horses were led to the bridge of timbers built down to the roadway.

The fallen statue blocked the street from the water filling the square, and people ran dry-shod toward the harbor. Garvan put Genessa on one of the horses, and gave her in care of Chote.

But Aristarchus turned back.

"My legion is here in this inferno," he said, grasping Garvan's hand. "I doubt that we might reach Misenum. My thanks for saving my animals. I had meant that you should ride one, and I the other. One more favor. If you should pass a shrine to Mars, burn there a candle for your friend."

"Rest on it," Garvan said. "Let my friend remember me."

They grinned at each other, weeping from sulphur. Aristarchus slid down the shoulder muscles, to an elbow, and jumped to a slab, and played steppingstones to the wreck of Vesta's temple, and on, climbing broken rafters on the roof of a house, and so, from sight.

"How shall it feel, towhead, to be boiled in a stew of your own sloth and the ruin of the city?" Khefi asked, standing behind. "Other streets going into the harbor spout the mountain's blood. See, it fills and burns the houses in between. Shall you ponder here? Or run?"

Garvan watched a boiling tide gush through a broken door and fill a garden and spew furniture.

"Run," he said.

They went to the bridge, and slid down, reaching the street. Water streamed, hissing through cracks between the statue and the corner houses. Garvan gave the marble a pat.

"Good Hercules, add another labor to those told of you," he said. "But this is true, for I was here to see!"

"With help of Lydia's God," Khefi said, trotting beside him. "She prayed, and so it happened."

"This was chance," said Garvan with no surety.

"Chance that a god was used to do a God's work," said Khefi. "What a woman is this Lydia that calls upon a God, and He sends a god to do her bidding!"

Apart from the Anointed trying to board Uriel's ship a crowd of townspeople along the quay's edge were fighting for room in any craft. Genessa stood by Lydia at the water's edge, helping people into skiffs taking them out to a vessel filled and ready to sail.

"Many ships are in the naval harbor," Genessa said. "But authority is needed to enter in."

"Authority?" Garvan stared.

"Rome is here," Genessa said. "No Roman consults himself whether he shall do this, or that. Authority must be got to take a ship."

"Enough of Romans!" Garvan told her. "How get these families on the water? What authority shall stand for us?"

"Here is one," Khefi pointed to Zetak among the crowd. "See him take his ease!"

Zetak sat, resting against a wall, with his feet on the neck of Julian Potitius, out of the net and squatting among bundles, and goats, and the scattered stuff of fright.

"Heed me, Julian," Genessa called. "By law, as children of our fathers, we are joint guardians of this city and all in it. Our citizens lack ships. The harbor men might give us craft on command. Will you go with me?"

"I will go with you as Aedile and city guardian," Julian Potitius said. "But when the ships are ours, I shall command you to surrender as criminals justly sentenced——"

"Khefi, ride a stallion and carry him in front," Garvan said. "Genessa, ride with me. Shelter yourselves, you others!"

A fine ash came with gusts of wind in the sound of steady rain, and the horses were frightened, and uneasy to mount. Ash burned the skin and sparked in clothing, and women shrieked fear for their children, and men tried to find roofing. Darkness was lit by reddish light behind the smoke of the mountain, and by the flames of houses on fire ashore.

Garvan sat steady, with his arms about Genessa's waist, but it took all his strength and her patting hands and soft cries to control the horse's fear. Khefi was harder put, for the Aedile sat as a sack. Garvan gave head, and the stallion beat sparks from the stone. He raced along the broad quay, almost awash with steaming water, scattering wide-eyed wretches begging help and bellowing terror that floated in their ears long after they were past. The high stone arch of the bridge puffed smoke from the lava pouring under it, and heat from the boiling river burned their faces. The stallion slid, refusing the approach, but Garvan turned him, and saw Khefi kick, and wrench, and send his mount over. But Genessa cried out to see the stallion's hoofs smoke in the passing, and cried again when their own stallion screamed pain, and leapt its way over, and splashed into deeper water on the other side.

The dockyard gates were open, and troops were trotting in from the high ground beyond the river. Galleys and smaller craft were loading troops and civilians, and floats were taking on stores.

Khefi was off and putting the Aedile down when Garvan brought his own mount to a halt. He helped Genessa down, and took both bridles, and led the stallions toward an officer at a gangplank.

"These Arabians belong to the Ensign Aristarchus Cornelius," he said. "Tell him they borrowed his courage, and share his breed. Deliver them into his hand, and say his friend was grateful!"

Garvan watched them curvet aboard the cooler wood, and turned to go back. But farther down the dockside he saw flame gleam in three silver fishes, and knew them for Lydia's sign fastened to the Ark of Tarsus.

The ship was empty, without crew, but her sails and tiller were in place and there was tide enough to take her off the berth.

He called the others aboard, and Khefi might have left the Aedile, but Genessa pleaded, and pushed Julian across the gangplank. Garvan helped Khefi to raise the anchor, and went aft, finding Genessa at the helm ready to steer.

"I know these waters as well as any pilot," she told him. "Cast off, and take my orders!"

The ship floated, and bumped, but current took her out, and Khefi raised a sail in ample gusts, and they rounded the end of the mole. A lighthouse shrine gave a steering point, and wicks fluttered leaves of flame among the wax drippings of years of rites by mariners seeking help of the gods. Tide was heavy and falling cinders burned the sailcloth.

Khefi found Julian Potitius in a place behind the deckhouse, and gave him a bucket, and ordered him to the crow's nest to throw water down and save the sail. But Julian Potitius ran to the bulwarks, and climbed, holding on to the stays.

"You will stand again before me," he shouted. "Make offering to any god for mercy in that day. From me, none!"

"Julian!" Genessa pleaded. "For memory of your mother——"

"Turn from me!" Julian Potitius shouted. "You saw me treated as a dog and made no protest——"

He lost hold, or he made attempt to dive, but he went into the water only a little way from the mole, and a few strokes took him to the stones. He climbed out, and turned to curse them, and they saw him step among the mounds of wax to reach the flat.

They heard him scream, and for a little saw that he stood outlined in gold by the massing wicks, arms apart as if in plea. But the shrine itself seemed to move, and countless tons of wax turned liquid in the heat overflowed, and, in falling, took other tons from higher tiers, and the shrine's canopy, and the effigy of Mars and all the marbling fell, and covered him almost to the neck.

Fire burst in yellow swathes about him, and they saw his shrieking face with flame for hair.

"See this, Aristarchus," Garvan shouted. "Here is the candle you were promised. May rats take the tallow!"

XIX

Wind freshened from the north, and a long gust blew the smoke thin, and they gaped at black sky above an opened gray parasol of ash. But the mountain spouted flame spreading deep red light over the countryside as if all were washed with blood, and a pink froth covered the city down to the harbor. A crowd waited along the deck, waving them on, and men dived in to climb aboard and help.

The Ark of Tarsus was tied up, and the Anointed people, last to leave, began climbing aboard under rugs and mattresses covering their heads against the ash. Lydia went first to the chapel next the deckhouse and made her prayer. Corbi came with the spaniels, but although Genessa held them, she was not over shock of Julian's death, and she sat apart.

"The box, Lord Prince," said Corbi. "That one with the crucifix from the house of the Pinarii."

Garvan took it to Lydia, and she saw it first with a wide stare of joy. But horror tightened her face, and she tore at her hair.

"Helpless, witless that I am!" she whispered. "I must go back to my house!"

"How could you go?" Genessa pleaded. "All these would follow, trusting only you. How many might perish?"

"The house is near," said Garvan. "If it can be reached, what then?"

"In the upper room," Lydia said. "Draw the altar curtains, and bring to me the other Cross that hangs there. Bind it against harm——"

Garvan kissed the length of Genessa's braid, and ended on the tip of her nose.

"Wait for me," he whispered.

"Ever!" she smiled. "Take care!"

He ran off the ship and along the quay toward Lydia's house on the high ground. Water poured down the streets into the fishing harbor, but it had thickened almost to a mud. Many of the streets were covered to the roof tops, and all the houses on the slope were under a bubbling lake. Loose planks made bridges across narrow lanes from roof to roof, and branches of trees gave power to his leaps across steaming gardens.

Lydia's house was filled to the first floor. A smell of burning wood stung his nose. He climbed along the roof top of the market hall, and up to the terrace. The tiles were hot underfoot, and the house shook as if monsters were at play in every room. He went over the roof to the other side of the atrium, and followed the garden around, and climbed through a window near the stairway.

He knew the voice coming from the upper room, and he went to the doorway, and stood, taking breath, watching Afra, thick with red mud, lying face down before the frame with the scarlet curtains.

"Afra," he said gently. "I am come in time."

"But wherever these hands touch is wet with blood of those betrayed," Afra whispered. "Where shall I go? My loom, and all my patterns are lost. That was my harp, my only music. Where shall I go?"

Afra sobbed as a child, and ran light hands over Garvan's arms, and touched finger tips to his face.

"How works this God, this Mighty One!" he whispered. "I turned to Him, and abased myself, and saw the shame in me from the sounds of my mouth. You will help me?"

"As you once helped me," Garvan said. "Let me find this treasure, and we shall go."

In small terror of a miracle he held his breath to draw the squares of scarlet silk.

But inside the frame a whitewashed wall was blank, and two pegs held a rough cross of splintered wood, the same as that he remembered in the cave of Uriel.

"A thief has been here," he said. "This is no treasure!"

Afra covered his blind eyes.

"This is part of the True Cross," he whispered. "Give it into my hands, and I will take strength."

He threw off his toga, and sought a place in the weave, and tore, and wrapped the Cross about, and held it up.

"Good!" said Garvan. "And now the loom. Come!"

Afra led the way swift to the stairway going into the atrium and garden. The loom stuck halfway out of red, steaming mud. Remembering his journey to the house, he had little hope of taking Afra to the quay, much less the heavy loom. But memory was strong of Lydia, and the God she praised was also in his mind.

The garden's outer wall cracked, and a gush of hot water spouted, and gouts of mud slopped through. In a little time even the top bars of the loom would be covered. He tipped bales to make a barricade behind the loom, and when they were high enough, he dug into the hot mud to unbolt the bars. But fast as he dug, the holes filled with water and left him as before.

In rage at helplessness he ran up the stairway to the terrace. Afra stood at the harbor end, with the bundle held to his chest.

"Let us go to the quay," Garvan said. "There we shall find help."

"The loom is too heavy," Afra said. "I tried. But can I go without? I was born to it. Who is Afra without his loom?"

"We can build others," Garvan said.

"Not for these," Afra laughed, showing his fingers. "To the finest distance, they know that loom, and none other. They never searched or learned. They knew, and know. Other looms? Other wilderness!"

"We must go," Garvan said, watching mud rising in the street. "There is little time, and many are waiting."

"My stick is lost, and the streets are filled with water," Afra cried. "Who am I now? If prayer has power, here is the time to pray!"

"Lydia said that never did she pray for herself," Garvan told him. "Then why should we? Let us hope, and have faith in Charity."

He saw the flash of steel not far away, and then he shouted and danced his joy.

"Khefi!" he sang. "Good Khefi! This way, war horse. Zetak! Stavros! Tadmon! Ho!"

Over the market roof they ran, carrying ropes, and planks, and ladders and tools.

"A fine stretch!" Khefi swore, climbing to the terrace. "Only towheads could dream such madness. We were almost a-swim, and the seaboard fills with lava. Come, weaver, your hand. Why do you wait?"

"What stands here is only shame, with a tongue," said Afra.

"Save the loom," Garvan said. "The loom is the man."

It took little time, with many hands, to dig out the big loom, and unbolt it, and carry it piece by piece to the terrace. Weavers' patterns of thin wood they found in boxes, and spooled thread, and hanks of silk in every color. Piece, box, and bale were taken to the roof, and carried over planks to other roofs, and pines were cut for makeshift bridges. Each man carried a load to a place, and went back for other, until the terrace was clear. Then he carried a load to a farther point, and so to the next. Afra followed all, holding the bundle before him. Never did he need help, and never did his foot stray from the narrowest plank.

The other craft had cast off, with Uriel's ship in lead. Garvan went to the gangway of the Ark of Tarsus, and Genessa came to him, and put her arms about him, and they listened to strong voices in a hymn from all the Anointed crowding the deck.

"Dearest Gaul, robed in mud," she whispered. "I thought it first in the garden, and dreamed it since. But now I know. You are first and only one. But I come to you with nothing. Not a lace to my shoe."

"I am wealthy beyond a dream in what is left," Garvan said.

"I think now only of you," Genessa whispered. "I fear what may come. How shall this be told to Caesar?"

"Far more he must be told," Garvan said, looking at the sea, red in the glare and wisping steam. "Think what less is here. I have many regrets, one, that this Roman city is no more."

"But you hated Rome and things Roman!" Genessa whispered. "How do you change moment to moment!"

"Only in moments when I stand beside you," said Garvan. "Then I change to deeper love of Rome, that fashioned you."

"Will you stand all night a-nibbling?" Khefi shouted from the deck. "The ship is low in water, and hands are needed at the oars. Back to slavery, shacklescar!"

Garvan laughed with Genessa, and saw her aboard, and ran after Khefi down to the oar banks. Men crowded all the benches, and the portside team worked to turn the ship under orders from Lydia.

Khefi took a place beside Stavros, and Zetak came on the bank behind with Garvan, and Tadmon made a third.

"We have our old places," Khefi grinned. "But no master, and no lictors. I work with all my heart!"

"And think what we have learned in this short time," Zetak said. "For me, all other gods may fiddle with that fat one, Nero. Who is more reasonable than the God of these Anointed? Only pray to Him, and the chickens stay in the coop, and the animals in the field. And your money stays in your pouch!"

"Remember, lardpoll, they work," said Stavros, grunting with effort. "And that Lydia needs no whip to drive."

A touch came soft on Garvan's shoulder, and familiar perfume made him turn. Genessa held up the oar-bench mallets, and went to sit at the raised table.

"The master of this ship wants speed," she said. "I learned the mallet stroke when I was little. Come, weaklings, your weight in this. One!"

The mallet fell, and the other followed.

Tadmon waited for the backswing and looked over his shoulder.

"Poor ragtail," he said. "See what like of woman is this, and think of marriage then!"

Garvan looked at a maenad mouth, and at eyes of a color he could never fix, that smiled in a glitter of love for him, and he watched a small, ringed hand lift a mallet, and he moved with it.

"She strikes us up to Gaul, and home," he said. "And I am well content!"

DATE DUE

DATE DUE			
AP 15 '66			
FE 27 70			
DE 9 '86			
GAYLORD			PRINTED IN U.S.A.